© Max Lamirande, 2022

Published by Max Lamirande

© 2022 Saguenay, Quebec, Canada

All rights reserved. No part of this book may be reproduced or modified in any form, including photocopying, recording, or by any information storage and retrieval system, without permission in writing from the publisher.

Credits:
Kindle publishing

Cover credits:

References:
Wikipedia, Wikicommons

FOREWORD

Dear readers,

I welcome you back to the Blitzkrieg Alternate Series. So much has happened since the first book. I can still hardly believe my success with the sales and the reviews.

Rest assured, I am still fully motivated to churn out a great story rapidly. The war in Europe is NOT over; I can promise you that!

Before I forget, I want to **thank you,** my dear readers, for continuing to read my work. It's what makes it all worthwhile in the end.

I believe you will like the change of pace that book 9 proposes on the Blitzkrieg Alternate Series. As one war is ending, a second war is slowly dawning. What remains to be seen is what will happen. Will it be like historically and evolve into the Cold War between superpowers? Or will Stalin take the plunge and try to take over the World? We will soon know.

But let's not count our chickens before they hatch, shall we?. There is still a Third Reich to destroy before any of that happens.

Read on!

*** Don't forget to review my work and also sign up to the mailing list at www.maxlamirande.com

P.S. The next book I am working on now is the second installment in the parallel story Pacific Alternate: **Battle Pacific**

PROLOGUE

Operation Tsar
Border between the USSR and Japanese Manchuria, January 12-22nd, 1947

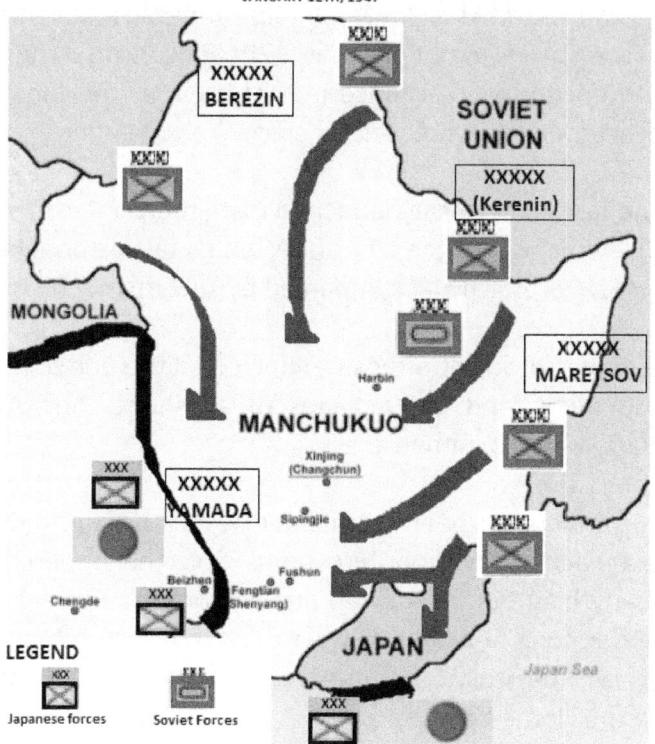

The quiet of the dying night was suddenly shattered by the most potent artillery barrage seen since the end of the war in the Pacific. From across the Soviet expanses, four massive armies started to attack the Japanese forces in Manchuria. Two mighty forces launched themselves from the area of Lake Khanka, near the Pacific coast. The 1st and 25th rifle armies, under General Meretsov, attacked frontally at demoralized Imperial forces. Within an hour, the shelling was over, and Russian tanks and infantry poured into Manchuria. Kwantung 1st Army under General Seiichi, responsible for the defense in the area, balked. Most men expected to be repatriated to Japan, not be attacked. Many amongst them had already discarded their weapons and settled into a more normal life. Discipline was lax, and the officers did the same. The units within the army group defending the sector were slowly disintegrating.

Another powerful attack was launched in northern Manchuria thru the Lesser and Grand Khingan Mountain ranges. It was led by Sergei Berezin's Transbaikal Front and his 12th Rifle Army. The Russians didn't even encounter resistance in that area, as the Japanese had already evacuated the whole sector since the surrender.

Finally, one last Soviet Army launched over the border to reach the central valley plains and the city of Harbin as fast as possible. It was Kerenin's 45th tank army, accompanied by several rifle divisions.

In all, the powerful Soviet offensive sported a little under one million men, 1500 tanks, and 1100 planes of all shapes and sizes. The artillery park was also immense.

Japan's surrender had been proclaimed weeks before in December after the nuclear attack on Hiroshima, and the Imperial soldiers expected anything but a renewed attack from the Allies. Of course, the surrender conditions had not yet been in effect in Manchuria as it was a vast territory, and the Americans were still busy just occupying the Home Country.

The Japanese government signed the unconditional surrender on board battleship Missouri. The ceremony had been quite formal, in Tokyo Bay of all places, with the entire American Pacific Fleet in view, planes flying above to show Allied might. It had not taken long after that for the Americans to land forces in Tokyo and other strategic points of the Home Islands. Several other strategic territories were also rapidly occupied, like Formosa, the oil installations in the former Dutch East Indies, French Indo China, and even limited areas at the tip of the Korean Peninsula (Pusan).

But Manchuria had thus far been left to its own devices. The by then 500 000 strong Army, supposed to guard the border with the Soviet Union, was numerous and in a backwater territory that didn't have much importance in terms of American strategic objectives. That army group had been the strongest in Imperial Japan before the war, but most of its elite forces had been taken away for the needs of the war in other theaters.

And so, the Japanese Army received the powerful and totally unwarranted Russian offensive with what could be described as total apathy. Within ten days, the Soviet forces were in Harbin and Changchun, and another five days later, they stormed Shenyang in the southwest.

Only the Chengde/Pekin area resisted since the former Commander-in-chief of the Kwantung Army, General Otozo Yamada, retained some semblance of control over about ten hodgepodge divisions. He established a precarious defense in that area, helped by other units from China that reacted in time to rearm themselves to face the Russian juggernaut.

The news was taken with utter shock in London, Washington, and other Allied countries. The Russian move had not been expected, nor any news or reports had reached the Allied military forces about Russian movements to the east. Everyone thought that the Soviets were concentrating on finishing the German forces in Europe.

And they were right, in a sense. But Stalin had entertained over 800 000 men on the Soviet-Japanese border to deter Imperial Japan from attacking Siberia. It didn't take a lot of reinforcements to make a coherent offensive force, especially since the Japanese Army was in a state of disintegration across the Pacific theater since the surrender.

The offensive shook the foundations of the Grand Alliance to its core and showed the World that all was not well. Officially, the USSR was coming to the help of the Communist forces of Mao Tse Tong in China, but no one was a fool about it. The lightning advances by the Red Army in what used to be the Japanese protectorate of Manchukuo, and its penetration of the Korean Peninsula could only mean one thing. The Soviets were making a blatant land grab.

Lake Balaton
Panzer Lehr Division on the attack in Hungary, January 12th, 1947

The Panzer gun barked again with all its might, recoiling slightly to the rear. The tank was at a dead stop, with its turret across its side, aiming at yet another enemy tank that was in sight. The 88mm high-velocity red tracer raced in a slight arc toward its unfortunate recipient, an IS-2 Stalin tank.

The round hit the Russian in between the gun mantle and the turret. It was a known vulnerability for this specific type of Soviet tank but a difficult place to hit— another superb shot by his young and very talented gunner, Hans Stromer. For a fleeting moment, probably half a second, it looked like the Russian tank would shrug off the shell. But only for that little moment. It didn't take long for the turret to disconnect from the tank's base and skyrocket in the air, followed by half of a body (probably the machine's commander) severed as well in the catastrophic explosion. Not much time elapsed after that for the rest of the IS-2 to burst into flame, with a giant pillar of fire bursting forth from the hole created by the turret's flying away.

The young soldier was not fazed in any way by his marksmanship.

Staying as sharp as a well-honed knife, he spotted another enemy in his targeting sight and yelled to the loader. "Quick now, load!" Walder looked rapidly thru the observation slit, and right as rain, another enemy was driving hard toward them, perpendicular to the by now fiercely burning IS-2 tank they'd just destroyed. He wondered how the kid saw the tank thru all this smoke and fire. He indeed had a gift.

The loader finished his job. "Ready to fire, Hans." And then the Konigstiger fired again. This time, it hit the opposing tank below the topside armor, right on the side where the tracks rested. Walder, looking thru his slits, couldn't believe the shot again. It was the only spot to aim at, and Stromer had again done it perfectly.

"Move to the right and backward!" Yelled Walder in order to get out of what looked to be a deathtrap. He'd been distracted since being too concentrated on the gunner's work. His job was to look at the overall scene, not just the destruction wrought by his gun. And he had not noticed the three T-34 75mm tanks rushing them from directly ahead.

The Tiger II was rocked by two powerful hits on its frontal armor. Fortunately for the Germans inside, the Panzer was one of the strongest in the German arsenal with its 185mm of steel plating. So apart from stunning everyone and getting their ears to ring profusely, the tank shrugged off the hits. But the three enemies were coming closer by the second, and if one thing was sure, it was that at short range, the T-34 would be able to penetrate the Panzer, thick frontal armor or not.

The tank lumbered at a surprising speed, even for the crew inside. They were still not used to the new Tiger II engine and transmission improvements. They'd just got the machine before the Lake Balaton offensive and had been told of the new Simmering Sla.16, a 1000hp+ engine (a significant improvement over the old 690 hp that the Tiger II used to have) and transmission derived from a ship's engine that the Kriegsmarine had developed in 1945 but never used because of the fleet's destruction. It had been adapted for the Wehrmacht tanks. This latest development came in handy for the famous Panzer, which had been plagued with low speed and transmission problems. The new gig was supposed to take care of the tank's main weaknesses.

So far, it lived up to its promises. The whole Panzer Lehr Heavy Panzer Battalion had talked about it at the start of the offensive and marveled at the new speed the tank could go - an average of 48km to 50 km- which was also a significant improvement compared to the 38-40 it used to do under the Maybach engine's power. Not even one machine had broken down during the advance to the frontline. It was a refreshing development for the Panzer crews since about 10% of the machines usually simply broke down just getting to the battle.

Erich had the tank backed up into a slight ditch that wasn't too steep nor too deep, but that enabled the Tiger II to get out of the charging T-34's line of fire. The Konigstiger rumbled down at full speed, plowing the soft earth deeply with its large and powerful tracks, splattering its side with brown mud. Several shells burst just in front of the Panzer, creating pillars of dirt and debris that then showered on the Royal Tiger. "Continue to drive backward at full speed," ordered the tank commander. A stream was at the bottom of the slight downward slope, and beyond it, a large rockface resided. They were right by the shore of Lake Balaton.

By the time the Tiger II splashed into the knee-deep water of the stream, scattering it in all directions and followed by smoke and some fog created by the movement, the first T-34 showed its underside at the top of the ditch. As sharp as ever and being ready for just that opportunity to present itself, Stromer fired. The shell hit the Soviet tank as it was tilting down. The 88mm penetrated cleanly thru the thin armor and even exited on the other side by the engine's compartment. Gutted, the enemy machine skittered to a halt sideways, sliding for a moment on the muddy, sloping ground.

That was when the other two T-34's decided to show up at the top of the ditch overlooking the small stream. They fired their rounds, but this time the Tiger II was able to dodge them since the driver expertly backed up the armored machine on the other side of the rockface. Again the tank splashed into the water (this time the Lake's water itself, but it was shallow depth), while the two Soviet rounds exploded in all their glory on the rock, splintering it in every direction.

The battle was far from over for Walder's crew and would still last a few more days. The Panzer Lehr was part of a German counter-offensive designed to save the Wehrmacht units trying to retreat from the Balkans and the rest of Central Europe. The situation had worsened gravely in the Balkans since December 1st. The Romanian betrayal had hurt the German strategic position, and the recent Western Allied breakthrough in Slovenia compounded the problem.

Bucharest and the Ploesti oilfields were gone, Bulgaria had surrendered the minute Soviet troops entered their country, and the Russians even occupied the Hungarian capital, Budapest. The attack's goal was to give the 500 000 or so men time to extricate themselves from the Balkans and other positions that would soon be cut off from Germany proper. So Walder and his men didn't know how long they would fight for and what city they needed to take, but they understood the odds. The longer they held and pushed back the Russian attacks, the more time they gave their beleaguered compatriots to escape and fight another day.

Bled Castle
141st Regiment (Lone Star Division), Slovenia, January 13th, 1947

As he was about to round the corner, a burst of machine-gun splattered the wall in front of him, making him stop dead in his track. An American soldier then fell backward, appearing in his view. The man fell to the floor with a heavy thud. The unfortunate G.I. had rounded the corner before Jack, and he received a ton of bullets in the chest and face.

Germans soldiers waited in the castle corridor that gave on the exterior courtyard they'd been trying to reach for the better part of the last four hours. The division had come up to a small town called Bled, in Slovenia, about halfway between Italy and Ljubljana, the Slovenian capital. In the last few weeks, they fought their way thru the defensive line hastily set up by the Germans, but their superior numbers and better-equipped forces had won the day in a couple of weeks. The battle had been hard, but it was a far cry from the Gustav Line a few months back. Then They'd broken thru in the Mount Falcone area (another Axis defensive line between Italy and Slovenia), which was by the sea. Several big battleships had also helped them with their big guns and bombarded the Axis positions to oblivion.

Since then, they had been advancing in Slovenia, trying to penetrate as deep as possible toward the Soviet forces battling it out with the Germans in Hungary and Central Europe. The Allied goal was to link up and thus seal the fate of over half a million Wehrmacht soldiers trying to retreat northward toward the Reich.

But while it was a nice wish, it was no easy feat. The enemy did not give up one inch of ground without a fight. Everywhere they advanced, the Nazis awaited them in some sort of ambush, minefields, or fortified position like this one.

The castle of Bled overlooked a tall rockface that towered over the town and a superb-looking lake. It was a great natural defensive position. With the added walls of the castle, it had, of course, been occupied by the damned Germans. The number of men they had bunched up inside was unknown. So, the artillery and the flyboys had shelled the place for a day or so to flatten it, but not much had been achieved in the end. The construction was well built and embedded into the rock itself. So, the Lone Star Division commander had been ordered to launch his men at it and storm the place.

So, Jack and his men climbed the steep slope that gave to the castle's main gate. There they'd fought a small group of enemy soldiers, nested in several machine-gun nests and hastily-made earthen bunkers. The firefight lasted for half an hour, and Jack had ended up calling the Lone Star supporting Sherman unit to storm the position since he'd determined that they didn't have any heavy ordinance.

After the tanks helped them take the entrance, they couldn't advance any further, the slope giving way to the steep walls and the area's rockface, so they continued their advance without the armored machines. They fought again for the inner gate, sending grenades and bazooka rounds at it and had charged.

And then, after that, the Germans had retreated within the castle tunnels. It was a difficult battle. Reminiscent of the Cassino ruins and bitter struggle for supremacy over the Gustav Line.

"Turnbull!" yelled Summers. Turnbull ran up to him (he'd been busy peppering the enemy toward another direction). "Anyone of your men still got grenades?" asked the sergeant. They were using the thing like they were snowballs, but contrary to a snow fight didn't have an infinite number they could carry at any given time. The battle was so tricky, and the tunnels were so packed with enemies and ambushes that they had no other choice. "I've got one myself, Sarge," said Turnbull, giving his superior a large smile. He gave it to

Summers. The sergeant removed the pin and threw it down the corridor.

Counting to three, he then yelled the order to charge thru. At the same moment, a loud, muffled sound was heard. The grenade exploded, showering the passage with splintering rock and smoke.

Jack stepped over the dead American soldier that had taken the bullets in his place and rushed the other side of the corridor, not before sending a couple of machine-gun bursts toward what he supposed were the awaiting Germans. The bullets ricocheted on the rocky walls, showering the area with sparks and dust. Arriving at the other corner of the corridor, Jack was pleased to see that the enemies (two German paratroopers) were lying in a pool of blood and gore. The grenade's explosion had badly mangled them.

He heard running footsteps further down and, in an instant, decided to follow. "Quick, boys!" he said, gesturing with his arm. His men ran after the enemy. Their group eventually arrived at the end of the medieval tunnel that gave to the inner courtyard. Apart from the four kaki-clothed paratroopers he could see entering the main building at the other end (there was no time to shoot at them), there didn't seem to be any enemies on the other side entrance since no one was shooting at them.

"Damned German Paratroopers," Jack said, sending a burst of his machine gun for good measure even if he didn't have any chance of hitting the soldiers that had already entered the building. The so-called "Fallshirmjagers" fought like demons ever since the 141st started exchanging fire with them on the Gustav Line. The American soldiers didn't hate them; they respected them immensely. But at the same time, they longed to be done with them since they were pretty good at killing G.I.s.

The courtyard was a broken piece of mangled stone and dirt. The bombings had seriously damaged it, and it seemed like half of the former floor had slipped away into the ravine on the lakeside. Bled castle indeed towered above the lake of the same name and gave a breathtaking view of the surrounding countryside.

Summers gestured for several of his men to fan out in every direction. Some went toward the final inner building where the German paratroopers had fled (it had probably been the noble's castle at one point in medieval times), and the rest toward the exterior walls and what seemed to have been small service buildings.

"Turnbull, Evers, Destasio," Jack pointed toward the men he named. "You're coming with me. We'll root out the Germans from that building. Get ten men each for the assault and join me back here in five minutes." The soldiers obeyed and went back into the tunnels to get more soldiers and fulfill their sergeant's orders.

Jack settled in a small hole between two demolished stones and waited for the men to come back with a couple more squads. It was going to be a long day.

American Command
Tokyo HQ January 15th, 1947

General Douglas Macarthur, commander in chief of all American forces in Asia and also temporary Governor of Japan for the military occupation, looked at the latest reports from the Manchurian offensive. The Soviet attack was in full swing against the Japanese forces and advanced like a hot knife thru butter.

There were even strong indications that the Russian forces had already entered the Korean Peninsula. Douglas was a fighting general and did not shy away from the new challenge that suddenly sprang up from the eastern reaches of the Soviet Empire.

It wasn't like he hadn't been challenged and won in the last few years. The Japanese Empire had given the U.S. a good run for its money. Macarthur had been sorely defeated in the Philippines and evacuated to Australia to rebuild Allied forces and launch a new offensive to liberate the Pacific.

He'd already had some correspondence with the President on the matter and advocated that America should take its distance from Communism, especially the USSR. He also proposed that the country needed to intervene in China to make sure the Nationalist Chinese, under General Chiang Kai Shek, would come out on top in the developing civil war against the Communist-led by Mao Zedong.

But he'd been overruled by Truman. The old and innovative war leader had an annoying tendency to be right about things, but people usually ignored him until it was too late. He'd warned the U.S. about their disarmament programs in the 1930s. They did not listen. He'd warned the U.S. about the coming storm in the Pacific. They did not listen. But when war came, they needed him. They finally did listen, and he delivered them a victory along with Admiral Chester Nimitz.

As he read the report and the bad news accumulated within it, he tried to imagine what the map would look like in a month from now. Stalin seemed to intend to take all of Manchuria and the Korean Peninsula. Hell, if the U.S. Navy wasn't careful, he could even try to take the Kuriles Islands for all he knew.

His first reaction as a military man was to send another message to ask for instruction from the President. But then again, he was the head of the occupation force and the overseer of the Japanese Empire's disarmament. He'd been given full powers to bring Japan back into the fold of free and democratic nations. The first and foremost order of business in his instructions from Truman was to secure the Asian theater and bring back peace and security.

The way he saw it, the damned Soviets weren't helping at all, and their offensive would destabilize the whole region, help Mao's Communists, and force the Japanese to take up arms again. There were already reports of the Kwantung Army commander in chief, General Yamada, issuing orders for all Japanese forces within mainland China and Manchuria to rally to his banner to fight the invaders. This was not good. Not good at all; the man was acting completely without orders from Tokyo or from him. And he could understand why. He couldn't let his Japanese General die without doing anything about it. The Japs were his surrendered nation. It had not surrendered to the Russians.

"Richard," said Macarthur, readjusting his pipe that he had in his mouth at all times. "Yes, General." An officer walked a few paces to appear in front of Douglas. The Americans were in the old Imperial Headquarters, now an American realm. Already, hundreds of Allied staff officers roamed the old Japanese palace. All Imperial officers had been either imprisoned (the ones that were suspected of war crimes) or sent back home. They'd only kept the ones that could be useful in helping them repatriate the overseas troops or make sure they would disarm properly.

"Send for Admiral Nimitz; we need to talk him and me. Also, make up the necessary paperwork to immediately transit the 1st, 2nd, and 3rd Marine Divisions to Korea. I want these men in Pusan as soon as possible. Get me General Rupertus (the 1st Marine Division's commander)." He seemed done, but Sutherland didn't move. He knew his man and expected more. "Ah and Richard, get me some kind of line with that Yamada fellow. If not possible to talk to him by radio, find an officer here or in our military prisons that I can talk with in Tokyo. " Yes, General." MacArthur continued: "We need to send some help to the poor bastard."

"Sir." And at that, Lieutenant General Richard Kerens Sutherland, Macarthur Chief of Staff since his arrival in Australia in 1942, left the room after his military salute. He has his orders and wouldn't question any of them.

Such was the General's men's devotion. They would all follow him thru hell. And the way it looked, he was sending them toward that since putting American troops on the ground in Korea was a perilous proposition, and it wasn't like it was under any type of presidential approval.

What if the Soviets decided they didn't like it? Macarthur was beyond caring about Stalin's sensibilities, and he was tired that no one listened to him in Washington.

Extracts from Von Manstein's 1958 book, LOST VICTORY
The worsening situation in January 1947.

As mentioned earlier in my book, the Alp Line was not the strongest defensive position I organized during the war. Well, that statement is only partially true. It was sufficient in the Dolomites, southern Austria, and the northern Alps.

There the Allies did not make one inch of territorial gains from December 1946 to mid-January 1947. The problem was more related to the portion that was supposed to defend the former border between Italy and Yugoslavia or, more specifically, access to the province of Slovenia.

There we didn't have the towering Austrian Mountains or the old World War One defensive positions built by our fathers. It used to be Austro-Hungarian territory before 1918, so not much fighting was ever done there during WW1. We had low hills, some higher elevations (but nothing incredible), and not enough troops to man such an intricate area. With, say, a couple of additional infantry corps, I would have been able to mount a decent defense of the place.

But Alas, in 1947, the Third Reich was scrambling for troops. Thanks to horrible strategic decisions by our Fuhrer and the OKW, we had hundreds of thousands of men stranded (or in danger of being stranded) in the Balkans and the Middle East regions. Even if warned that this would happen, Goering still clung, during the last six months of 1946, to the pipe dream of somehow redressing the situation. The sensible move should have been to completely evacuate Turkey and the Balkans when the Dnieper Line was broken. But the decision was too drastic for our Fuhrer to take, so he did nothing.

By the time it would have been opportune to send reinforcements to the Alp Line an d try to hold it with superior forces like I had been able to do with the Gustav, it was not possible to do so, for lack of troops. The situation got desperate in the Balkans proper, with the Romanian treachery, the Bulgarian surrender, and the mighty Soviets armies pushing hard toward Hungary. A counter-offensive was well executed by Heinz Guderian's Army Group Center in Debrecen, Hungary, in December '46, which ended in a pretty reasonable success. But with the size of the forces arrayed against the German Ostfront army, it was only a momentary reprieve.

So the forces that should have been available to defend the Italo-Slovenian were instead sent to Hungary to block the advancing Russians. The main objective was to give enough time for the 500 000 or so Axis soldiers trying to extricate themselves from the Balkans to rejoin the main defensive line in Austria and Germany proper. These men came from Yugoslavia, Greece, and our so-called allies (Romania and Bulgaria). Even more came from Rommel's command in the Middle East, where an airbridge had been organized to ferry as many men and equipment as possible before it was too late. It was, however, certain that over a quarter of a million able Axis soldiers would be left stranded in Anatolia once the Soviets completed their drive to the Bosphorus Straits. There just wasn't enough time to have a chance to get them back before it was too late.

Many more had already been lost, being cut off, destroyed, or simply encircled by the advancing Allies. So the American-British breakthrough in Slovenia was due to all these factors simultaneously. It would have been great to hold the line and send the necessary assets to make it work, but what would have been the use of that if it entailed letting the Russians cut off so many troops and anyway arrive at our rear thru Hungary?

And thus were the conditions by which me and Heinz Guderian, the commander-in-chief of the Eastern Front forces, came to meet in secret on January 18th in Vienna, Austria.

The time was not for half-measures, and also, one could see that the war was over and that Germany would lose. Prolonged fighting only killed more people, with a similar end result. While there were still those in Germany clinging to the hope of getting some negotiations together with the Allies, I was not part of them. But I must admit that I was greatly intrigued by the electrifying news of the Soviet offensive in Manchuria. This meant a significant rift between the Soviet Union and its allies in the West since Japan had already surrendered, so the Russian offensive could only be seen in London and Washington as a blatant land grab.

Hence why, upon his urging, I agreed to see Guderian in Vienna. The meeting was held in the old Palace of the Hofburg, the former principal imperial residence of the Habsburg dynasty. We both flew with false names and were only flanked by one bodyguard each. We left our respective commands for only 15 hours.

There we talked for a while about the worsening situation on all fronts and what should be done about the future conduct of the war. As leading generals, we both felt we were obligated to Germany and not the Nazi leadership. While a lot of our discussion was about several operational aspects of the battle underway to save the Balkan forces, we also discussed what should be done if the government continued its stubborn stance in the face of the Allied nuclear power.

Of course, Goering and the Nazi leaders would not surrender. They first had too much to lose, but second, they probably did not want the Allies to discover their crimes and corruption. So if it were up to them, they would fight on to the end.

For us professionals, it was more about the survival of Germany and the safeguarding of our men. Nothing was decided nor discussed in specific details about what we would do, but we both agreed that we were of the same mind. We would not let Germany sink into the dustbin of history for the sake of the Nazi leaders and their crimes.

Little did we know that we were about to be handed out an opportunity to change things, if not for the better, at least to avoid the worst. In short, fate had not yet abandoned Germany.

In between two battles
Galileo Galilei Airport, *Pisa, Italy January 16th, 1947*

He hit the ball so hard in the right-center field that it crossed the distance in no time. Looking at it for a fleeting second, he knew that the ball would land in fair territory, and he was in at least for a double.

The scene was in Pisa, in Italy (Tuscany province). The venue was a friendly baseball game between Americans and a few Canadians. Every Sunday, they played like that, had some downtime, and smacked a few beers. Well, at least the U.S. airmen did, for the other Allied nations had no such luxury in the war.

The United States' prodigious capability to supply its troops with ammunition and supplies also rang true in terms of food supplies and other commodities. So the G.Is could have some comfort food like beer, natural beef, or even chocolate bars.

Lamirande understood the game of baseball. In fact, he was one of the pioneers in his hometown for the game. It was an American sport, but many in Canada had picked it up, Gaston being one of them. When he was young, he even convinced the factory boss in Isle-Maligne to build a baseball field so they could play.

Not many non-Americans could play in the traditional Sunday baseball game. Only the ones that were good enough. Because there were several professional players in the US Air Force, many were located in Italy. So you were included only if you were good enough. And Gaston was. He was even one of the "star players" on his team.

He'd even discussed with one of the officers, who was a coach for the Brooklyn Dodgers back stateside, about a professional tryout when the war was over.

Lamirande liked the game all right, but he was coming every Sunday to play because there was real food to be had. Instead of the dreadful SPAM canned beef and other not-so-tasty British commodities, he would be one of the boys and get real steaks and beers. While he enjoyed them every time, he also brought some back to the British side of the airfield after the contest and evenings were over. It was a nice setup for him.

As he ran hard toward second base, the centerfielder threw the ball at the shortstop to try and get him out. Lamirande slid under the other player's glove. "Safe!" yelled the referee (another pilot that acted as the on-base referee for the game). He stood up, and several of his teammates applauded him. He was 4 for 4 in the game, with several RBI's.

The game lasted for about half an hour more, and Lamirande's team won. They all got together after the game, and he got his excellent food, putting some more and leftovers in the large backpack he'd brought to get some to the boys later that evening. He first stopped at the mechanic's barracks, as these guys were the ones taking care of his plane and deserved some good stuff. It also didn't hurt that they loved Gaston for it and consequently worked hard to make sure his plane was always in perfect working order. Then he went directly to his commanding officer, who distributed the rest to the men.

After a good night's sleep the following day, his Gloster Meteor took off from the Pisa runway and rapidly took up altitude. Their mission that day was to escort several squadrons of Hawker Typhoons, the British ground-attack planes. Their objective was the Slovenian city of Ljubljana, where the Third Reich entertained a large concentration of troops to block the advancing Allies on both sides. It was fast becoming one of the last places that the retreating German forces stuck in the Balkans could use to filter back toward the Reich. Some room was still available in Hungary proper as well, as a powerful German counter-attack was underway. Nevertheless, the Allies needed to block everything, and the lead elements of Allied forces (a unit called the Lone Star Division) were in Bled, about a day away. He hoped that it would be again an easy mission.

As of late, the Luftwaffe had been a lot less noticeable in the skies above the German forces. It was a tell-tale sign that things were not going too well for the Third Reich; it was a welcome change for Allied flyers like Lamirande. It meant that their missions were less risky and that their lives would not necessarily be in jeopardy every time they went up in the sky and over enemy territory.

For a moment, he wondered where his rival was. He had not seen the skulls and crossbones plane for weeks on end and wondered if he'd been shot down or transferred to another front.

Getting everything ready
Kehlstein *Mountain, Southern Germany, January 14th, 1947*

The SC 1000 (Sprengbombe Cylindrisch 1000) was a giant air-dropped general-purpose thin-cased high explosive demolition bomb used by Germany during World War II. Weighing more than 1,000 kg, the Germans nicknamed it the Hermann in reference to the portly Luftwaffe commander.

The bomb had a body of drawn steel to which a heavy pointed nose cone was welded. At the other end was a base plate, just forward of which the magnesium alloy tail was tack welded onto the body and bolted to the tail attachment brace.

A metal ring around the bomb's nose, triangular in cross-section, was designed to prevent ground penetration or stop forward momentum when hitting water. The bomb was intended to be attached to an aircraft horizontally by a suspension lug.

In this case, it wouldn't be dropped from any German planes. Nor would it fly at any given point. The device had been chosen for its size (so it could house the necessary uranium and machinery going along with it) and because it could also be used with a Type 17 mechanical clockwork time fuse. It was a time-delayed fuse able to be set from between 3 and 195 minutes. While it had been part of the original weapon's design, it had never really been used by the Luftwaffe, that sort of needed its bomb to explode on impact when they sent it at the enemies of the Reich.

As he looked at the scientists clothed in protective gear play with the refined uranium and work on the inner parts of the modified SC 1000 bomb, Skorzeny thought that his latest daredevil operation had a reasonable chance of success. After the meeting with the Fuhrer back in December, following the dreadful news of the Allies' nuclear bombing of Wilhelmshaven, he'd been hard at work to find a way to deliver a working bomb on the enemies of the Reich. He'd taken on the project with his usual enthusiasm. He first consulted with Heisenberg, the lead German nuclear scientist. The man had told him that the bomb they could detonate was not as powerful as the one dropped by the Allies on the German North Sea coast city, but it would be close enough if used well. The next part of the problem of exploding it on their enemies was that the German scientists had not net finalized or worked really hard on a delivery system for the device.

Only a manual detonation was possible at this point, so the Wehrmacht and Luftwaffe could not envision any possibility of sending an airstrike like the Americans and dropping a nuclear bomb on the enemy's heads.

But Otto was not about to be discouraged by tiny unimportant details. He'd visited the Luftwaffe arsenals near Berlin and found the perfect device for his daring plan, the SC 1000 bomb, the biggest bomb that the Reich had. Since the scientists had not been able to work on getting anything to a decent size(miniaturization), he'd needed to find a bomb big enough to house the weapons components. Also, the timer fuse was a blessing since it meant that he could activate the bomb and leave before he was vaporized by the blast, a welcome possibility, in his opinion.

"Herr Skorzeny," said Heisenberg, that stood beside the SS commando. "The bomb will be ready within the week." The modified Hanomag armored carrier (Sd.Kfz. 251) is also ready to house the bomb." The scientist shook his head in bewilderment. "I am still wondering how you are going to pull this off." Skorzeny turned his head to look at the man and smiled, his scar-laden face showing in its full glory. "You worry about making the bomb, Herr Heisenberg, and I'll worry about exploding it in our enemy's ass."

CHAPTER 1

White House
Washington D.C., January 15th, 1947

"Well," said President Truman, dropping the telegram from his hands. "This sort of had to be expected, I suppose..." he added, moving back in his chair to press his back against it.

Present at the meeting in the Oval Office was General Marshall, along with Cordell Hull, the Secretary of State, and Admiral King, commander-in-chief of the Navy. The time was early morning in Washington, and it was around that time that the four men held a bi-weekly meeting on the general conduct of the war in military and diplomatic terms.

The President had received the telegram some time ago, for the difference between the Eastern Time zone and the Japanese one was 9 hours. So the message announcing MacArthur's orders to send American troops on the ground in Korea arrived the same day that the Oval Office meeting was being held (on January 15th). At first, Truman had not been pleased, for he was woken up in the middle of the night by Hull himself that had called him in great urgency. He hadn't slept much after that, but instead put a lot of thoughts into the matter. He'd paced back and forth for the whole night, trying to get a sense of unraveling events. So MacArthur had not waited for instructions or orders to send troops to Korea and confront the Soviet forces that were sure to come down south after they defeated the weakened Kwantung Army. Truman did not know what it meant or if he was comfortable with the fiery General's move, but one thing was certain. He was not against it. He'd always been skeptical of the Russian Alliance and had never fully trusted the dictator leading the USSR, Joseph Stalin. The man was a butcher, and the President suspected that he was not in the good guy's camp.

The Soviets had blatantly attacked the Japanese in Manchuria on January 12th, and their offensive was still in full swing. The whole affair was a serious problem because the Japs had already surrendered, so there was no need to attack them unless another motive other than the end of the war was at play.

On the morning of the attack, he'd immediately sent for the Russian ambassador to the USA, Andrei Andreyevich Gromyko. The man came rapidly enough a few hours later.

But what he'd had to say about the whole affair was not encouraging. He only had a pre-prepared answer to give the U.S. leader on some bullshit story about Japanese provocations and that the Kwantung Army was not surrendering. On Russian historical rights to the area. On the border clashes in 1939 and 1938 and the fact that a state of war existed between the two countries for a long while. And, most importantly, the matter of the USSR not being included in the peace talks with the Japanese Empire. Of course, they weren't included in the peace deal! They had not been part of the whole war against Japan. They had not helped the American struggle for the liberation of the Pacific. Not even a little.

"Mr. President," started Hull. "If we let MacArthur send troops to Korea, this might mean war with the Russians. The risk of a clash between the two forces is high, especially since Douglas is not what you could call a peacemaker...." The Secretary of State let his words hang in the air for a moment. Truman didn't say a word, wanting Hull to continue to speak. "Need I remember everyone around this room that the war is NOT over with the Third Reich, our main enemy in this war?" Hull looked around the room as he found no support for his words. Not from Truman, not from the fiery King or Marshall either. The President had never been known to be a Communist lover, and the other two were military men and understood only one thing. "What would you have us do, Cordell?"

intervened King. "Bend over and ask for more?.... This is a blatant act of war against us. There is no mistaking the signs. The Soviets are already making a play for the World after the war and are positioning themselves accordingly...." Truman didn't say a word again but couldn't agree more. Marshall just nodded his agreement to the Admiral's statement.

"I understand what you mean, Admiral. But this isn't a simple matter. The USSR is our ally, and we simply cannot afford to make the situation worse by letting MacArthur play hardball diplomacy."

Having already made up his mind on the whole matter, Harry Truman had had enough of the developing argument. "Cordell, I understand what you say, but there is also a need to show Russia that we aren't pushovers. But we are going to have to take some sort of risk here to show Stalin that we mean business." He hit his desk hard with his fist. "By God, we haven't fought this war to remove a dictator and have it replaced by another one. I told Roosevelt it was not the greatest of ideas to get too cozy with the Reds." Truman stopped for a moment, hesitating. His mind wandered a little the implication of the decision he was about to take.

"You know what? I am of the mind to show this Communist that America doesn't back down from a challenge." Truman said in a convincing voice. He'd made his decision. "General Marshall, please confirm to General MacArthur that we fully support his decision. He is to advance as fast as possible thru the Korean Peninsula to occupy as much territory as possible and face the Red Army as soon as possible." Cordell Hull was speechless. "But...." Added Hull. Truman continued unfazed: "He has no authorization to attack the Russians. You need to make it clear to him that I will remove him from command if he is the first to fire a shot." "Yes, Mr. President," answered Marshall, evidently happy with what Truman had just ordered him. "Admiral King, please show our Soviet friends some naval muscles. I want the Yellow Sea, the Northern Japanese Islands, and the Korean coast to be patrolled heavily. Make certain they see that we are serious about this." He then turned toward the Secretary of State, who remained unhappy about the decision but fumed silently. "Cordell, I need you to accept the decision and also to send a note to this Gromyko ambassador that America will defend the ground we occupy, and the Russians are not permitted to advance further than what they conquer by force of arms. And convey to them that we do not support nor approve of their attack on Japanese Manchuria."

He gestured for the three men to leave. "The meeting is over." The group started going when Truman talked again. "Cordell, can you stay a moment, please?"

And the President talked some more about him wanting to organize a summit with the United Kingdom as soon as possible. The Western Allies needed to make a concerted effort in Europe as well, for if Stalin was known as a butcher, he was also known as a great strategist. The Manchurian offensive was only the opening move in something that Truman suspected was a grander design.

Stalin's bluff
Office of the USSR's General Secretary, January 17th

The small office of the General Secretary held a pretty select meeting comprised of five people. First and foremost, Stalin then Marshal Zhukov, the Red Army's commander in chief. Also present was Malenkov, one of the top officials in the Russian state. Also present was Nikita Sergeyevich Khrushchev, another one of the main Soviet officials. The last man in the room was the USSR's Foreign Minister, Vyacheslav Molotov.

The men had gathered in the partially rebuilt Kremlin, made almost as a replica of the former, completely destroyed building. They all marveled at the intricate details that had been put in making Stalin's office that was practically identical to the old one.

It was the middle of the day, and the mood was festive amongst them. The Manchurian offensive was in full swing, and nothing seemed to be able to stop the red tide from sweeping the Japanese territories. The major city of Harbin was already in Russian hands, and it looked like the rest of the Imperial forces were in a state of disintegration. No wonder, since they'd already surrendered, and the last thing they expected was to be attacked again.

In Europe, events were also finally unfolding in the Soviet Union's favor after many deaths and sacrifices. The Reich was buckling under the pressure, and victory was near. While the final outcome of who would win between Axis and Allies was already pretty obvious, this didn't seem to be the end of it for Stalin and his dream of "World Revolution" or, more simply said his lust for conquest and power.

The dictator was now as busy vanquishing the hated Nazis as he was about the plotting and planning for the territory he would control once the last bullet was fired.

So under the happy façade that reigned in the room that day, everyone was a little wary of what they were doing. Well, everyone except Stalin, the whole mastermind of the affair. Their moves were going entirely against their alliance with the USA and the United Kingdom. It was not clear where this would lead.

But then again, not one of them, and probably not even one person in the whole Soviet state, was crazy enough to challenge so momentous a decision by their leader. The man was known for not really appreciating diverging opinions.

"Great Stalin," started Zhukov, with his usual brash approach. "The troops are doing quite well on all fronts. We think we will be done clearing out Manchuria and Korea within a month." "Good, Marshal. Good," said Stalin, taking in some of his tobacco from his pipe he always had in his mouth during meetings.

"What of the other plans we have discussed?" said Stalin, now looking at Khrushchev. "The device is in working order, great Stalin. We have made all the necessary analysis and, of course, retrieved it from the American bomber and are now ready to use it for our own purposes." The men in the room had had some more discussions earlier on what they were planning and what the American reaction would be. It was anticipated that they would use their newfound power (the nuclear weapon) if Russia decided to do anything other than finishing the war and go back home. But after the U.S. bold call for the Reich to surrender or else another city would be destroyed, they had not followed up on it, and the only explanation was that they were out of bombs. Some limited form of supply and production was at play here, and the Soviets had been lucky enough for the last American bomb to land in their lap.

Before that event, Stalin had had thoughts of making an ending to the war as advantageous as possible for the Russians but had been wary of the Western Allies and their new weapon. But after he providentially received a free one for his use, an idea had started to take shape in his mind.

What if the Russians exploded their atomic bomb against Germany? If used properly, this would shorten the war against the Hitlerites (against a large army group concentration, for example) and also have another interesting effect.

Stalin was to fake that he had the atomic bomb as well. Once exploded, they would announce to the world that they also had several more in reserve. The whole thing should make the Americans ponder and wonder if they indeed had them. The dictator was confident it would make them blink and let him do whatever he wanted in Europe and elsewhere.

Indeed. Stalin was about to try one of the biggest bluffs in history.

Wolfchanzze
Masurian Woods, January 19th, 1947

Whatever were the Grand Alliance's problems and Stalin's plans, the war they were fighting (not the one they were planning for or trying to avoid) was far from over. Indeed, a man and his sycophants in Berlin had no intention of whimpering away from the epic fight that was still being fought everywhere in Europe.

The Third Reich still entertained millions of soldiers. They were well-armed and well-supplied. The Germans had towered over large swaths of lands for years and, as such, had accumulated a lot of resources and power. They had oil in significant quantities in their secret bases in Austria and Southern Germany. The Wehrmacht possessed more machines of war than men to use them. Germany indeed started to run a little dry on manpower, but things were looking up in a weird twist. As Nazi forces retreated and lost territory, they withdrew to a smaller area to defend themselves and got closer to their primary supply sources in Germany.

The Reich suffered several disasters in 1946, chiefly the final defeat (or more like what could be called a strategic withdrawal) in Russia and the potential loss of half a million men in the Balkans. Another quarter of a million was already lost if not surrendered in Turkey and the Middle East. The Italian surrender and occupation of its territory up to the Alps. France was attacked and penetrated on all sides by the Western Allies. The Romanian/Bulgarian betrayal had also hurt the German position, outflanking a whole frontline and the Balkan defense plan.

It started to look like the Axis forces would compress into a wide semi-circle around Germany, Austria, and parts of Bohemia, Moravia, and Poland.

Another meeting was being held at the Masurian Wood's bunker H.Q. of the German Armed Forces. The men gathered in the stale, reinforced concrete bunker were not meeting to talk about successes and victories.

The last two months had been difficult on the Reich, and the leaders in the room on that cold Eastern Prussia day of January showed it. First and foremost, Hermann Goering, the leader of Germany, looked worn, tired. His usually immaculate white uniform was wrinkled and dirty, showing signs of having been on him for the whole evening – and night following it. The Fuhrer was not what you could call in one of his good spells and been in that mood since the news of the November and December disasters in Romania and Africa the year before. He'd shown some of his old spine again after the dreadful news of the nuclear attack on Wilhelmshaven at the beginning of December, but in these early days of 1947, he could be either one of two: the German leaders of the Buffoon he could be. His health also seemed to be degrading by the day, for some reason, but probably because the man had lived a life of too-much-of everything.

Also present around the large table was General Frantz Halder, the commander-in-chief of the Wehrmacht(OKW). The man retained all his outward composure and seemed as sharp as ever, but most knew that he was out of options in terms of solutions. The Germans were done fishing out magic tricks from their sempiternal bag of acrobatics and tactical prowess.

General Von Leeb, again just back from an inspection on the French theater, appeared tired (no wonder he'd just traveled for ten straight hours). He'd reported continued retreats for the German forces that reeled back before the Western Allied powerful armies.

General Von Paulus, for his part, was also back from an inspection tour in Hungary, where the Lake Balaton offensive was in full swing. Things there seemed to be looking up, with Guderian's forces dashing thru enemy lines. Paulus even believed that the German troops would retake Budapest within the week.

Albert Speer, the Minister of Armament and production, was also there. The industrial mogul was his usual calm self, sitting quietly on the table, with one hand laid nonchalantly on what was Turkey on the map. He seemed bored.

"So, General Halder," started Goering, in a coarse voice (the night seemed to have been eventful for him). "Talk to me about the Balaton offensive." "Yes, Mein Fuhrer," answered the commander-in-chief. "Guderian's forces are well into their 9th day of the attack and are advancing steadily toward the Hungarian capital. Me and General Paulus," he gestured with a quick look toward the man in question, "believe that the forces should be able to get to Budapest with little difficulty, now that they've broken thru the frontline Russian units. We even have to report that the 7th guard tank army has been destroyed as a fighting unit by our brave forces." "Good good," said the Fuhrer, seemingly satisfied.

Since he didn't add anything else (there were much more happening than that needing attention), Albert Speer, worried about his Austrian, Polish, and Bohemia-Moravia factories, intervened. "General. What are your thoughts on the follow-up to the Lake Balaton offensive? I hope we are not planning to evacuate beyond the line I have discussed with you and your staff?" The Minister had indeed drawn a line on the map with Halder regarding how far he could retreat without dangerously undermining the Reich's capability to produce weapons and supply its troops with the necessary supplies. Germany had stockpiled a lot of stuff while it towered over the gigantic empire it conquered, but there could only be so much done with it while the armed forces fought intensively on every front.

"Minister Speer, rest assured that the Wehrmacht will do its utmost to hold the line where we said we would. If we can succeed with extricating the number of soldiers from the retreating Balkans and Turkish forces, I believe that we will be able to operate a strong defensive line and keep the enemy at bay for an indefinite period of time. "Good," answered Albert, seemingly satisfied with the answer. He was neither an expert in military matters nor interested in them, but the production aspects needed to be defended, so he was happy with Halder's answer.

The General then continued. "Speaking of the retreating troops, we have already been able to get the 64th corps out of the Hungarian plain with the last push west of Budapest. Once we take the city and hold it, we'll be able to trickle thru at least 20 000 men a day, perhaps more." "What of the Americano-British offensive coming in from Slovenia?" asked Goering, again interested in the discussion. "Very good question, Mein Fuhrer. This is the tricky part. We expect that the Balaton offensive will also have to split its forces after storming Budapest and send several strong elements toward the American 12th Corps that should be near or beyond Ljubljana by then." Before everyone could ask more questions about his claim, Halder held up his hand to stop them from doing so since he wasn't finished talking. "Obviously, this raises the matter of our capability to do so. In this, I can assure you that Guderian has all the necessary firepower to attack in two directions. Need I remind you that most of Army Group Center and several other units from the Baltic States recently evacuated have been concentrated in a narrow space, comparatively speaking with the Russian immensity," said Halder adding a smile. It was a fact that German forces, which had been covering a lot of land while in Russia and a frontline several thousand miles wide, were now defending a very tiny fraction of land compared to even six months earlier.

The Lake Balaton offensive had been launched with 450 000 men. Experienced troops, fully mechanized, and boasting over 2000 powerful tanks. "And don't forget that we don't send the forces retreating from the Balkans on vacation when they join the main body in the Hungarian plains. We rearm them or make sure they have what they need and send them right back to the front. Just yesterday, the total number of men of the Balaton offensive is now close to 600 000 men." Halder hit the table with his fist in clear enthusiasm. For once, in this godforsaken conflict, we have more troops attacking than the Russians have trying to defend against them. They will unavoidably send reinforcements, as we all know, but for the moment, we can continue to attack and take on the Western Allies as well. In two weeks, things will be different, but now is the time if we want to save the half a million soldiers still in danger of being trapped."

Everyone assembled in the room seemed to be entirely happy with this news. "French Front, Von Leeb?" now asked Goering directly to the General. "Mein Fuhrer, General Rundstedt has the situation well in hand. While we have suffered several setbacks since the British landings and the French offensive from the south, we have been able to process a fighting retreat up the French territory. Our forces are now concentrated in Alsace Lorraine, the Vosges Mountains, and thru half of the Netherlands. The General thinks he will be able to stop the enemy cold within a week or two when they advance to his main line of defense."

Again, good news of a sort, so everyone seemed okay with it. Goering even grunted in approval. Halder, however, had some less-savory subjects to talk about. "The Middle East is now lost; Rommel's forces have completed their retreat to the Turkish border mountains (Taurus Range). The rest of our forces have also retired to the Armenian Highlands and entered the prepared defensive positions east and west of Lake Van. The situation, as we all know, is not ideal. Still, Rommel was forced to retreat as fast as possible and not defend on the Suez as originally planned because of the Russo-British offensive coming from Persia and the Iraqi plains that would have outflanked him. From the moment Auchinleck pierced thru our Persian defenses, the game was up for our forces in the Middle East." "What about the Turkish government's position and the population's will to fight?" asked a worried Goering. "Everything is holding, with that. The Turkish military is concentrating its strength against the Soviets in the east. The defenses they have are quite formidable because of the mountains there. We do not think that the enemy can break thru, and besides, they aren't trying really hard."

The door in the back of the room opened, letting thru Joachim Von Ribbentrop, the Reich Foreign Minister. "Ah, Joachim!" said Goering, clearly happy about the man's entrance. Having the diplomat at any kind of strategic meeting was not usual, but in this case, it was warranted with the recent incredible news of the Soviet Manchurian offensive. "Have a seat," added Hermann. "Thank you, Mein Fuhrer," answered Ribbentrop while gesturing everyone in the meeting with a quick glance. "So, what do we know of the Russian attack in the Far East, and does it represent any kind of opportunity for us?" "Mein Fuhrer, I believe it does. My sources within the diplomatic channels I have access to talk of a growing rift between the USSR and the rest of the Grand Alliance. It seems they are already bickering over the spoils." "Well, the Reich is not dead! So they should know better," said Goering enthusiastically. The Minister continued, unfazed: "However, our overtures to the Western Allies have again encountered deaf ears. For them, nothing has changed. It's unconditional surrender or nothing. They also still threaten to drop another atomic bomb on us." "So far so good," added Halder, referring to the fact that since the December attack on the Baltic Coast, the Allies had not followed up on their threat.

"So for now, nothing different, the Allies seem unmoving on their demands, and we can only stay the course," concluded Ribbentrop. "Very well, Joachim. What can a man do but continue to fight?" said Goering, spreading his hands in a gesture meaning he was powerless in the developing situation.

And the meeting continued a little bit more on the diplomatic front but not for long since Germany was now alone in the war. Every one of its friends except turkey had either surrendered or joined the Allies.

Things then rapidly moved to other matters, like the most vital aspect of the Reich's first nuclear detonation and Skorzeny's progress on the subject. It appeared that the man was almost ready to explode the device that Heisenberg and his scientists were finalizing at Kelstein Base in Bavaria. What remained to be decided was on which enemy and where it should be used.

The Fuhrer, and almost everyone in the room except Halder, Leeb, and Paulus (for genuine strategic considerations), wanted their revenge on the Americans and wished to target the U.S. forces.

But events soon to unravel would change their mind – and the target of their bomb.

Extract Of Heinz Guderian 1952 Book, Panzer Leader
The Lake Balaton offensive and a secret meeting, January 1947

By the time the new 1947 year kicked in, the Soviets had driven deep into Hungary. After a two-week-long and bitter struggle, Army Group Center/South forces (both army groups were somewhat mixed after the southern debacle) again had to retire from the battlefield. The battle of Budapest was a costly affair for both sides, and while we again inflicted a lot more casualties than our enemies did to us, we still lost a good 124 000 men (dead or injured). As always, the damned Soviet numerical superiority played its role, and we eventually got overwhelmed.

By December 28th, I ordered a full withdrawal from the Hungarian capital. This saved my men, but at the same time, we had to abandon any chance of keeping the Hungarians into the war on our side. The Russians hastily put the new government in place. The so-called "Alliance for democracy and liberty" (nothing else than Communist puppets working for Moscow) hastily agreed on a full cease-fire with the USSR.

Unfortunately, this meant that we had to scratch several additional divisions from our order of battle. Granted, they were under-equipped and under-trained, but the Hungarian soldiers were nonetheless valuable since we were such at a disadvantage against the Russians and their innumerable hordes of men and material.

The overall situation was not great, as one could surmise by a simple look at the map and the discrepancy in numbers. Furthermore, a lot of troops were stuck in the Middle East for the duration (roughly 750 000 Axis soldiers, including German, Turkish, and other auxiliaries). But there was still one group of men that were salvageable from those.

Over 500 000 men were trying to extricate themselves from the Balkans, moving up from Yugoslavia to Hungary and ultimately to the new defenses we wanted to establish along the Austrian Mountains and the Polish plains. After our defeat in Budapest, it was clear that we would not be able to give them enough time.

So, I mounted another desperate counter-offensive, with everything left in terms of mobile forces. The Soviets, in their headlong advance, had been sloppy to a certain degree, exposing their northern flank near Lake Balaton, in the extreme western part of Hungary itself. I guessed that the Russian field commanders believed that the Lake would serve as a shield to their exposed flanks, or else maybe they thought they were finished with Hungary and that we'd given up on our beleaguered men trying to save themselves.

In any case, and for whatever reasons, the enemy advance gave me a new opportunity. Not that I could win the whole war with my move, but more or less, my goal was to slow them down significantly and force them to turn around and face the force exploding their northern flank.

With the Lake Balaton offensive, I hoped to give more time for several divisions to slip thru before it was too late and the Allies (both Russians and Western) linked up somewhere in southern Hungary, thus sealing the fate of all the brave men that would still be south by then.

The attack went quite well, both initially and with the several days afterward. In fact, it stopped the Soviet western push altogether, giving enough time for many Wehrmacht soldiers to be saved.

During a certain lull in the operational planning of the Balaton operation, I sort of "escaped" from my command to have a secret meeting with Erich Von Manstein, the Italian/Austrian theater commander, to discuss the worsening German situation. We met at the Hofburg, the former winter residence of the Austrian Habsburg dynasty. While we were not yet totally committed to any type of rebellious planning, we nonetheless discussed the very fact that the war was lost and that, as commanding Generals, the lives of our men were paramount. We both agreed to keep the communication channel open – and secret - for it would not be good for us if the Gestapo eventually found out the essence of our talks.

We both left each other on the same day, under the same secrecy, and back at our command. The time was not yet for action, but things were not looking good. If one took the time to listen to the propaganda machine, the Nazis leadership clearly said that Germany would never surrender and fight to the last bullet. Such was definitely not our intention.

The Balaton offensive
From the Lake to Budapest, January 12-25th 1947

The Lake Balaton offensive started with a bang as the Wehrmacht pushed deep into the Soviet front, eliminating several units right on the northern shore of the freshwater lake, where the attack started.

Guderian's offensive was well supplied with men and equipment. A whole army was sent forward, and the units that formed it were still in relatively good fighting shape. Since the Romania debacle in November 1946, the Germans retreated ever backward but were never really defeated or seriously weakened by Soviet advances and offensives. By the time they were back into Western Hungary, having lost most of their former ally's country and capital, a new problem arose for the German OKW.

The rapidly advancing Allies (east thru Hungary and west thru Slovenia) threatened to completely cut off the Axis troops trying to move up north and out of the Balkans. Over 500 000 men needed to get back to the Austro-German lines of defenses being built to defend the country.

So Guderian proposed and got the go-ahead from OKW to launch himself forward once again. His forces included (at the start of the offensive) 450 000 men, 2000 tanks, and total air coverage with

ME-262's and several bomber squadrons. "Army Group Balaton" was thus created and sent to the attack.

Within three days, the German forces cleared out the northern bank of the Lake, pierced thru southward, and drove hard, cutting lines of communications for the Soviet 561th Rifle Corps at the southwestern tip of the Lake. Also, a large section of the west bank of the Danube was rapidly secured south of Budapest, and the Germans then turned north and northwest, threatening to link up with other forces attacking in the north and to cut off an entire Soviet Front.

After 11 days of the offensive, Army Group Balaton, with valuable assistance from several new units that trickled into the battlefield during their retreat northward (the units coming from the Balkans), recaptured over 600 square kilometers of territory, inflicted 88,800 casualties on the Red Army and cleared seventeen infantry divisions and a Guard Mechanized Corps from west of the Gran River to Budapest, all for the loss of only 20,989 casualties.

On January 23rd, the first lead elements of the Panzer Lehr Division, which had been driving hard at the tip of the offensive since its start, rode into Budapest almost unchallenged. Some fighting was still in order as many scattered Russian units tried to resist as hard as possible, but on the 24th, the city was German again, and the Pro-Communist government fled the scene, right in the Red Army's wake.

The Russian forces were finally able to rally back to the attack on the 25th, and a titanic battle for the Hungarian capital ignited, with Army Group Balaton, now almost 700 000 men strong with the Balkan reinforcements, faced the whole Ukrainian and Voronezh Fronts, boasting a staggering 1.2 million men.

The OKW and Guderian fed everything they had available into the battle, as the longer they resisted there, the more troops they would save from the Balkans.

Also, as a follow-up operation, once Budapest was in Axis hands, Guderian sent two corps (67th Panzer and 12th Mechanized) toward Slovenia to take care of the other pincer that threatened to cut off the brave Axis forces moving north.

Budapest
Lake Balaton offensive, Panzer Lehr Division, January 24th, 1947

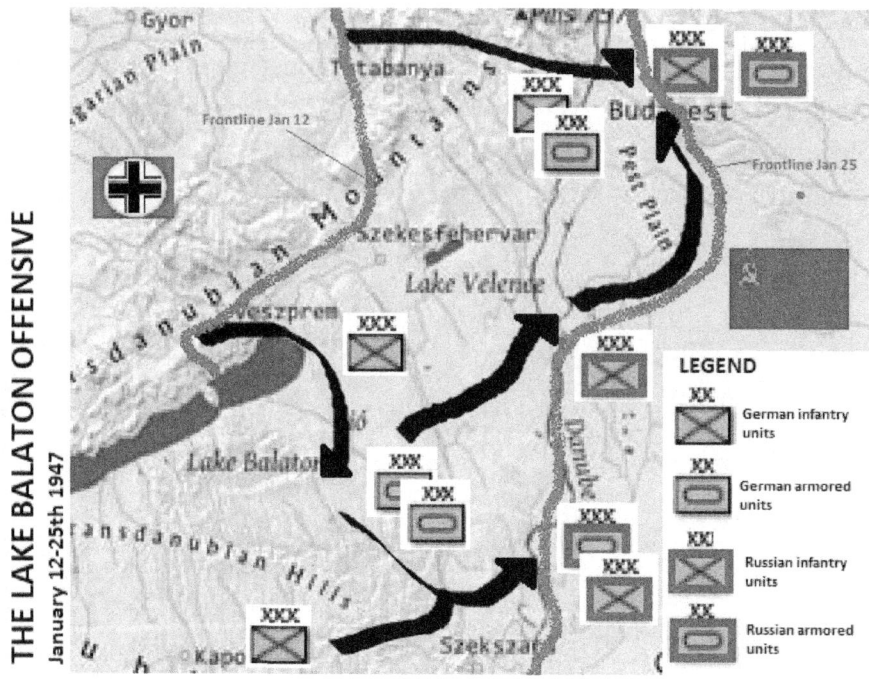

The Tiger II rumbled on the rubble-strewn street as its engine created a great echo between the still half-standing buildings. Broken pieces of constructions, resulting from the destruction wrought by the intense fighting of the last few weeks, were laid about in the tank's path, and the engine stained hard to either push the blocks or rocks away (some were big). A few minutes back, the Konigstiger had even rolled into a large crater, the result of some enormous explosion. Walder even wondered what could have created such a blast. Probably an ammunition dumb or gasoline tank or something similar. He'd seen such mayhem with his own eyes in his long years of battle experience across European battlefields that nothing surprised him anymore.

The Panzer advanced slowly since it trailed several infantry squads behind it. Several other Tigers were doing the same across the length of the ample open space they were moving thru. A persistent fog hung into the air. It wasn't a humidity-created fog but more like a dust-riddled one. No wonder, thought the tank commander, since the whole of Budapest was being leveled back to the ground by the constant fighting and bombings.

Of late, the Germans pounded it to a fine powder with their successful Lake Balaton offensive. The Panzer Lehr and several other units from the Army Group entered the Hungarian capital a day ago, but not before the Luftwaffe had executed several destructive raids at the place. Weeks before that, it had been the Wehrmacht on the receiving end of a Russian artillery barrage worth a story in itself. The Soviets had concentrated a lot of firepower to take Budapest and had done an excellent job killing German troops and demolishing the building within it.

Erich was looking thru the observation slits, and his gunner Hans was doing the same, for they were pretty nervous. Their Panzer was at the tip of the German advance within the city. While the Russians had largely vacated the place in the last day or so, several pockets of resistance stayed and ambushed them at every possible opportunity. While the small arms fire and machine-gun nests were of no consequence to the armored behemoth, a hit from a 122mm field gun could damage it badly. Walder and his tank crew had been privy to the last ambush earlier in the day, where one of the giant Russian guns barked one of its mighty shells at an unfortunate comrade, another Tiger II. The shell had hit the tank in the gun mantle and killed everyone within the machine as it burst in a towering pillar of flames. The resulting explosion had also hit several men that were using the Panzer for protection. Quite a gory spectacle.

To avoid a repeat of that disaster, Erich ordered several of the Panzer Grenadiers following the Heavy Battalion to advance ahead of the Konigstiger. These men moved slowly and, of course, not in any open way. Their job was to crawl and approach at a different angle, between the buildings, and undercover to see if Soviet ambushes lay ahead waiting for the Germans to walk right into it. These men were equipped with radios and ordered to report anything suspicious or that they spotted.

Walder almost jumped when the radio crackled to life in the tank. It was one of the recon unit reporting. "Commander. Two 122mm setup dead ahead, with several machine-gun nests with intersecting firing positions." The soldier finished with coordinates for the artillery to know where to fire or the Luftwaffe.

"Got it, thank you," Erich answered rapidly. He then immediately called an air raid over the radio and ordered the all-stop for his forces. The artillery unit supporting his advance also acknowledged the enemy's dispositions and said they would fire a couple of salvos.

A half a minute later, while the whole of Walder's group (Panzers and Grenadiers) were stopping and putting themselves in the best defensive stance possible, several loud whistling sounds were heard flying overhead. They almost sounded like alarms ringing their tunes. Such was the ignominious sound of an incoming bombardment. Fortunately for the German soldiers, it was headed further down and not on their heads for a change. The 25th SS Artillery Regiment had just fired. A few heartbeats later, loud explosions rocked the ground and soundwaves in front of the Germans. Bright flashes made the day seem even brighter, and several large plumes of dust rose in the air while more buildings crashed down.

Walder awaited news from his recon elements over the radio. "All clear, commander. Soviet positions destroyed." And then he gave the order for everyone to resume advancing toward the last part of the city that the Wehrmacht was in the process of taking back from the damned Yvan's. The plan was not to keep it forever but for long enough to give a chance to the large numbers of troops trying to move northward from the Balkans.

The tank commander sighed deeply. He loved to be in the attack, and defense had a less savory taste for him, especially when fighting the damned Soviets that always brought so many men and machines to battle that it inevitably ended in retreat. And that was precisely what he'd been ordered to do. Finish storming the city's section he'd been tasked to take, and then put his forces on the defense as a Soviet counter-attack was expected soon from the intelligence reports and also the numerous overhead flights that told of a large body of troops coming right for Budapest.

Cammel Laird Shipyards
Birkenhead, UK, near Liverpool, January 25th, 1947

Three days after the Soviet had taken the major Manchurian city of Harbin and even penetrated into the Korean Peninsula, brushing all feeble Japanese resistance before it, Truman arrived for urgent discussions with Winston Churchill, the leader of the United Kingdom.

The two men had much to talk about, and telegrams, subordinates, and the likes did not replace two heads of state talking and planning. They needed to completely re-assess the strategic – and political – situation.

The USSR had started to act on its own by the end of 1946 and was giving clear signs of jockeying for territory and power as if the war with the Axis was already over. Most of it would have been accepted by men like Truman and Churchill as the next fight to process, but only after they were done with the Third Reich. Yes, they had not liked Molotov's approach and declarations in their last conference on the matter of Eastern Europe. Still, they had sort of accepted the concept that the Soviets would be advancing and conquering some lands before they were done. They'd loosely expected to be able to discuss zone of influences with the Russian dictator after the war.

But with the Manchurian offensive, they were unwilling to continue and let Stalin do what he pleased, for it was now clear to both men that the USSR was up to no good. Japan had already surrendered, and the Soviets had still attacked. A nation bent on peace did not attack a vanquished nation that was already laying down its weapons, which was precisely what the Imperial Japanese Army had been doing in Manchuria and China.

The Americans were still three months from having another operational nuclear device and could not end the war in a simple stroke with Germany. And besides, events had clearly shown that wanting to bomb Germany and actually succeeding in doing it were two different things. The Luftwaffe had thousands of jet planes, rocket aircraft, and ground-to-air missile defense systems called the Wasserfall that could destroy any bombing raid that decided to attack any German cities. The Allies had succeeded in Wilhelmshaven because it was a coastal town, and the Germans never had a chance against a large air raid coming from the sea. But bombing a major city like Berlin or Hamburg in the Reich hinterland was a very different matter.

And so Truman had proposed to Churchill to fly to the United Kingdom for urgent talks. He thus boarded a B-29 Superfortress directly in Washington and flew direct on a non-stop flight to Liverpool. The meeting was not held in London or any other place in Southern England because there were fears of German commando raids and also V1 and V2 missiles still falling down on London proper, as if the city wasn't rubble already.

The city of Liverpool had been chosen for the conference. The plane that flew to England included Cordell Hull, the US Secretary of State, and General Marshall, the military commander-in-chief. Dwight Eisenhower (Us overall theater commander in Europe) and Bernard Montgomery were also invited to the talks once the political aspects were done but moved to Liverpool overland (train and jeeps).

The city of Liverpool had not been hit as hard as the southern part of the UK in the war. Sure, it suffered heavily in the 1940-1941 struggles against the Germans but had been left mainly to its own devices after that. Even during the liberation campaign, there was not a lot of fighting in the area since the Wehrmacht mostly evacuated the British Islands in 1944 during their strategic withdrawal.

The meeting proper was, in fact, held in the Cammell Laird

Birkenhead shipyard, the giant shipbuilding company that produced famous ships like the Prince of Wales.

The two delegations met in the large factory complex that had been rebuilt since the liberation and that produced the brand-new Wellington battleship. The yards were currently working on a new aircraft carrier, the Auspicious, based on the USS Midway design, the world's then-largest flattop. So, the leaders had decided to meet there in honor of the unique working relationship between the two allies. A visit of the great ship was planned during a half-day recess of the three-day conference.

The room where the talks took place was towering above the shipyard and offered a great view of the Auspicious being worked on. The men in the meeting could watch thru the large room's windows and see welding sparks flying around, large cranes lifting and lowering armor plating and guns, and all the necessary parts that a modern aircraft carrier needed to have to be what it was. It wasn't the most beautiful view, but it showed Allied industrial might, and the gloomy, smoky ambient air reminded everyone that the war was far from over. It wasn't all shiny and beautiful, exactly like the real world.

The talks on the first day were heated, and much debate flew around about what the Western Allies should do about the Russians and their intentions to grab as much land as possible. There were two factions during the talks. The cool-headed, like the Cordell Hull, some high-level British diplomats, Montgomery and Eisenhower, that believed in trying to make do with the Russians and not provoke another war.

Then Churchill, Truman, and Marshall were intent on not letting Stalin get away with anything. As Churchill said smartly near the end of the first day, the Free world had not fought a war of such proportion only to have one dictatorial and totalitarian regime replaced by another. And so, the first day ended in favor of the

Allies doing something about the USSR's aggressiveness because the two leaders willed it.

On the second day, the talks moved on to how they should stand up to Russia and how far they should enforce their will and determination on the Communists. After much debate, it was decided again with Truman and Churchill's impetus to advance as far as possible in Europe and take control of as much territory as possible before hostilities ended with Germany. The question of atomic weapons was again discussed on that day, and another bombing of Nazi Germany agreed upon the moment a new device was available.

By the third day, both heads of state went on to visit the Auspicious and on other talks, while the military men stayed in Birkenhead to discuss the details on how to finish the war with Germany, which was far from over. Several decisions were also made to give full support to MacArthur and Nimitz in their choices in the Far East, and more troops were authorized to Korea, including British reinforcements.

Things were not looking like peace in these early days of 1947.

Low Hills near Trento, Italy
Air superiority mission, January 27th, 1947

The extreme temperature created some comfort difficulties for Gaston. He was freezing his butts off and was constantly cold. His 'seat' was the parachute, with the dingy underneath, which made for a very uncomfortable mission once again.

Once in a while, he pulled up his oxygen mask and let the condensation drip out, rolling around on the plane's floor... and it froze almost instantly. On an airplane, the temperature was reduced with altitude by 10 degrees Fahrenheit every 3000 feet. Thus, it was freezing at the 20,000 feet he was currently flying, and also because of the time of the year (middle of January).

The Gloster Meteor designers had built an excellent plane, and as such, Lamirande was grateful to be flying one against the fast German jets. But unfortunately, no thoughts had been invested in terms of crew comfort. All airmen were supplied with special cold-weather clothing (sweaters, string vests, sheepskin jackets, trousers), and Gaston was thus fully clothed for his mission. He'd learned from experience that one is never warm enough in a plane at a high altitude. The B-29 (and its variants like the B-50) was the only WW2 aircraft designed with HVAC; the cockpit pressurized so that the crew could work at altitude without oxygen masks.

Besides, jet engines became more efficient as you climbed, so the higher, the better for the Meteor in handling, maneuverability, and speed. The reason was because the air concentration thinned, so there was a lot less wing drag. He was flying an air superiority mission. The squadron's objective was to remove any German fighter presence above the American divisions advancing into Slovenia.

A strong enemy concentration had been reported operating from several airfields north of the Slovenian provincial capital. So high command had sent the flyboys toward the area to battle it out with them. The whole Allied formation was flying at a comfortable altitude which wasn't ideal for engaging enemy aircraft, but with the cold, they left long and dense white jet exhaust contrails so they could be spotted from far away. Being at 20 000 feet enabled them to avoid being surprised by the Axis pilots.

They flew for about two hours when the first German fighter was spotted over the low horizon. Another great aspect of winter fighting, the sky was usually quite clear, and one could see from miles away. One of the pilots in front of Lamirande had spotted it, but it did not take long for him to see several dark dots appear in the blue sky.

"Enemy formation at twelve," announced the squadron leader over the radio. His announcement was quickly repeated through the pilots and the other squadrons. "Stay in formation," added the commander. The Allied fighters were all in a fingertip formation for this mission, one widely used by both sides during the conflict.

The fingertip formation was named so because it looked like the fingertips of a human hand. The formation consisted of a flight of four aircraft, with a "lead element" and a "second element," each of two aircraft.

The lead element was made up of a formation leader (Lamirande was the one for his four-fighters group) at the very front of the formation and one wingman to his rear left. The second element was composed of an additional two planes, the element leader and his wingman. The element leader was to the right and rear of the flight leader, followed by the element wingman to his right and rear.

Both the flight leader and element leader had offensive roles in that they were the ones to open fire on enemy aircraft while the flight remained intact. Their wingmen had a defensive job — the flight wingman covered the rear of the second element, and the element wingman covered the rear of the lead element.

The Allied thus presented a large formation to the Germans, and they flew head-on toward the ME-262s that approached quite fast. Gaston was ready for his job and prepared to fire as the enemy fighters grew bigger in his targeting sight. The plan was to take the Germans from the front, pierce thru their aircraft line, and then turn around for another pass.

He fired away when it was time, followed by his lead element wingman, August McIntyre. Their shells were followed by grey tracer's wakes that arced in long, slow curves. The extreme cold made for exceptionally visible shell contrails. The enemy did the same and opened fire, so Lamirande saw them zipping by (or more like he saw the tracer lines). The plane covering his rear was hit head-on by a 30mm shell and exploded mid-air. Gaston's plane rocked from the blast, but he could keep it steady.

With no time to check or mourn for his comrade (at least it wasn't August), he continued to fire, adjusting his aim. He finally was rewarded with a hit, one of his 20mm connecting with a German ME-262's wing, splintering it in a million pieces. The German fighter banked hard toward the ground, flaming and trailing a large contrail, spewing dirty smoke.

And then, the two formations thundered past each other. Additional aircraft were hit. Turning back again, Lamirande saw that several men from both sides had at least been able to bail out and had opened their parachutes. "Lami, got a break off from the fight," said McIntyre over the radio. Looking thru his plane canopy, Gaston was not surprised to see the reason for his friend's message. His left engine was trailing a fine white vapor, an unmistakable sign that it had been hit in some way. "Okay, August." Try to speed off the airspace. We'll cover you on your way. Lamirande's friend broke off banking hard right and turned his plane away back toward their

Italian airfield.

But the Germans had other plans than to let a wounded Allied plane get away. And one, in particular, had taken a special interest in Gaston's group. Luftwaffe ace Adolf Galland. The men's exceptional side view noticed the hockey sticks on the French-Canadian's plane as his Me-262's flew by in the first pass and veered back toward Lamirande, along with four other ME-262s that he'd called to the fore. Adolf made sure the other planes he called to the attack knew their role. "Remember, men. As I told you, the hockey stick pilot is mine. You guys take care of the rest and isolate him from his wingmates." He paused for a second. "Happy hunting, Galland out."

The Axis pilots did as they were told and fired away at Lamirande's colleagues. The fact that they were superior in numbers helped them scatter the neat Allied formation now that it was two planes short. While the large air brawl exploded all about them, the two pilots groups kept busy trying to kill each other and edged away from the main fight.

The first to fall was August McIntyre's plane. His Meteor had lost a lot of speed after being hit, so it was caught up by two of the ME-262s that fired away with their cannons. The Allied plane lost its rear tail and received damage to its engine, sending it into a nose-spinning dive toward the ground. However, the British pilot was able to bail out at the last second and opened his parachute while his plane crashed catastrophically on the ground.

A few minutes later, the other British plane in the fingertip formation was also shot down, this time with the pilot killed instantly when a shell burst thru the Meteor's canopy. All the while, Lamirande got quite busy dodging Galland's attack, flying low in between high, rolling hills. He roared near the ground, pushing his engines to the maximum, while his German enemy peppered the ground about Gaston's plane with explosions, showering it with dirt and debris.

Trying to shake off his pursuer (by this time, he knew that his archenemy was on him, as he'd started to recognize his flying style), he pulled hard on his flight stick and veering right and left, so to roll his meteor while doing it. The maneuver was quite risky, but he'd practiced it a little in the last few weeks. So he climbed fast while his Meteor seemingly tumbled in the sky. The unexpected maneuver threw Galland's aim off. It wasn't the best idea for a pilot to start doing this kind of acrobatics at low speed and while dogfighting, but the simple fact that the German ace had not expected it saved Lamirande's life. The German shells went wide by a big margin.

Once back up in the air, he tried to find out where the main body of the Allied other squadrons was. "Safety in numbers" had been one of the things he'd learned while training on the Bonaventure a few years back near Quebec City in Canada. Galland wasn't playing it fair this time. He was using other pilots to isolate Gaston for their fight. Well, the French Canadian had not become an ace because he was stupid. He would not continue to play Adolf's game and rejoin the rest of the Americano-British planes.

He pushed the engine throttle to its max and picked up some distance from the Nazi fighters tailing him. The improved versions of the Gloster Meteors were faster and now sported pretty much the same speed as the ME-262s. Several more tracer contrails raced by his aircraft, but he was never hit until he joined back the main dogfight, some distance from where Galland's group maneuver had sort of isolated him.

It would now be impossible for Galland to box him in again with his other Axis friends with Allied aircraft surrounding him. He turned the plane back and set his sights on finding the German ace. After a few seconds, he was rewarded and spotted him. Eight ME-262s approached fast toward Gaston and the main dogfight. They had not followed him right away and had seemingly taken their time maneuvering for some reason. The German ace plane towered above them all at 20 000 feet, like a bird of prey waiting to plunge. The group of fighters dropped toward the dogfight. The battle involved over a hundred planes, so no one noticed the newcomer's approach, as it did not matter; aircraft were crisscrossing in every direction.

But Lamirande knew they were coming for him, so he picked up as much altitude as he could, pushing his engine to the limit while doing it to the point that it shook and groaned. He never looked back and climbed. After about four minutes and a half, he was nearing the plane's ceiling above 40 000 feet, which was a little higher than what the Germans could do. Furthermore, the British climbing rate was a lot faster than the German one, so he was all alone by the time he was up in the rarified air. The main fight happened below, with some rare aircrafts trying to duel it out at these altitudes.

Once he was done climbing and his engine started showing signs that it would stall, he turned it around and dove. His goal was to meet Galland as the German was still climbing. And rightly so, the moment he faced the ground again, he spotted several dark spots coming toward him. He let his machine pick up more speed, making him feel dizzy with the G forces he was thus submitting to himself.

By the time his vision blurred and he was starting to see weird colors in front of his eyes, he pulled his stick toward him, just in time to level the Meteor with the incoming German planes. He fired away with everything he had at the Axis pilots, and several of his 20mm shells hit two different ME-262s. One burst in flame and arced down, trailing a long, dark smoke contrail, while the second one was only hit lightly near its port engine. To Lamirande's luck, he'd shot Galland's plane, and the German ace immediately went into a tumble to dodge the rest of the French-Canadian ordinance. By the time he took control of his plane again, his engine was stalling and dying, forcing Adolf to head home.

"Once again, this damned man eludes me," he said, muttering softly. "Damn!" and then he punched his plane control panel before directing his jet back to base. The fight was over and in another draw.

Gaston looked at Galland flying away and decided that he would not pursue the German, for his enemy's squadmates boxed him in and protected him. He decided that the ace was done for the day and that he'd better get back to the primary fight.

The Last Axis redoubt in the Middle East
Gaziantep, January 1947

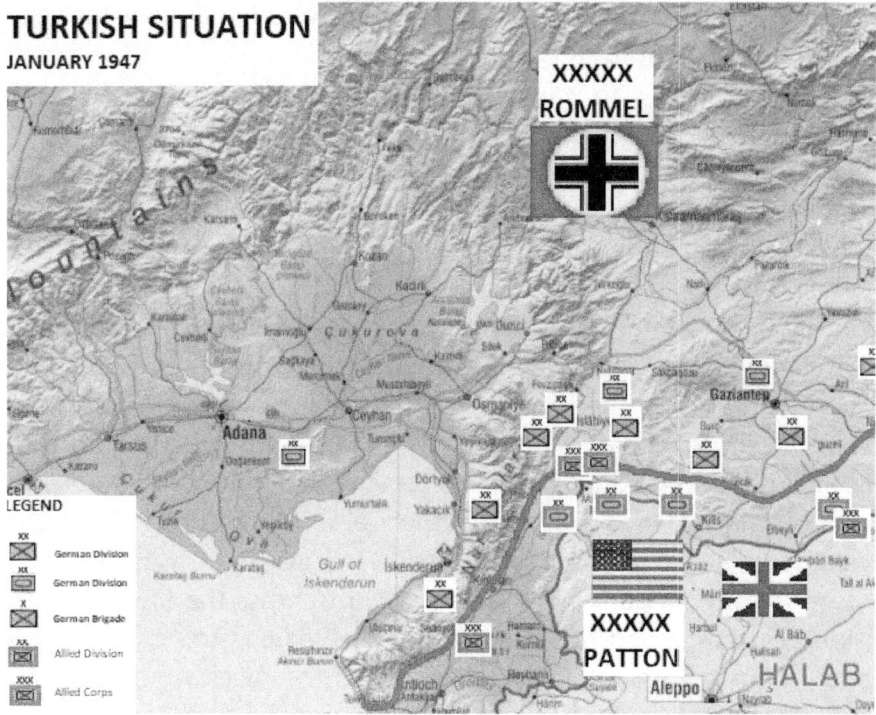

Gaziantep was the capital of Gaziantep Province, in Turkey's southeastern Anatolia Region, approximately about 185 km (115 mi) east of Adana and 97 km (60 mi) north of Allied-occupied Aleppo in Syria.

Erwin Rommel, commander of the Afrika Corps, towered above the city from his vantage point. The fortress was a castle first built by the Hittite Empire as an observation point and later built into a main castle by the Roman Empire on top of a hill at the city center. The circumference of the round-shaped castle was 1200 meters. The walls were built of stone, and the castle sported 12 towers.

While it wasn't much of a modern base, the Desert Fox had decided that it would do for the time being. It was built sturdily and stood the test of time. And it also gave a great view of the surrounding countryside. The 123rd Flak battalion was also installed within its walls, as it protected the city and the neighboring airfield that the Luftwaffe had built for the coming campaign.

The city of Gaziantep was far behind the frontline and probably not the best place for a commander, except that it was what it was. Rommel had had a choice between that city and Adana, west of the frontline, but that major city was even further back from the front.

Rommel HQ city sported great roads going northward and commanded the only way for modern armies to enter central Turkey. The rest of the front (toward Adana) was protected with the towering Nur Daglari Mountain Range, right on the Golf of Iskenderun's coast. So if an enemy attack came, the German General was certain it would come thru the Gaziantep gap and then turn west thru Bahçe pass in the Osmaniye Province. It was the best route for any modern army that wanted to cross the lower Taurus Mountain range and flood into the plains leading to Adana. It was also where the only rail line operated, so the Allies would want to control it before continuing to move north in any efficient fashion. The railroad went down to Bagdad and also forked into Syria, which would greatly facilitate the enemy war effort in moving supplies and troops northward toward Turkey and beyond.

Basking in the gentle wind and bright sun of the lovely Mediterranean weather, Rommel, hands crossed behind his back, looked down at Gaziantep's streets, where Germano-Turkish forces moved about.

The men looked confident enough and seemed to be about their business. It was always surprising to the German commander how soldiers kept on going even after defeats and reverse—especially German soldiers. For the last few weeks had not been easy. In just over a month, most Axis forces in North Africa had retreated northward, executing an epic fighting retreat.

After his troop's defeats in Cyrenaica, where he was outflanked and overwhelmed by Allied numbers, Rommel had first decided to retire to the Suez Canal Defensive line, which already had been worked on by his predecessor, Von Arnim. His general plan there was to use the Suez Canal, and the bunkers/trenches built a year before.

But the simultaneous collapse of the frontline in the Zagros Mountain (Central Persia) and subsequent British breakthrough into the Iraqi plains changed his plans. If he'd chosen to resist on the Suez, it would have meant that the other Allied forces could have moved from behind him and cut him off from the Wehrmacht's Turkish bases.

And so, once crossed over the Canal, he just ordered his forces to keep going. Roads were not the most modern in these areas, but the weather was always clear, and apart from dust, the Afrika Corps did not encounter many difficulties in retreating to Turkey. A few battles had been fought to slow down the aggressive American General Patton, who had continuously probed his forces to find a weakness. First, in Jerusalem, a sharp counter-attack from one of his Panzer divisions saved the day and enabled the rest of the Army to move northward before being too deeply hooked in a fight with the fast-moving Allied troops. Then there were a few more fights in non-descript towns and one last major scuffle in Damas. After that, the Germans had been able to move into the defenses that the Turks prepared for the better part of the month to resist and defend their country.

And then the Afrika Corps settled in what would probably be its last battle. The reason was simple. There was obviously no more retreating to be had since the Soviets occupied the Balkans. The Germans were stuck in Turkey for the duration. The Axis command for the whole Turkish theater was over a quarter of strong Germans and another quarter of a million Turks. It included Turkish, German, Iraqi, Egyptian nationalists, and a few more divisions of Ukrainian volunteers and some Croats battalions. Thanks to a robust Turkish economy and burgeoning industry, the troops were well-supplied, fueled by the critical German investments in the country since 1941. Vital were the military production factories that would continue to churn out ammunitions, anti-tank guns, and some replacement parts. The Axis would run low on gasoline at one point as the Axis fighting forces in the theater depended on the Reich for its supply, but Rommel figured that it wouldn't be that big of an issue now that his Panzer divisions were more or less on the defensive.

So the Allies would not have an easy battle, especially since Turkish terrain was quite rugged and mountainous. The only question mark for the Desert Fox was the possibility for the Turks to surrender, as persistent rumors on the subject abounded.

36th US Infantry Division
141st Regiment, January 27th, 1947

It has often been said that artillery was the God of war. Overbearing and potent, its attack shattered everything, obliterated all, and shell-shocked even the best of soldiers.

As Jack ran as fast as he could for some sort of cover, the loud, siren-like whistling sound of falling artillery shells approached faster and faster. There was another sound as well, the sound of rocket artillery, also about to fall on the American positions. The combined might of the German 210mm *Nebelwerfer 42* rockets and the 150mm *schwere Feldhaubitze 18 or sFH 18* heavy field guns were about to rain hell on the Allies.

The significant number of shells came from the 93rd and 123rd Infantry Divisions, the 33rd, 37th, 47th, and 78th heavy artillery regiments, and the 101st, 42nd, and 56th Rocket Artillery Regiment. These units originated from Guderian's Balaton Army Group and were dispatched by the General to blunt the Americano-British advance into Slovenia, which threatened to unhinge the Balaton offensive success gained so far. In order to get enough time and space for the retreating Balkan forces, the Western Allies also had to be stopped. In addition, a couple of Panzer divisions advanced at incredible speed toward the Allies.

Summers was able to jump at the last seconds before the German ordinance started to explode all around the 36th U.S. Division. He landed hard on a small stream bed about two meters deep. On falling, he hit some rocks and broke his rifle. He lost his helmet and was knocked out cold. It was sort of a blessing since the first few minutes of the enemy bombardment was so intense that it felt, to the soldiers still awake or alive, like hell itself had descended upon the earth.

The Americans, or British for that matter, were not used to this kind of heavy artillery shelling since it was usually kept in store for the Russians on the Eastern Front. The war there had an ignominious level of brutality that it didn't have in the west. Combat between the Third Reich and the Soviet Union was on a scale that was not comparable to the struggle fought on the more civilized parts of Europe. Heavy troops concentrations, untold numbers of shells and weapons fired at each other's soldiers, casualties in the millions that could not be assessed because both sides had stopped counting a long time ago.

The Germans had seen an artillery attack of that magnitude countless times. They sent many mightier ones toward their enemies regularly. They endured much worse in a repetitive fashion from the Russians with their innumerable artillery guns. The Yvan's loved nothing more than softening up their German enemies with them. In fact, the Soviet Union could mount even bigger artillery barrages than what the Axis forces were raining down on the 36th Infantry Division on that cold day of January.

Be as it may, the Western Allies were used to having some form of comfortable superiority in everything when faced with their Axis enemies. No wonder since, to date, they'd faced only a tiny portion of the Wehrmacht. The Reich operated over 60% of its army against the Russians. It was a war of a totally different proportion.

By piercing thru Slovenia and joining the theater that the Nazis and the Communists were raging against each other, the Western Allies would learn a different level of conflict. One several notches higher than what they thought already was pretty intense violence.

The Lone Star Division (and so Jack's 141st Regiment as well) had advanced thru a forest in the low hills between Slovenia and Italy. The forest itself was not too furbished in heavy undergrowth, so the going was not too hard on the Allied soldiers. A few hours earlier, they'd watched as a great air battle unfolded just over their heads. A fight that the Germans won, again. This had been the first blow to the unit's morale that day. It seemed that the Luftwaffe would never run out of those damned jets. At least they hadn't seen any bombers yet and so would be scot-free in terms of being bombed. Or so they thought.

The shells that were exploding catastrophically all around them splintered the trees, made short work of the Division's mobile armored units, and killed hundreds of soldiers. It melted and scattered the snow and almost made winter disappear. It even landed on some of the Sherman infantry support tanks that advanced on one of the excellent forest trails that the recon guys had found. It burst the wooden area aflame, obliterated humans and machines alike. And the shells kept landing. Only the lucky or the quick-witted ones survived the intense blast that seemed like it would go on forever.

Summers woke up from his predicament after a few minutes. One could hardly blame him for doing so (it would have been better for him to stay unconscious in a sense) since the noises and explosions were so loud that a man was bound to wake up. He opened his eyes with a terrible headache and wondered where he was. His vision was jumbled, and his face was resting in dirty, red water. He wondered why it was that color. His vision was blurry, and he sat up with his legs crossed, putting his head between his two hands. A 15 cm shell landed just on the small stream bed's lip, not five meters from him, catapulting dirt and water all around with a resounding boom. That event finally woke Summers up, and he instantly came back to his senses. He suddenly realized where he was. The red water wasn't just water. The stream ran red with blood from his comrades dying by the dozens. The water was also damned cold. It was January, after all. His fingers and the part of the face that had been in the stream felt numb. Turning his head left to right, he didn't see anyone, so he decided that he was better off lying flat on the ground to avoid any splinter or other shrapnel hitting him.

The Axis attack was worst than the craziest bombardments he'd been thru, even the ones where the naval guns (battleships) had attacked the fortified position across the Strait of Messina the year before. Jack had thought then that the big 300mm+ shells explosions had been impressive. Apparently not.

He decided that he could survive the ordeal if he was lucky enough to avoid a bomb falling directly on his head. Being in a two-meter hole, he had a chance. He spotted his broken rifle and wondered what happened to it as he lay flat. No time to worry too much, he decided, since there would be many intact weapons available after they were done counting the 141st death toll.

From Jalalabad to Mosul
Euphrates-Tigris front, January 1947

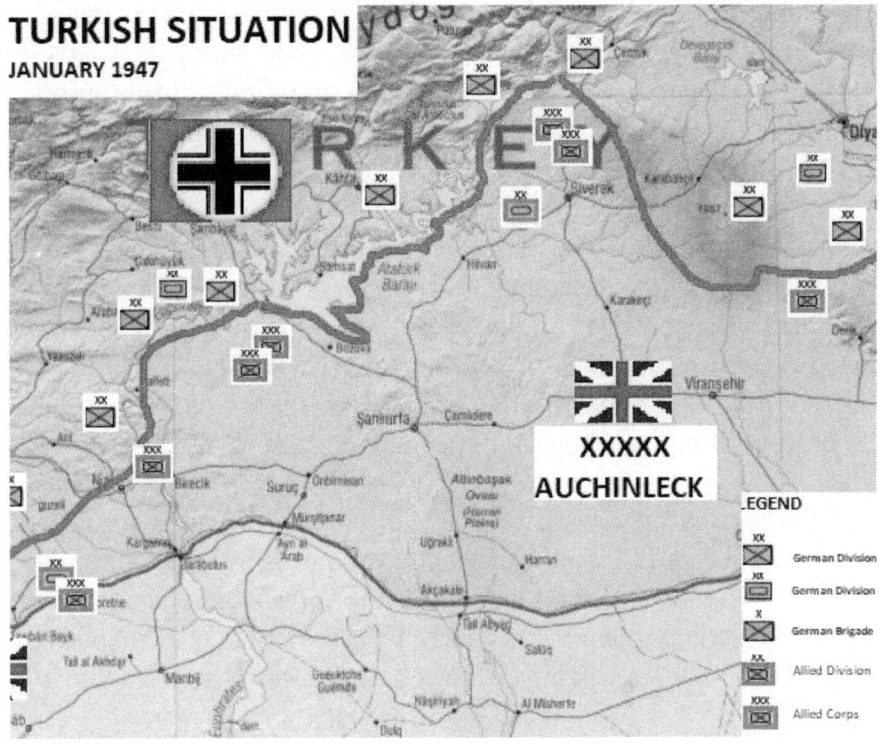

The Kurds were a mountain people with all the characteristics of mountaineers—love of freedom, violent passions, and a clannish feeling of pride. These primary traits disposed the Kurd to fly to arms at slight provocation and engage with zest in bitter blood feuds. In short, something that General Auchinleck was used to seeing.

As he sat in front of the numerous tribal chiefs (nine of them) from the Mosul area, he knew better than to interrupt when they yelled at each other and settled some sort of dispute. He'd learned that it was better to let them wind down about it or else propose them something totally unrelated that would stop them bickering over some water well, goat, cow, or something trivial. The arguments could also be about the blood feud existing since immemorial times between families and clans, and that was definitely not a good idea to get involved in, as he'd learned not even ten days after he'd left Jalalabad and entered Afghanistan in 1946. He knew that he wouldn't get anywhere by trying to solve these issues because the Kurds themselves sort of didn't want them to be solved. He saw a lot of similarities between these men and the ones he'd learned to deal with in Afghanistan.

What he needed from them was their cooperation. He didn't anticipate too much problem with supplies and ambush like with the Pashtuns in the rugged mountains of central-south Asia, but one could never do too much to soothe these proud men. And besides, German rule had been very lenient toward the Kurds, letting them do pretty much what they wanted, so he needed to tread lightly.

As they argued over his proposal, he wondered if they would get what they wanted. The British needed the Kurds to help them in the attack on Turkey, and the thing made a lot of sense since about half of the Kurdish population resided in Turkey proper. Perhaps they could finally have an independent country after they defeated the Axis...

Auchinleck's mind wandered far away from the sizeable colorful tent they were having the meeting in. Thru the flaps, he could see the beautiful mountains of the rugged northern Iraqi countryside, and the whole thing made him remember the campaign he'd fought and how far they'd advanced. The going had been tough at first, not because of Axis forces trying to attack, but because of severe supply issues. He'd even had to garrison most cities and towns on his journey thru Afghanistan and Eastern Persia.

Then had come the battle in the Zagros Mountains, where his army stormed Isfahan. They eventually broke thru into the Iraqi plains and spilled everywhere while the Axis forces retreated. They'd taken

taken Baghdad almost without a fight, and the rest of the area had fallen like a ripe fruit because the Axis forces evacuated it as fast as they were able to. The only thing left were giant POW camps containing a couple hundred thousand Italian soldiers kept in custody since their country's surrender. He only regretted one thing. He had not been able to initiate a battle with the Axis forces. Now Germano-Turkish armies were solidly entrenched in Anatolia, where the rugged terrain made their defense relatively easy.

Auchinleck's forces were arrayed on a large front, facing Lake Van's south shore, and it looked like it would be a hell of a fight to try and force their way into the Axis defenses. German and Turkish units were entrenched in the mountains overlooking the area and were well supplied in artillery and anti-tank guns. The Germans were cut off from their home country, but that didn't mean they weren't well provided by the Turkish industrial infrastructure.

A tribal chief, yelling louder than the others, yanked the General back to the present. The argument seemed to have reached a crescendo. Maybe, he would see the end of it before sundown.

36th US Infantry Division
Slovenian low hills, 141st Regiment, January 27th, 1947

The relentless artillery barrage eventually died out after what seemed an eternity. In the end, the rugged 141's sergeant even curled into a ball like a child and blocked his ears with his hands. He was wet, cold, and miserable after the time he spent in the streambed. He felt frozen, dirty, and disgusting, for he'd been wholly soiled with the blood that ran in the small stream. The cold was also overbearing. He was shaking like a leaf.

After half a minute of complete, utter silence, Jack picked himself up and lifted his head to peer out of his hiding place. What he saw shocked him. What had previously been a forest was now a lunar landscape, and fire still burned fiercely everywhere. The trees, laden with snow before the attack, were mostly gone, replaced by ash, blackened stumps, splintered wood, and a smoking pile of embers.

A persistent foggy smoke hung everywhere, giving the whole scene a look of horror. It was then that he noticed the bodies on the ground. Some mutilated, several missing many body parts, others were lying flat on their bellies, burning slowly. A Jeep, completely gutted, was split in two, having probably received a direct hit. There, an armored personal carrier (the M3 half-track model) was nothing more than a pile of molten and broken metal that would not have been recognizable if Summers hadn't known what it was.

And then, the seemingly dead and burning land started to move. Several soldiers jerked themselves up from other hiding places, or some had been simply lying flat and been lucky not to get hit. Many were injured. Jack hauled himself out of the streambed and tried to shrug off some of the crusted blood he'd accumulated while trying to hide. Looking back upstream, he saw the reason for the blood. Two soldiers he knew well (Stevens and Devers) had been opened like tin cans by shrapnel or other wood splinters. And they probably either fell in the stream or had been in it when they got it.

"Sarge!" someone yelled behind Jack. It was Blair Turnbull. The sergeant was happy that his friend survived the ordeal. "Turnbull, your alive!" he said as he turned and shook the G.I.'s hand. "Damn, sarge, you look like shit.", exclaimed the soldier. Indeed, Summers looked like he'd been swimming in a pool full of blood, gore, and mud. "Yeah, I know, but not even a scratch," he said, giving the soldier a wary, uncertain smile. And it was then that Summers heard a low rumble coming from the east. Turnbull wanted to talk some more, but he gestured him to shut up. As Jack concentrated, the sound grew louder, and he even perceived several German voices thru the ambient noises. He gave a sharp look to Turnbull and gestured him to move and pick up the rest of the men. The soldier didn't argue. He'd heard it as well. And so the American ran westward, picking up their injured (only the light ones, as the gravely wounded could simply not be taken with the time they had). "Hurry up, men!" one of the surviving captains yelled over the running men. Jack started running, but not before picking up a sub-machine gun and a rifle from a dead man.

The men ran back about 500 meters, at which point they started to hear gunshots. The Germans had reached their former positions, and some left-behind U.S. soldiers decided to strike back. However, the whole affair didn't last long, and after a minute or so, it was over.

The rumble of tanks and loud German voices continued to get closer and closer as the American soldiers got busy organizing makeshift trenches or cover. Several bazookas and other anti-tank ordinances were brought forward since, luckily, some of them had survived the shelling. Summers, flanked by Turnbull and a few other surviving members of the squad, installed themselves in rock that had a large fissure. It was a great cover since it was almost like a trench and was solid enough to withstand small arms and even, probably, enemy shells.

An eager young private ran forward to Summer's position with a Bazooka in hand. It was the common name for a man-portable recoilless anti-tank rocket launcher weapon, widely deployed by the United States Army, especially since 1944 and 1945. It had been heavily used during the terrible battles up the Italian Peninsula.

Also referred to as the "Stovepipe," the innovative bazooka was amongst the first generation of rocket-propelled anti-tank weapons used in infantry combat. Featuring a solid-propellant rocket for propulsion, it allowed for high-explosive anti-tank (HEAT) warheads to be delivered against armored vehicles, machine gun nests, and fortified bunkers at ranges beyond that of a standard thrown grenade or mine. The 141st Regiment had used it more than once to storm an enemy position. The weapon had been particularly handy during the Monte Cassino battle.

The universally-applied nickname arose from the vague resemblance to the musical instrument called a "bazooka," invented and popularized by a U.S. comedian in the 1930s.

The M1 bazooka was not very useful against the heavier Panzer versions like Tigers and Tigers II or even the powerful mobile guns like Jadgpanther or Jagdtiger. Summers and his comrades had tried it many times without much success. It, however, fared much better against infantry or on the rare occasions when it could be used against the thinner armor typically fitted to the lower sides, undersides, and tops of enemy tanks.

To hit the bottom of an enemy tank, the bazooka operator had to wait until the tank was surmounting a steep hill or other obstruction while hitting the top armor usually necessitated firing the rocket from the upper story of a building or a similar, elevated position. They were pretty much on a level footing with their enemies in their current predicament, so that option was out of the question. Jack gestured for the young private to give him the Bazooka. He'd decided he would aim for the tracks of whatever tank would show up in front of them. Even the heavy Konigstiger tank could be stopped in its tracks were destroyed.

The sergeant put the weapon down directly on the rock to keep a steady aim and waited. After a few minutes of unmoving coldness (he was still wet and miserable and so realized it when he was idle), he was rewarded with the first sight of an enemy tank.

The thing rumbled into view, crashing everything before it. Most of the trees were already half-burned stumps, but the Panzers bulldozing over burning wood, splintering fires and embers, made for a fantastic sight. "Look, Sarge. Some big bastards moving, and infantry behind them. They're coming right for us," said Turnbull, a moment before he started to fire with his submachine gun.

Summers spotted the first tank and aimed at the front right side, where the track was, and fired. The rocket exited the tube with some flame spurting out in the weapon's back, and it fizzled noisily toward the German tank. In a fraction of a second, it hit the lower side armor of the Konigstiger. It made for an impressive explosion that splintered in every direction in a star-like fashion, but the Panzer rumbled right thru the smoke and fire created by the shell.

Another little novelty had protected the Tiger II Jack had just fired on. One that the Allies had not seen very often on their frontlines. At the time of the German invasion of Russia in 1942, the Russian 14.5 mm PTRD and PTRS anti-tank rifles were very effective against the side armor of all of the Reich's tanks. Even the side armor of the Panther was easily penetrated at very short ranges. And as in every army in World War Two, the tank tracks were very vulnerable to side attacks in the vast Soviet expanses.

To increase protection against anti-tank rifles, 8 mm steel sheets,

"Schürzen" (skirts) were hung on rails along the side of the tanks. The things were invented by some enterprising Wehrmacht soldiers that applied good sense to their combat experience. It did not take long for the whole Panzerwaffe to ask for the modification because it added top-quality armor protection. These steel sheets caused the shots to tumble, preventing them from penetrating the tank's armor. The Schürzen were divided into sections, allowing a single section to be easily replaced if damaged or lost.

The other reason the Allies had not seen this development yet was that they'd been facing Konigstigers that didn't have the engine to take up the extra weight that the 8mm plates entailed, as the Maybach powering them had been barely enough for the already extraordinary weight of the machine. But with the new Simmering Sla.16, and its staggering 1000+ horsepower, it had no trouble with the added weight – and, of course, the protection coming along with it.

So the American rocket just exploded against one of the protective plates. And then everything exploded around the already beleaguered American units. The Germans attacked with superior numbers and firepower, while the U.S. forces were stunned, diminished, and without heavy ordinance to fight the heavy Axis attack.

The regimental commander didn't take long to call the retreat, and Sergeant Jack Summers did not mind. The whole affair did not look good, and it was better to regroup further west.

The French theater
January 31st, 1947

German General Gerd Von Rundstedt was busy writing up the next set of orders and filling out the mountain of paperwork that came with a theater command. That type of generalship posting was prestigious and exciting, but it entailed a lot of stress and a lot of working hours. The old soldier looked at the two towering stacks of papers and despaired. He already felt pretty numb about the last few weeks and months.

The ordeal had started when OKW stupidly emptied the Pyrenees defensive line to bolster its Ostfront Citadel offensive. The thing had been a resounding success but had created weaknesses all along the German defenses where the troops had been taken from. Southern France had been so weakly defended that the Reich's only hope for defense had been to cross its fingers for the Allies to forget to attack it.

But, he surmised, that faulty line of thoughts had not taken the French into account. While the rest of the Allies had been quite content in continuing their push northward in the Italian Peninsula, General de Gaulle and old Petain stayed fixated on the Bordeaux region. They had the troops and left them there, waiting for their opportunity. Rundstedt had tried to convince OKW to take troops anywhere BUT from the Pyrenees Line (as it had already been weakened by earlier successive troops removal). But it had been to no avail. Goering had been intent on counter-attacking the Soviets. The exalted Nazi leader continued to hold on to the pipe dream of a victory in the east.

What had been forecasted came to happen. Under the excellent and energetic General Alphonse Juin, the French forces had launched a decisive surprise attack near the town of Hendaye, near Biarritz, and south of Bordeaux. It didn't take long for the brigade-sized defenses to be pushed away. No wonder Von Rundstedt didn't even have enough troops to operate all the bunkers and the trenches in the area!

Once the defensive line was broken, all hell broke loose. Since the Germans had emptied the theater of frontline AND reserve forces, the Allies poured into Southern France, outflanking the rest of the Line's positions and rapidly pushed to Bordeaux.

OKW finally reacted and rushed divisions upon divisions to the old General for him to organize a counter-attack. However, by the time he launched his forces south of Marseilles, the Allies were already advancing up the Atlantic Coast and sending more and more reinforcements to exploit the breach in the Fortress Europa. His counter-offensive had initially encountered a lot of success. Still, an Americano-British landing north of his position un-hinged the whole affair, and he had to retire his troops with all due haste.

All of Southern France was thus abandoned to the Allies, including the Alps defenses between Italy and France since the enemy was also coming up that way after it broke thru (in succession) the Gustav and Gothic Lines.

The German forces mounted some stiff defense in Lyon and fought valiantly against superior odds in Normandy and south of Paris. At the end of November, the Axis forces also mounted a successful counter-offensive in Besancon against the Anglo-Saxons forces. While it permitted the Germans to have more time to retire in good order and save two great divisions from encirclement, it did not change the overall strategic picture that the Reich was being overwhelmed in the theater.

In the end (after several other sharp counter-offensives by the men under the old General's command), it had been to no avail since the Allies attacked from too many directions and with too many troops compared to what Von Rundstedt had available.

His conclusion had been obvious and logical, and he'd pushed hard to get OKW to accept them. From the moment the Pyrenees Line was broken, added with the British landings in Calais, France became un-defendable. The only course for the Wehrmacht was to try and re-establish a defensive line along the old Maginot or else the Siegfried defensive works on the German sides of the old border.

It was not what the Fuhrer wanted, but the Third Reich was beyond trying to fulfill its leader's wishful thinking or pipe dreams. The country could no longer afford stupid decisions or weird leadership. Therefore, he'd retreated and moved his forces toward Germany, with the full support of Halder that took care of Fat Hermann's susceptibilities on the matter.

Therefore, he'd spend the last two weeks getting the troops into the posture he needed to stop the Western Allies from entering Germany. The high command, finally recognizing the danger of losing the main German industrial node of the Ruhr region, supplied him with strong reinforcements and great Panzer Divisions. The Reich's retreating stance on every front rather helped his predicament in the sense that there were now many units available for less ground to cover. It was a simple equation. As it retreated, the Wehrmacht was stronger. There was, of course, a critical point where the country would lack the resources it was extracting from its Empire, but for the next few months to a year, Rundstedt figured that they were in a good position. If the Americans did not drop too many atomic bombs on their heads...

Pre-war planning had determined that the Germans needed twenty-five full-strength divisions to man the West Wall (Siegfried Line). The old General now had over forty strong units, supported by thousands of jets, artillery, and several powerful Panzer Division. Finally, most of the V1's rockets had been transferred to his command, following the loss of their launching bases in Belgium and the Netherlands. There were even rumor s about Goering finally relenting on his insistence to continue to pound the Southern English cities into rubble. Since they already were fine dust, everyone but Hermann thought it logical to employ the mobile V2 launchers in a tactical role. The fearless German leader was slowly coming to the same conclusion and seemed ready to use the magnificent weapons tactically.

All in all, the more he thought about his order of battle, the better he felt about being able to resist and keep the invaders away from the Fatherland.

CHAPTER 2

Oak Ridge Nuclear factory complex
Near Knoxville, Tennessee, January 31st, 1947

The K-25 Plant in Oak Ridge housed the massive gaseous diffusion apparatus used to partially enrich uranium before it was sent to the nearby Y-12 Plant, responsible for the last part of the process into the uranium refining that made it possible for military use. "K-25" came from Kellex Corporation, the contractor that designed and built the plant, and uranium-235, often shortened to "25."

The K-25 plant was an enormous building. A mile-long, U-shaped structure, the K-25 plant was the world's largest roofed building at the time. The factory's job was to separate the isotopes of U-235 from U-238 by turning uranium metal into uranium hexafluoride gas and pumping it through a barrier material with millions of microscopic holes.

K-25 cost $512 million to build. The mile-long, U-shaped plant covered forty-four acres, was four stories high and up to 400 feet wide. Engineers developed special coatings for the hundreds of miles of pipes and equipment to withstand the corrosive uranium hexafluoride gas that would pass through the plant's 3,000 repetitive diffusion stages (together making up a cascade essential to get the Uranium enriched).

The entire process was hermetically sealed like a thermos bottle, as any moisture could cause a violent reaction with the uranium hexafluoride. Even minute pinhole leaks and contamination from fingerprints were major concerns. A special leak detector was invented, and every component of the entire system underwent a "cleanliness control" procedure before it was installed.

Instead of producing fully enriched uranium 235, the new gaseous diffusion plant would provide around fifty-percent enrichment for use as feeder material for the Y-12 factory. The decision to use both plants was part of the larger design to double the capacity of Y-12 and fit with Groves' strategy of utilizing a combination of separation methods to produce enough fissionable material to make as many bombs as was humanly technically possible at the time. In short, it was the proverbial and typical American way of making sure things could be built in an assembly-line fashion.

As he walked the perfectly polished floor of Y-25, flanked by several white-robed scientists, Groves wondered how in hell the damned military had been able to squander one of his precious bombs. Did they understand how much work went into building it? Did they gauge the level of risk in trying to bomb so deep into German territory? Damn Truman. The man was now calling Groves every day to get progress reports on when another bomb would be ready. And every day, the General answered the very same thing. "March, Mr. President. Not a day earlier than that." For making Uranium was the most complicated process in the World at that moment in time in 1947.

Proof of that was that only the United States had developed a bomb so far. There were reports on the Third Reich being busy making one and having a pretty serious undertaking on the matter, but as of yet, the Germans had not been able to explode one. The same could be said of the other Allied countries. Apart from the United Kingdom that possessed the knowledge to make one but didn't have the capability, the rest were not even at the starting line in terms of research and infrastructure build-up. Or so the reports said.

Groves was skeptical about what the so-called nuclear expert said on the subject. If the Germans were working on a bomb, why the hell not the Russians? There had even been a project in Japan. General Macarthur, the commander-in-chief in the East and governor of Japan, had sent him everything the military found on the subject. It was called the Riken Complex Project in the town of Komagome. But it never went beyond the early research stages, and most of the buildings (and scientists along with it) were killed in one of the American firebombings attacks in 1946.

"So, you say that everything has been done to optimize production and nothing short of building another Oak Ridge complex will speed up the process?" "Yes, General," answered the blank-faced scientists walking beside him. They were in a large room, supplied with a high ceiling, filled with tubes and large steel canisters. The floor was spotless. Tons of workers and other scientists milled about their business. "We were already operating at full capacity before the request to work faster," Groves Grunted at the last words from the man. Of course, they had been; he was the man that pushed most of them to the brink of exhaustion to make the three bombs Truman claimed would end the war in one bold stroke. "Okay." Were the only words from the General's mouth after that.

The group continued walking, but Leslie wasn't listening or looking at anything in particular. He was thinking about the report he would send to Truman, asking for the funds and the manpower to make a second complex to quicken nuclear production. He inwardly smiled at the face the arrogant President would make upon reading his words.

Konigsberg, Eastern Prussia
Model arrives back in Germany January 31st, 1947

The first mention of the city of Konigsberg in history indicates it as the place of a village of fishermen and hunters. When the Teutonic crusaders began their Baltic Crusades, they built a wooden fortress and later a stone fortress called "Conigsberg," which later morphed into "Königsberg." In old German, the literal meaning was 'King's Mountain,' in apparent honor of King Ottokar II of Bohemia, who led one of the Teutonic campaigns.

Not many cities in Germany embodied the Aryan will to conquer or defend against the east than the city that Walder Model, the new commander in chief of all German forces in Eastern Prussia and Northern Poland, put a step on as he exited the Kriegsmarine cruiser Courland.

The city had been the center of the Teutonic Knights crusades against the Slavs in the east and the heart of Prussian expansion thereafter. The first Prussian King, Frederick the 1st, had been crowned in this very place in 1701.

For the dream of the Reich of a thousand years, as promised and prophesized by the late Fuhrer Adolf Hitler, Konigsberg needed to be held at all cost. For its fall would mean the invasion of the Bolshevik hordes into the German historical heartland. The very crucible of the Fatherland.

Model, turning back a moment to look at the ship that brought him here, gave one last nod to the ship Captain, Hans Lutherman. The man was again leaving for Helsinki to pick up more of the last few soldiers still there in Finland.

OKW had ordered the complete evacuation of Finland at the end of September 1946, so it could use its fifteen divisions to bolster the defense of Germany proper. Model had approved the move and had put to the task immediately. The trick had been to make an orderly evacuation without having the Soviets know about it. He'd kept his frontline north of Leningrad as sturdy as possible for a while, compensating for the troops he was moving out of the country with planes transferred from other commands and all the artillery he could muster. He'd bombed the enemy around the clock, so they first would never have time to get a serious attack organized, and second, keep them busy surviving.

The strategy had been possible because of the Luftwaffe's dominance of the skies against the Russians. While the enemy was getting stronger every day now because they also had jets, most of their air force was still predominantly propeller-driven, so Model had been able to keep the sky above his troops throughout the evacuation.

His stepping on the Konigsberg dock meant that the evacuation was almost complete. Some men had been chosen to be sacrificed, but most of them were now back in Germany. The ones left were the artillery operators, which kept the Soviets busy until the last minute.

As he sailed thru the Russian-infested waters of the Baltic (several air raids were fought against, and a couple close calls with enemy aircraft dropping bombs almost on the Courland), he'd received the telegram naming him commander in chief of Army Group Prussia, tasked with the defense of Northern Germany. Guderian was now responsible for the so-called Army Group Balaton and busy with an offensive to push the Soviets back in Hungary and southern Poland.

As he read thru the whole message, he'd been completely baffled by the staggering number of divisions he would have under his command. In fact, it probably would be one of the most potent concentrations of Wehrmacht units in the war to date. Over 60 units, some full strength, some depleted, but it didn't matter. In a minimal area (compared to the damned Russian expanse), he would command an army so powerful that the Russians would be faced with at least numbers equal to their own for once in the war.

Given the German tendency to inflict double the casualties than the Soviets inflicted with their superior machines and training, he wondered how the enemy would be able to break thru. Probably never, he thought to himself.

As he walked to his armored staff car (modified Hanomag SkL1), he decided that he could not see any way the Red Army could break his forces. If only he'd known what Stalin had in store for his forces, he would not have felt so confident.

Panzer Lehr moving back west again
Exiting Budapest, February 10th, 1947

Walder, jutting out of the tank's hatch, looked beyond the horizon. A cold winter wind blew his blond hair in all directions, but he didn't care. He didn't notice the cold. Or the scene of smoke and fire-laden destruction his Tiger II was leaving behind. In his pocket was the last letter from Ingrid. The girl of his dream was seriously injured. At least she was alive. Erich had wondered why she was not writing to him by the end of December 1946. She explained in the letter that she had been in a hospital ward for three weeks, unconscious and unable to send him any message.

She'd described the last powerful attack on Berlin. It had been weeks since the last one before that, and Berlin seemed to be able to recover finally. And then, a new, mighty bomber raid had come over the city. It had been repulsed by the flak, Wasserfall, and other jet/rocket planes, but not before dropping its powerful bombload on the city. As a flak battery operator, she'd been injured by one of the B-29 bomb's blasts.

For a while, she just blacked out with a severe head injury. She was finally back to her senses only in January. By the time the damned mail caught up with the Panzer Lehr (the Division was in the middle of an offensive, so it was normal that it took some time).

The unit stopped at Budapest and had already been there for eight days, finally enabling the letters and other supplies to catch up with the frontline.

He'd read the thing over and over again until he finally knew every word by heart, so he didn't need to read it anymore. He now simply rehearsed it in his mind.

The Konigstiger shook as it caught a large pothole in the mostly destroyed road leading out of Budapest, jerking Walder out of his thoughts about Ingrid. "You okay, commander?" asked Hans, his young and talented gunner, that was sitting just in front of him by the turret. The kid was smoking a cigarette. Erich signaled him to give him a puff. He extended his arm, and Erich picked up the cigarette and took a long drag, inhaling the smoke slowly to try to relax. "Yes, Hans," he said, handing back the smoke stump. "Just thinking of home and if we'll have something to get back to." "I hear ya, Sir. My parents were killed in 1944 in one of those damned Allied raids." The teenage soldier was from Cologne, one of the hardest-hit cities in the Reich. "Sorry to hear that, Hans," he said, putting a hand on the younger man's shoulder. "Same here, kid, same here...." He didn't say anything else, as both men went back to their meditative state, looking westward.

The Panzer Lehr Division was evacuating Budapest. But this time, it wasn't because it had been defeated or encircled, so it had to retreat. No, they had been successful with their Balaton Offensive. They'd given enough time for almost half a million soldiers to seep thru the line and evacuate the Balkans. These men now boosted Army Group Balaton's own force. Guderian's command was about to be renamed back Army Group Center, while the northern part of the front would be handled by a new, excellent commander, General Walter Model.

Erich was confident they would keep the invaders at bay. The commander had sent down the information that the Army Group would be at least 40 divisions strong, and that was a comforting thought. In a very narrow space, they would defend with what was thought to be the same numerical ratio than the damned Red Army. Walder was confident that they could give the Yvan's a good whipping.

The scene the Lehr left behind was a leveled Budapest, with long, towering dark columns of smoke rising high in the sky, while squadrons upon squadrons of the Luftwaffe ME-262s patrolled the skies above the brave German forces. A gigantic explosion rocked the only bridge left standing in the city. Walder turned his head slowly to look at the event. The Széchenyi Chain Bridge, a symbol of the union of Buda and Pest, was flying to pieces into the Danube river in a shower of fiery pieces, scattering across the water's surface only to sink immediately. The affair brought memories back to the old tanker. Memories of Kiev and of a better time. A time when Germany was still towering as a behemoth over Europe.

The Goltap Offensive part 1
Minsk, Liberated Bielorussia, February 14th, 1947

Russian troops moving to the frontline in Bielorussia, January 1947

General Ivan Cherniakhovski was in a good mood as he waited for his other commanders to arrive. Born in July 1906 in the city of Uman, he joined the Red Army in 1924. In 1936, he trained in the Red Army's mobile force, eventually becoming commander of the 28th Tank Division in March 1941. With the outbreak of the war, his rise thru the ranks was meteoric, not because of political connections but through his actions.

From December 1942 to June 1943, he commanded the 241st Rifle Division, formed from his depleted tank division after the difficult battles during Operation Barbarossa. Promoted to major general in May 1943, he was given command of the 18th Tank Corps for a month before commanding the 60th Army. His troops recaptured Voronezh the year before, and promotion to lieutenant general followed. The 60th Army then took part in the Battle to liberate Smolensk, Bryansk, and other cities. He was also part of the subsequent offensives against the Dnieper-Volkhov-Lovat Defensive line.

Promoted to colonel general in March 1945, Cherniakhovski became the commander of the Western Front north of the Pripet Marshes, making him the youngest front commander in the Red Army at age 38. He retained command of the front when it was renamed the 2nd, 3rd Belorussian, and 1st Baltic and was promoted to general of the army on June 26, having received the Hero of the Soviet Union designation twice.

During the Soviet summer offensive and counter-offensive of 1946 after Operation Citadel, Cherniakhovski smashed through the lines of the German forces, taking Minsk and pushing on to Vilnius, Lithuania. By the end of October, the 3rd Belorussian Front had crossed the Nieman River and taken Kaunas before moving farther west. In November, Cherniakhovski's troops stopped to regroup and resupply. They had achieved great victories, but replacements were also needed before continuing their advance.

It had been a good run for the general. His men had helped liberate Bielorussia while inflicting heavy losses on the enemy. Now, in the early days of January, the 3rd Belorussian Front stood on the border of East Prussia—the first province of Germany proper to be threatened by the Red Army. Some of his advance units had already crossed the border in small probing actions. But the going announced to be quite tricky. The German forces had executed a successful fighting withdrawal and avoided disaster or encirclement. They also did not get caught in large attrition-like battles that the Red Army so loved.

And finally, as they'd retreated, their forces became more concentrated to the point that they now had an almost equal number of soldiers than the Russians facing them.

Cherniakhovski had first wondered how the Soviets would break thru that solid enemy barrier of steel and might, but then overall commander-in-chief, Marshal Zhukov, had visited the General on February 13th with a proposed solution.

During the great commander's visit, he discovered that the Soviet Union also had an atomic weapon. His theater had been chosen for the first detonation against the hated Germans. Given the extraordinary damage stories from the Wilhelmshaven and Hiroshima bombings, the General was inclined to think, as the Marshal did, that exploding a bomb at the right place could unhinge the whole German defense plan.

He'd called a final meeting to plan his operation, taking into consideration his new trump card. Cherniakhovski had called everyone to the House of the Red Army and Fleet in Minsk(also known as the Army Palace). It had been the headquarters for the Bielorussian front in 1942 before the German invasion and also a school for officers in the 1930s and 1940s. The building was heavily damaged during the Wehrmacht Minsk Offensive. Three floors were severely damaged due to fires that started due to the explosions. After the liberation of Minsk a few weeks earlier, the restoration work of the building was underway. The adjacent territory was cleared of debris; some makeshift wooden structures were built to house the staff people to help the General organize and lead his forces to the attack.

As his commanders filed into the room for the crucial meeting(they were in one of the old ballrooms, still damaged but acceptable for a gathering), Cherniakhovski greeted each one before directing them to the map table. The maps showed a somewhat detailed area of the East Prussian border and the province's interior.

Stavka's (Soviet Army Command) orders were somewhat loose. Given his earlier successes against the German forces, it seemed that it might be possible for Cherniakhovski to drive his forces straight through the German lines to the province's capital of Königsberg. However, Soviet aerial reconnaissance showed that the Germans had prepared a series of defensive lines and strongpoints to prevent such a move. And as said earlier, they had plenty of men with which to handle their formidable defenses.

While he wasn't permitted to tell his officers of the actual bomb itself, he knew it would create a large hole in the enemy front and one that he would have to exploit. His idea was to initiate battle across the enemy positions and see where they had the strongest or most numerous units concentrations. That would give him the indications on where to use the bomb. Zhukov approved of his idea and gave him "carte blanche" to use it as he saw fit.

Once the initial breakthrough occurred, Cherniakhovskii could weigh his options as the battle developed. If the German defenses collapsed quickly, the possibility of a quick drive to Königsberg was still in the cards. If not, the 3rd Belorussian Front and the 1st Baltic could penetrate as far as possible and dig in to await support from its neighboring fronts. Cherniakhovski could also swing his armies north to the Baltic Sea, cutting off several German divisions defending positions along the coast. Whatever the initial outcome, the Soviet general would be inside East Prussia, and by then, the Reich would have all the difficulties in the world to kick him out.

Pointing out these possibilities, Cherniakhovski unfolded his plan of attack, which would become known as the Goldap Operation. His finger moved from the Soviet frontline positions through the initial German defenses to the town of Gumbinnen. From there, he followed the Gumbinnen-Insterberg-Königsburg highway to the East Prussian capital. That would be his main axis of attack initially, and he would see from there what the Germans did.

His speech to the officers that day was inspiring to all, and the unit leaders left with a high confidence level. Had they not ousted the Hitlerites from the Motherland? They would now go to the heart of the so-called Fatherland and wreak havoc on the birthplace of German militarism.

The Eupen Rocket strike
First tactical use of the V-2. Bonn, Germany, February 14th, 1947

A peculiar group of trucks and their processions rumbled out of the German city of Bonn on the early morning hours of the 14th of February. Hundreds of troops and specialized vehicles were involved in the movement. It wasn't the typical armored formation, nor the Infantry one. It sort of looked like an artillery unit, but not quite. The curious Wehrmacht soldiers around the town did not distinguish the things well in the dark of night. Ostfront veterans declared that they were Nebelwerfer Artillery (rocket artillery) mainly deployed against the Soviets to date in the conflict. The curious troops and other onlookers had their answer by first light as the full view of the impressive artillery units was finally revealed.

A hundred rocket-mounted trailers lifted their weapons slowly to point at the sky as the hundreds of men and vehicles around them prepared the launch. A low, grumbling noise was starting to be heard as the flying bombs were slowly starting up. Smoke and the morning mist fused together to give the casual observer an eerie feeling of dread and excitement.

These were the famed V-2 Rockets, the Wonderwaffe that had bombed London, and countless other British cities to smithereens. They recognized them because they had seen the things in propaganda movies at the theaters or in the Army magazine "Signal," regularly distributed to the troops.

More soldiers, tankers, and even airmen assembled near the field west of Bonn to see them in action, attracted by the lights and loud noises. Civilians that by now had seen too much of war and wanted no more part in it were also won over by curiosity.

The hundred rocket launchers had rolled into the thin snow-covered ground, and now the watchers understood why so much work had been put in the previous days to get the ground plowed and level.

Some trucks had even come and dropped gravel. Pilots near the town had thought that the Luftwaffe was building a new airfield, but they found the chosen site a little peculiar. Too many trees around, for the field used to be old farmland now dotted with vegetation all around.

In the early days of rocket operations and before the Luftwaffe finally won back the sky over the Reich, the ideal firing sites were those that provided heavy camouflage. Now it hardly mattered, as most Allied air raids were stopped well short of the launching sites. The mobile V2 rocket system also needed to be along with a flat, firm footing for the firing table. Usually, the crews preferred to launch near dusk in the late evening hours. Still, they'd been overruled by General Rundstedt, that needed their timely tactical bombardment for a sharp counter-attack he planned on the very same day.

A long line of Opel trucks and their large trailers also lined up the Bonn streets, containing more rockets that would indeed be mounted by the fifty or so large mobile crane that came with the units surrounding the rocket mobile firing platforms.

The rest of the weapons, the liquid oxygen, and alcohol needed for the V-2 launch had been delivered to the firing area by railroad. The warheads were then be delivered via truck (explaining the long line of Opels), while the rest of the supporting men and special purpose vehicles had driven to the town.

The Meillerwagens (mobile V2 platforms) raised the rockets vertical on the firing table. The firing crews performed the various duties they were tasked with for the firing. The missiles were aligned, fueled, with the electronics and gyros set and armed. From the time the rockets were raised to the time they were ready to fire, about 90 minutes went by.

All personnel and vehicles around the launch sites were cleared away, for the weapon's exhausts were terribly dangerous and destructive. Then every one of the unit's commanders entered the firing control vehicle, the only one that stayed close to the V2's.

Then at some pre-determined time, they all pushed the fire button. In every missile, the liquid oxygen and alcohol flowed by gravity to the exhaust nozzle, where they were lit by the igniter, which resembled a pinwheel, sparking as it rotated. The burning in itself was not sufficient to launch the rocket, but it did give the control officers a visual indication that the missile was functioning correctly. Once the launch control officer believed the weapon was ready to fire, an electric command was sent to start the fuel pump. The fuel pump steam turbine reached full speed, the fuel flow reached its full value of 275 pounds per second, and the engine thrust blossomed in a flash to 69,000 pounds of pure power.

Almost in unison, the cone-shaped flying bombs lifted in an earth-shattering noise that rumbled as if Thor, the God of thunder himself, had descended upon the earth. The onlookers were momentarily blinded by the gigantic flash of light produced by the epic coordinated launch.

And then, in an instant, the V-2 Rockets were away, climbing unbelievably fast, almost straight up. Twenty seconds into the launch, they were but tiny specs on the horizon.

Four minutes and a half later, they exploded catastrophically amongst the poor 45th British Infantry Division, which got caught in the bast like hell itself had hit it. By the time Rundstedt men arrived on site, they only had to mop up the dazed Americans and stormed their objective, a small town in the Belgian district of Eupen.

Extracts from Von Manstein's 1958 book, LOST VICTORY
From the Swiss border to Austria (The Alpine Wall), February 14th, 1947

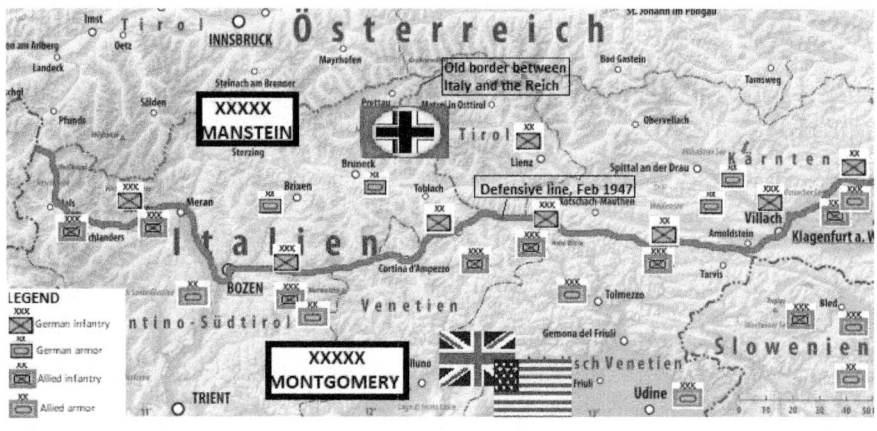

By the middle of February, our southern frontline was finally stabilized. General Guderian's offensive in Hungary and Slovenia had pushed back Russians and Western Allies alike to give enough time for the rest of beleaguered forces to extricate themselves from the Balkans. We bolstered our defenses with the new troops and had plenty to fight the Allies with.

All the while, my command, now including a little over fifteen divisions, was entrenched all along the heights from the Swiss border to the Austrian heartland. In the valleys below, the Allies were definitely not in the best of stances to launch an offensive. We prepared our defenses well and were helped by our forefather's defenses a generation before. As mentioned earlier, the installation had been in a state of disrepair and abandoned for years. Still, my forces and the excellent work of the military engineers (pioneers) were able to get them operational.

In addition, we were able to use the old Italian *Vallo Alpino* (Alpine Wall) for our designs. The fortifications were an Italian system of defenses built along the 1,851 km (1,150 mi) of Italy's northern frontier. Made in the years leading up to the war at the direction of Italian dictator Benito Mussolini, the defensive line faced France, Switzerland, Austria, and Yugoslavia. While we left the Swiss, French, and Yugoslav sections of the Italian builds alone (in any case, many were already occupied by the enemy), we re-purposed what could be and modified them to face the other way. It wasn't always possible since the work's original design had been to defend against invasion coming from the north and not from the south. But in the end, enough had been modifiable for our needs to bolster our defensive potential significantly.

The *Vallo Alpino* line was similar in concept to other fortifications of the same era, including the Maginot Line of France, the Siegfried Line of Germany, and the National Redoubt of Switzerland. The mountains were enhanced with lookout posts and fortifications. The defenses varied between three designs: prominent mountainside forts, rallying points and bunkers, and point-defense fortifications.

Italy's land frontiers were mountainous and easily defended in most places. Due to the Alps rugged nature, the *Vallo Alpino* defenses were confined to passes and observation posts in accessible locations. So we had to make sure we filled in the blanks with new bunkers and trench systems to complete our preparations.

With the magnificent work and the added strength of the new divisions saved from the Balkans, I felt that the Alpine wall was stronger than the Gustav Line the year before.

The final result was impressive if you added the fact that they were nested in the towering Alps Mountain range. All the valleys were flanked with defenses to enfilade any enemy advance along the valley floor, and works within the valleys were constructed where they were wide enough. Anti-tank guns (PAK 44 and PAK 45), artillery (Hummel II, Nebelwerfer rockets), and machine guns were trained on prepared and pre-registered fields of fire, with observation positions at higher points. Shelters for infantry were located farther to the rear, and a system of communications links and roads or, for higher locations, ropeways, were provided for communication and supply.

In many places, we either used the old World War One positions or made new ones typically built into the rock on the valley sides. Where this was not feasible, concrete to a thickness of 9.8 to 16.4 ft (3 to 5 m) was used for protection. The fighting compartments were located at each fortification's forward section, with ammunition rooms to their rear. Underground galleries connected the combat blocks and their support areas, including utility rooms, barracks, storage, command centers, and the main entrance was located farthest to the rear. Combat areas were isolated from the rest of the structure by gas-tight doorways. The Italian and the Austro-Hungarian areas were all (except for a few) designed for independent operability without externally supplied power and other utilities. They made a great addition to or setup.

The whole system was camouflaged as best we could with nets or other natural-looking features to help defend against air raids. We also re-purposed the Italian equipment already included in the Alpine Wall (The Royal Army never bothered to remove any of it, apparently) – Fixed machine guns works, several artillery guns already on steel slab (much could be said about the Royal Army, but they certainly made great guns). In addition, about twenty heavy mortars and over two hundred flamethrowers, complete with bunkers and angles of fire, completed our protective setup.

The Allied commander facing me, General Bernard Montgomery, would not have an easy time against what we all considered the Reich's last line of defense. From there, the enemy could invade Germany and Austria from the south and put an end to the Fatherland. So our Fuhrer's order, as well as mine, was that no retreat was allowed. We would either win or die defending.

The Battle of Eupen
Eastern Belgium, February 14th, 1947

The rockets flew over the determined men of the 4th Panzer Corps. As they passed by, the soldiers heard them coming and saw them fall amongst the enemy, which was just in the process of gathering its men to receive the German counter-attack.

The place: the town of Eupen, capital of East Belgium, a city and municipality only fifteen kilometers from Liege and from the German border on the other side (Aachen). The area used to be part of the German Empire, but the district was given to Belgium as war reparation after World War One.

Rundstedt had chosen to attack over his prepared defensive position on the Siegfried Line because he wanted to save the last two divisions trying to retreat to the Reich. The two units, having been caught in fortress battles and several close-call with being outflanked, were the last of the Wehrmacht on French soil, and the old General would not let them get destroyed without trying to save them, as he'd done countless times since the German retreat from the French theater had begun months earlier. He'd been successful at places like Besancon but had failed in other instances, like at the Battle of Paris, where a similar operation (to save German units trying to retreat) had been attempted.

For the operation, he'd decided to engage an entire corps, namely the 4th Panzer corps, one of his best units that had been under his command since the days he gathered his forces in Marseille for the counter-attack in mid-1946. The units included three full Panzer Divisions, the SS Nordwin (Norwegian SS volunteers), the SS Aryan, and the 53rd Panzer Divisions. He supplemented them with three heavy tank battalions and three Panzer Grenadiers' mechanized infantry. The plan was to hit hard and fast, right on the heels of a powerful V-2 strike, followed by a conventional artillery barrage.

The tough German soldiers, that thought they'd seen everything in the dreadful war their country was involved in, could not help but stop for a moment (even if ordered not to) and watch as the epic-proportion destruction unfolded in front of their eyes.

The V-2 Rockets and their 2,200 pounds of Amatol high-explosive impacted the small town where the enemy was trying to find some sort of cover with the fury of an unchained maelstrom. First, the warhead itself was powerful in its own right. But it was increased tenfold by the supersonic speed of the rocket (2880km/seconds).

The impact simply vaporized everything within a twenty meters radius. Hits on buildings meant that they were atomized. Even bunkers were destroyed by anything resembling a glancing blow. Trenches did not save the poor British soldiers cowering in fear under the German weapon's wrath.

If that attack in itself had not been enough for the poor sods on the received end, Rundstedt then launched his conventional artillery attack that finished the job. By the time the 4th Panzer corps rolled over the still-smoking debris of Eupen, the 45th British Division was in full flight to the rear.

The SS Nordwin Division was then sent ahead toward Liege, where the German divisions they came to save were moving. Contact was made by the end of the afternoon. It took another two days of fighting for the brave German forces to move back to their starting point in Aachen. But by the time they crossed back over their Siegfried Line defense, they'd saved their comrades. And the V-2 rocket artillery played no small parts in the battle. For the better part of the two days the struggle lasted, they unleashed over eight hundred additional rockets at the bewildered Allies.

Far east American HQ
Tokyo, February 16th, 1947

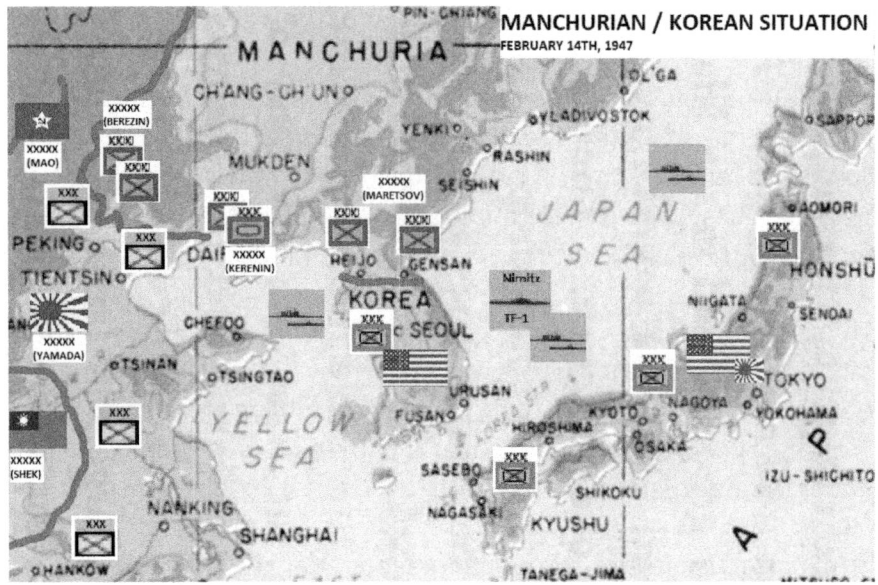

"So, this is Yamada's answer to our messages?" said General Macarthur, re-adjusting the proverbial pipe he always had in his mouth. The Allied force's eastern command overall commander was dressed in his usual wrinkled General's uniform that looked worn to the bone. No wonder, since he insisted on having the same sets of clothes since the Philippines campaign. He cleaned them, of course, but they didn't look new. It didn't matter to the man. He was of a superstitious nature, so nothing would make him throw away the uniforms that saw him thru the worst of the Pacific War. And so they'd trudged along with the General since 1942.

"Yes, General," said Richard Sutherland, his chief of staff. "General Yamada gladly accepts our offer of supplies and weapons. He also insists that something needs to be done about the Russian offensive since his forces will be overwhelmed at one point." Macarthur grunted loudly. Both men were in the old Japanese Imperial Headquarters, now fulfilling the same function for the American victors. "Proceed with what we've discussed on the matter, Richard." The chief of staff nodded. The U.S. forces would start supplying weapons and supplies to the Kwantung Army's beleaguered troops, now confined to China, having been mostly pushed out of Manchuria by the Red Army. They anyway had mountains of confiscated Nipponese guns and ammunition.

So far, all requests for explanation or discussion with the Russian field commanders had failed miserably. In fact, the Americans had been trying to talk to them since the start of the offensive at the beginning of January, but they were being ignored. To Macarthur, this did not bode well, and so he'd decided to rearm the Japs. He didn't have any authorization from Truman to do so as obviously as he was about to, but to hell with politicians. To hell with the Reds. They acted as aggressors and invaders, and Douglas had not liberated the whole Pacific theater just to see it all crumble in front of the Communist hordes.

Having already either executed or imprisoned most of the Japanese High-Command, most leaders in the Imperial Army and Navy hierarchy, he'd then had to do the unthinkable. Consider using the Japs for some help. He'd already organized an audience with the Emperor of Japan, which had been kept in place even after the surrender. The Nipponese spiritual leader gave him his ascent to organize what must be in front of the Russian aggression. Anti-USSR sentiments were already rampant within the Japanese armed forces, as the country had almost decided to attack the Soviets instead of launching its Pacific Blitzkrieg. Only the late President Roosevelt's moves, namely the freezing of Japan's financial assets, plus the embargo on steel and oil, had made the Nipponese change their objectives.

Some political fallout was expected with the Nationalist Chinese, who wouldn't like it. Chiang-Kai-Shek, their leader, had been one of the U.S. best allies and fought Japanese aggression since the 1930s. Hell, he'd give weapons to him too and see what comes out on top.

One thing was sure, the Russians were advancing into China, and the Red Chinese followed in their wake from the north. The Nationalist leader wasn't of the stupid sort, had decided Macarthur. He would see the value in slowing down the Soviet offensive, for there was no guarantee that the Soviets would stop once they reached Shek's lines in Central China. The enmity between the Communists and Nationalists was well known, and the two forces were fighting a civil war simultaneously as the Japanese invader. With the Soviets being Reds, it was easy for everyone to see which side they would back.

"Sutherland, what about the news out of Korea?" asked the American commander in his commanding, calm voice. "The Soviet forces are stopped along a line from Heijo and Gensan and are not moving an inch further south." Macarthur walked a little from his chair to the wall where a pinned map of the Korean and Manchurian areas was hanging. Putting his fingers on the two cities his chief of staff named, he turned back toward the other man. "So they haven't moved an inch since we came up to the line to confront them, have they?" he added, with one of his rare smiles. "Exactly, General. The Soviets have entrenched and set up defensive positions as we did, but so far, everything is quiet on that front." Richard also walked up to the map, right beside his commanding officer. "What should we do now, General?" MacArthur took a drag from his pipe re-adjusted his cap before talking.

"Nothing, Sutherland. Nothing. We wait for the Reds to make their move and see if they have the guts to pull it out....." He turned back toward his chair to sit back down. "In the meantime, let's discuss these troop's dispositions." Most American land forces were either still in Japan or else on the various Pacific Islands they'd conquered. MacArthur wasn't sure it was the best of ideas to send too many soldiers into Korea. He wanted to stand up to the Russians but not necessarily provoke them. "Ah, and what of the reinforcements I've requested from Washington?" "The president had accepted to send a couple of armored divisions with the new tanks, as per your request." The Eastern Allied commander had indeed requested some armored formations since the Americans had nothing close to the numbers of tanks the Soviets had, all assembled into fighting divisions and corps. They had simply not needed them in their Pacific campaign since most of their battles involved amphibious landings and the Japs had no heavy machines with which to oppose even the U.S. Shermans.

"Well, Richard," said MacArthur, clapping his hands. "Things seem to be well in hand for the moment. Let's go have a bite!" Sutherland nodded with a smile. His General was happy, and things looked somewhat better than they had a couple of weeks ago.

Somewhere between Munich and southern Bavaria
Atomic Convoy, February 15th, 1947

The convoy rode into the night with lights on but under a good tree cover. It was moving thru one of the thick southern Bavarian forested areas. It had been decided to avoid the autobahn that ran from the old Austrian border to Berlin for security reasons. While Allied air raids were rare these days because of the excellent Luftwaffe air cover, they weren't unheard of. The enemy did try to attack convoys, trains, and the likes once in a while.

A lot of traffic was going on the autobahn, but the convoy speeding through the darkness (it only moved during nighttime) was too important for even the slight risk of Allied attack. Its cargo could simply not be lost or destroyed by the enemy.

In front and back, several Opel supply trucks drove hard and were also full of soldiers in case something happened along the way. Right after (in front and rear of the convoy), a total of four Flak panzer IV "Ostwind" mobile flak guns flanked the procession. The machine was the best the Reich had in mobile anti-aircraft guns. It had been developed in 1944 and by 1947 equipped most Wehrmacht divisions in several variant forms. The Ostwinds (Eastwind in English) were fitted with a very effective 3.7 cm Flak 43 gun. It could, of course, down planes but had shown its uses against ground forces like light vehicles and infantry.

And in the middle of it all stood a modified Hanomag armored carrier (Sd. Kfz.251). The thing seemed too big to be a standard infantry carrier, and indeed it was. Skorzeny had to modify the thing by removing all armaments and everything inside. No more crew space, no more ammunition storage. Just an empty steel shell. Even so, some more modifications had to be welded on top of the Sd. KFZ to house the components needed to make the atomic bomb workable.

The SC 1000 device was two meters long and almost the same in width. But what made the whole thing complicated was all the add-ons that the Kelstein base scientists had to install to transform the Hanomag into a rolling bomb. Detonator, enriched Uranium, casing, other components.

The only space was for the driver and the helper in the front. And as sure as the sun sets every day on the horizon, the two most famous commandos in Europe stood in it. Marco Sturm was at the wheel and driving. Beside him, Colonel Otto Skorzeny, the man behind the most daring operations of the conflict to date. Together, they'd even infiltrated North America twice and succeeded in coming back to Europe. They'd killed Tito, the Yugoslav partisan leader. They'd rescued the Italian leader in a difficult glider operation, Benito Mussolini.

They even survived a major Allied raid after attracting the Brit's full attention in their failed attempt at Churchill's life. The English had launched a full paratrooper division at their main base in Friedenthal, just to try to get rid of them.

They even went back to the Russian front for a stint as snipers, where they'd been quite successful. And now, they had been tasked with exploding the first Nazi atomic bomb. As the Fuhrer explained to Otto, the operation was critical for the Reich's survival. Detonating a device would supposedly show the Allies that Germany also had atomic power. Goering hoped it would make them think twice about dropping more bombs on the Fatherland since their own soldiers could also be killed in nuclear fire.

Another intended benefit would be that it would also make the Soviets pause and ponder if it was the best of ideas to continue attacking the Germans. All in all, Skorzeny understood that his mission could very well change the course of the war and give better winning odds for the Third Reich.

Both Marco and him had finally found a way to trigger the bomb without dying in the process and now only waited for the Fuhrer to point them in which direction – and against which side – they needed to explode the weapon. OKW was still undecided about where to use the thing. The hardliners amongst the Navi leaders simply wanted revenge on the Americans, but the smarter, more moderate ones figured that it could have not one but two consequences. Yes, it would make the Americans wonder if the Reich had more, but it could also fill them with a terrible resolve for revenge, and they could drop more and more atomic weapons on Germany. And since the Reich didn't have anything left after that, well, it was a risk that even crazy Hermann had not yet decided what to do.

The other option they had was to trigger it on the Russians. A far more enticing prospect in Skorzeny's opinion, it would have the double effect of killing a lot of Yvan's (that was always good) while still delivering the same message to the USA.

As he pondered the options in his head, he yawned. It had been a long day. He decided that he would close his eyes, for there were still several hours of darkness ahead of them, and anything else than what concerned the actual success of his mission was irrelevant to him. His job was to detonate the thing. Everything else was above his pay grade.

General Maretsov field HQ
Gensan, North Korea, February 17th, 1947

"Comrade General," said the soldier handing out the telegram to General Kirill Afanasievich Meretskov. The man was the commander of the 1st and 25th rifle armies or the so-called Far Eastern Front. He was a decorated officer from the war for the motherland and during the Winter War of 1939–1940 against Finland, where he had been tasked with penetrating the Mannerheim Line as commander of the 7th Army. He was awarded the title of Hero of the Soviet Union shortly afterward for his actions.

The NKVD arrested Meretskov at the start Barbarossa in 1942. Released two months later, he returned to command the 7th Army in the battle in the Volga Uplands and the Moscow front. He was later called to the Volkhov Front during the 1945 operation that saw the Soviets finally pierce the vaunted German defensive line of the same name. He commanded the Karelian Front from December 1945, notably the Petsamo–Kirkenes Offensive against the Germans in Finland from August 1946. From October 1946 onward, he was assigned to the Far East, where he was to take part in the top-secret operation against Japanese-occupied Manchuria.

The message from the overall eastern commander in chief, Aleksandr Vasilevskiy, was quite simple. To Maretsov's inquiries about what he should do against the Americans that now blocked his forces in Korea, the answer was a simple: "Do not engage the U.S. Forces. Dig in and entrench. Observe and report on their movements. Under no circumstances is there to be any provocations, incidents, or attacks on our Allies." And the last line of the message was a bit hard if he wanted to make sure the first part was to be ordered to the letter: "Do not communicate with the Americans in any circumstances."

Well, there he had it. After the resounding success by his forces, he now had to stop, while the other two fronts under Kerenin and

Berezin could continue to attack the enemy in China. At least he could console himself in thinking that in mere weeks the Far Eastern Front had achieved what had been talked about in military circles for almost twenty years. The Soviets finally ousted the damned Japanese from Chinese territory and avenged the 1905 defeat.

He turned toward his command tent that was a few paces back from where he'd read the telegram. He headed to it under a slow walk. He quickly gestured his main staff officers to drop the orders down to all the units. Their active campaign was done.

He would congratulate his deserving soldiers later, but for now, he would brood over what he could have achieved if that damned MacArthur hadn't decided to meddle into Russian greatness.

Ministry of Armaments and Production
Berlin, February 17th, 1947

The building that housed the Ministry was located at Berlin's heart, near the chancellery. It was a grand Nazi construction completed in 1937. It boasted a floor area of 56,000 cubic meters, spread over 2,100 rooms. The maze-like corridors had a combined length of almost 6.8 kilometers, with some corridors up to 440 meters long. The underbelly of the gigantic building has space for 250 cars. Seventeen staircases and seven lifts connected the different levels in the confusing complex, which was designed to achieve one main aim. Concentrate and optimize the Reich's military production.

Albert Speer's black Mercedes stopped in front of the building, flanked both in front and back with two Hanomag armored carriers full of soldiers. Before he got out of the car, the soldiers jumped out of their vehicles and spread out in a protective net around the building's entrance. The Ministry's master then stepped out, leather case in hand. He wore a long grey coat and was dressed in civilian clothes. In this fashion, he set himself quite obviously apart from the rest of the Reich leaders, almost all military or former soldiers who always wore their uniforms. He also harbored a hat and smoked a cigarette that he was keeping loosely between his lips. As the soldiers lined up toward the entrance, a neat-looking staff officer walked up to him from inside the ministry. "Herr Minister. Good morning." "Good morning, Colonel Weinzel," answered Speer in his good-humored tone. "Lots of work today, I am afraid." "Yes, Herr Minister. I have a full schedule for you."

And both men walked into the building. The hall was grandiose like all Nazi buildings built in the 1930s, with marble floors and a gigantic central stairway that climbed up the twenty-story building. Large paintings of Adolf Hitler and Hermann Goering adorned the walls on each side. Dozens of men in civilian and military clothes walked the place and went up and down the stairs. Several black-clad guards also looked sharply in every direction with their watchful gazes. The minister's office was on the last floor, so they walked to the right side, where the main elevator was located.

When Speer became Minister of Armaments and Production early in the war, he was charged not only with armaments builds, transportation, and placement but also with final authority over raw materials and industrial production. With this authority, Speer had created and then expanded a system that fueled the Reich's war economy. It was a fine mix of transportation infrastructures (the exploitation of the Nazi empire's considerable resources), stockpiling when possible, and a lot of conscripted (like French) and slave labor (like Russians), supplied primarily from prisoners of war, that maintained production of war material for Nazi Germany.

With his decisions, roads and railways had sprouted out of nowhere. Defensive lines had been financed (the Todt Organization was also under his responsibility), planned, and executed with millions of slaves workers. Panzers, guns, and jet fighters had been made in numbers greater than the manpower to operate them. In fact, at one point in 1943, he'd even thought that Germany could pull it off and extricate a victory against the Allies. But then the high tide was reached, and the Wehrmacht started retreating from some of the conquered territories. Slowly at first, and then in a landslide.

So it was all coming to a crashing end. The Third Reich was almost back to its original borders in 1939 before it invaded Poland. According to all his simulations and analysis, the country would eventually run out of resources to make its ammunition, machines of war, and gasoline.

The whole time the elevator climbed up to the last floor, he was lost in thoughts, trying to think back about what he could have done differently. And, when he thought about it, there wasn't much he could have done otherwise. The Reich was a collection of realms within the realm. Every top man in the government had their own little petty interests, starting with Hermann Goering himself. They all had their production priorities and fought each other for them, with Speer in the middle of it all, trying to be the arbiter. So he decided he'd done enough there.

It wasn't like he could have done the job the generals were paid to do. They were the ones who got defeated in the Soviet Union, in the UK, Africa, France, and Central Europe... Granted, they were overwhelmed by so many enemies that it was baffling how Adolf Hitler could have blundered so miserably into a war with the rest of the World.

The doors to the elevator opened the way to his destination: his office. The grand hall leading to it was also made of marble, and a nice black rug adorned its floor. More painting along the walls, with this time several pictures, most of the time of Speer himself at some ceremony of with the Fuhrer. On the way to the minister's desk, they walked by dozens of offices, filled with staff and secretaries already busy doing their workloads for the day. Running a war economy took a lot of people.

Weinzel and the minister finally walked into the richly decorated office with an oak desk. The two men sat down, with orderlies bringing them their morning coffees. The order of the day was to allocate steel resources and evaluate how much Chromium was left for jet fighter production. While some air cargos still trickled into the Reich from Turkey, it was not enough to replenish the stocks accumulated in 1944 and 1945.

They would also talk about other resources needed to keep the Wehrmacht fed. Several large stockpiles had been gathered at secret bases and warehouses across Germany, so Speer wanted to have their inventory status. Most of these caches were located in the Bavarian Mountains and quite strongly protected (like in the oil's case). The unrefined steel ore was just accumulated in giant piles by the factories themselves.

The end result they were looking for was to give OKW commander-in-chief, General Halder, how much stock he had to fight his war. The Wehrmacht had retreated on every front, but now that it was ringing Germany, it was stronger than ever, and many military people within the Reich believed that they would hold for a long time, provided they had enough ammo and supplies.

Speer would try to make it work with what he had. "So... Weinzel. how's the report I asked you for yesterday?......"

Austrian Alps
Kranjska Gora, Slovenia, February 18th, 1947

Jack Summers, a sergeant in the 141st Regiment of the Lone Star Division, grumbled as he walked up the steep road. He was not in a good mood. His squad had been tasked to recon the enemy defenses by the captain. The whole Division was bivouacking in the small, beautiful town of Kranjska Gora. It was located in northwestern Slovenia, on the Sava Dolinka River in the Upper Carniola region, close to the Austrian borders and the new German frontline.

The place harbored a decent-sized village with cozy houses and even a large hotel, built at the turn of the century. Most men had thus been housed in the warm buildings, while Summers and his men again had the shit job of advancing thru the snow. The weather wasn't so bad for the middle of February, but it still made the rest of the men feel miserable, as they were all wet (the snow was slushy, the roads muddy, and a little snow fell from the sky.

The hard-fought battles of the last few weeks had been brutal for everyone. The Regiment had again lost a lot of men when it was counter-attacked by several strong units from Guderian's Army Group Balaton. And again, Jack and Turnbull had had to welcome new, green soldiers. About half of the squad had been killed or injured enough to be removed from the frontlines. Having fresh troops was a mixed blessing. Sure, they had fresh meat with guns, but that meat tended to be raw and untrained to actual wartime operations. Consequently, their survival rates in the first few weeks were minimal at best.

Summers was a hard-nosed son of a bitch and wasn't the kind of feeling too emotional at a few deaths here and there, but after a while, losing so many youngsters still ended up affecting him. He felt sort of responsible, even if he tried to give the new kids all the chances in the world. But the German soldiers weren't pushovers, so it was challenging to keep the new arrivals out of trouble, especially since they tended to do stupid things and fought against outstanding soldiers.

Jacks' nine men and him (ten being the typical number for an American squad) walked up a large mountain path that was one of the mountain road access to Austria. The border was somewhere on top of the reasonably high mountain. The area was heavily forested with pines and tall trees. They walked in two ranks on each side, alert to any enemy activity. Since there was snow on the ground, their feet crunched as they stepped on it.

The road ahead was undisturbed whiteness, so to Jack and the rest of the men, it meant that at least the Krauts had not been anywhere near where they were currently advancing on the road. The men moved in silence, as any noise could give them away. They also needed to be quiet so they could listen to any the enemy could make.

The higher they got, the heavier the snow falling from the sky. The men could hear birds, which was a good sign, for they weren't afraid, so there wasn't anything ominous waiting for them on the sides. Jack was more worried about the front. The enemy was quite good at ambushing them with a well-positioned machine gun nest and entrenched anti-tank gun. Every time there was a bend in the road where they couldn't see where the path turned represented a potential spot for a German surprise attack. Being thorough and careful (there was a good reason he was still alive in this crazy war), he always stopped to be certain and take his time.

The drill was the same one at each bend. He sent his men in the forest to crawl and recon ahead with a better angle to see what lurked around the corner. So far, so good. No enemy had shown themselves.

One of the local men in the town had given them the information that the Nazis were entrenched right on top of the path, where the old border buildings and forts were located. Since it was pretty logical for the Germans to use what was already border defenses, he'd believed the man, especially since he had been a border guard before the war and seemed to know the area well.

While the Italians had had their Alpine Wall fortification, the French their Maginot Line, and the Germans their Siegfried Line, the Yugoslav were not about to ignore the trend in the 1930s. Called the Rupnik Line, it was a defensive system of fortifications and weapons installations that Yugoslavia constructed along its terrestrial western and northern border. The construction of the line, named after General Leon Rupnik (the designer and lead project manager), was a safety measure taken to counter the fortifications built by Italy on the other side of the border. It also was out of fear against the imposing danger of a German invasion following the Austrian Anschluss.

As was the case with the Italian fortifications, the Wehrmacht repurposed the Rupnik for its own use, turning the defenses around by pointing the guns and bunkers southward. It wasn't a perfect design, but it was a hell of a lot better than just trenches and improvised strong points.

So Jack's job on that damned cold day of February was to go up and recon the German positions. He was to report back as soon as possible on the enemy dispositions. As he continued his walk-up, he thought for a second that he heard voices. He took a few more steps. He heard noises again and was almost sure that it was the distinctive rumble of a tank or something mechanical. He lifted his hand in a gesture to the men behind to stop.

He quickly ordered them to spread into the forest on each side. By the time he was all bundled up on a hole full of snow, the noise was now obvious. An enemy vehicle was coming their way. He tapped Turnbull on the shoulder (his best soldier was just beside him) and whispered to prepare the Bazooka.

And then the squad waited. Another few minutes and a German Hanomag appeared into view. The Krauts were also on a recon but in an armored carrier. Summers again whispered to Turnbull to wait before firing, as the German truck was still far. For a fleeting moment, he hoped that the enemy would just pass by. But then he remembered that their tracks would be easily spotted in the snow, and the Germans would see that they'd fanned out into the side forest.

As forecasted by Summers, the Hanomag didn't need a lot of effort to spot their tracks in the snow and mud underneath it. The officer on top of the Hanomag barked orders, and soldiers started to jump out of the armored vehicle. Jack tapped Turnbull on the shoulder for the man to fire the Bazooka. The round fizzled loudly, shooting straight toward the target to hit the German half-track right in the middle of its armored side. The explosion opened the machine's inside and killed everyone still there. The men about to or already jumping got hurled into the air, some whole, some in shredded body parts. For a moment, the sergeant wondered why the explosion was so intense, but he then noticed that the other half of the squad's men had also thrown several grenades almost at the same time.

And in a few seconds, it was all over. The Hanomag and its men were no more. "Quick, boys!" he yelled. "Find me a prisoner if there is still one alive!" And the ten men squad fanned back onto the road. Most of the Germans were dead or critically injured, except one. A lucky son-of-a-gun had survived the explosion almost unscathed apart from having been knocked out. "Let's go back down and bring this one," said Summers as calmly as he could. Two men picked up the unconscious Wehrmacht soldier.

The way Jack saw it, they got what they came for. Information. After their little stunt in destroying the Hanomag, he wasn't about to to continue his "pleasant" little stroll up with roused up and angry Germans waiting for them.

The captain would want to know if they'd been all the way up to the German defenses, and he would tell him no. The expected officer's answer would be followed by anger, but at that moment, he would fish out the prisoner and give him to the Captain. The man would be happy with that, and Jack and his squad could get some warmth in the lovely hotel at the town's center.

CHAPTER 3

Stavka Meeting
Moscow, partially rebuilt Kremlin, February 20th, 1947

The important gathering was being held in the partially rebuilt Kremlin in New Red Square. The city was slowly re-taking shape after being destroyed almost entirely by the successive battles to storm it in 1942, 1943, 1944, and again in 1945. Moscow was one of the most fought-over pieces of land in all the Motherland. The Nazis had wanted it for their glory, and the Communists had thrown everything into retaking it for their pride.

Now it was back into Soviet hands, and this time for good (the Germans had been completely ousted from the USSR in February 1947). The Kremlin, the ultimate symbol of Russian power, had, of course, not been spared the incredible destruction. In fact, the Hitlerites had specifically targeted it in their first raids on the city. The fighting in the two following years and Skorzeny with a commando operation finished the job.

So Stalin had ordered its reconstruction, prioritizing it over several other more critical infrastructures for the war effort. The Russians, he felt, needed the Kremlin back on its feet for their prestige to be completely restored. So the half-reconstructed building was surrounded by scaffolding, giant cranes, and over a thousand workers. Several parts had already been completed (without the cosmetic aspects, of course). The Secretary-General of the Soviet Union's area (office, meeting room, Stavka operational quarters) was already housing the country's war leadership.

That day, the Stavka meeting was being held in the big operational room below the building. It was a giant bunker system equipped with everything needed to run a war from underground.

The air was stale, and most men present that day would have preferred to avoid the rank smell permeating the place, but Stalin liked it so had decided to hold the gathering there.

Present that day were Georgi Malenkov, Chairman of the Council of Ministers of the Soviet Union (sort of Stalin's deputy), Nikita Khrushchev, top political officer of the USSR. Followed several minor players that wouldn't dare speak during the talks. Marshal Zhukov rested on the opposite side of the table to represent the military.

Stalin, for once, was the one doing the talking at the Stavka meeting. "Zhukov, when can we launch the offensive in Eastern Prussia and Central Poland?" "Great Stalin. The Goldap offensive toward Konigsberg will be launched at the beginning of March while the attack on Guderian's forces will happen a few days afterward." Stalin grunted his approval. "And General. Have you discussed the special dispositions with commander Cherniakhovski of 1st Baltic and 3rd Bielorussian fronts?" asked the Soviet dictator, looking straight up into his military commander's eyes. "Yes, comrade General-secretary. As discussed, the device will be brought forward to be used at the greatest concentration of enemy forces."

Khrushchev intervened. "Marshal Zhukov, how will you achieve this? It's hardly like the Germans are known to be stupid". Zhukov gave the man a tiny smile. But Comrade Khrushchev, they do not know we have the device." He paused and put his big finger on the map laid in the middle of them all on a table. "We will attack here and toward Konigsberg. The Hitlerites will have no choice but to put themselves into our path to try to push us back," Stalin interrupted the commander. "How many casualties are we talking about?"

"Well, great Stalin, all of that is a matter of suppositions at this point," he answered as best he could. "But all indications point toward a complete destruction within several miles radius, so if we time it right, we can bag a lot of Germans with this explosion." He paused with a severe look on his face. "Of course, some losses will have to be expected on our side as for the enemy to be concentrating against us; we have to send something forward to push them hard…." He let the words hang for a moment.

The Soviet dictator barked one of his rare laughs. "Well, we have plenty of men to go around, so I don't care if we lose a ton. As long as we pierce the German lines and finish them in Prussia, I will be fine with it."

He stood up and walked around the table, behind the men sitting down. "We need to break the Nazi's backs, but at the same time, the bomb's explosion will send a clear message to the Americans." He walked over to the other side and put a hand on Zhukov's shoulders. "We will make them believe that we also have nuclear fire."

Stalin's bluff was so outrageous it might just work. The man's grand designs stretched far beyond the end of the conflict with the Axis powers. It ranged far into a future where Communism dominated the world.

"Zhukov, don't forget to stress to all military commanders that they are to avoid conflict or armed incidents with the Western Allies at all cost," the dictator said, tapping one more time on the Marshal's shoulder before continuing his round table walk. "Yes, Great Stalin."

Coming back to his seat at the head of the table, he sat down and stuffed some fresh tobacco in the pipe that he fished out of his side pocket. Everyone in the room waited for him to finish. They'd learned from experience that it wasn't a good time to interrupt the man.

"Malenkov, will you get Foreign Minister Molotov in here so we can give him his instructions on what we want him to tell the Allies," he said in between two puffs of his foul-smelling Georgian pipe tobacco. "Yes, Comrade General-Secretary." And Malenkov got up and walked the distance to the door to get the diplomat in the meeting for the next part of the discussions.

West wall
Germany's defense in the west, February 1947

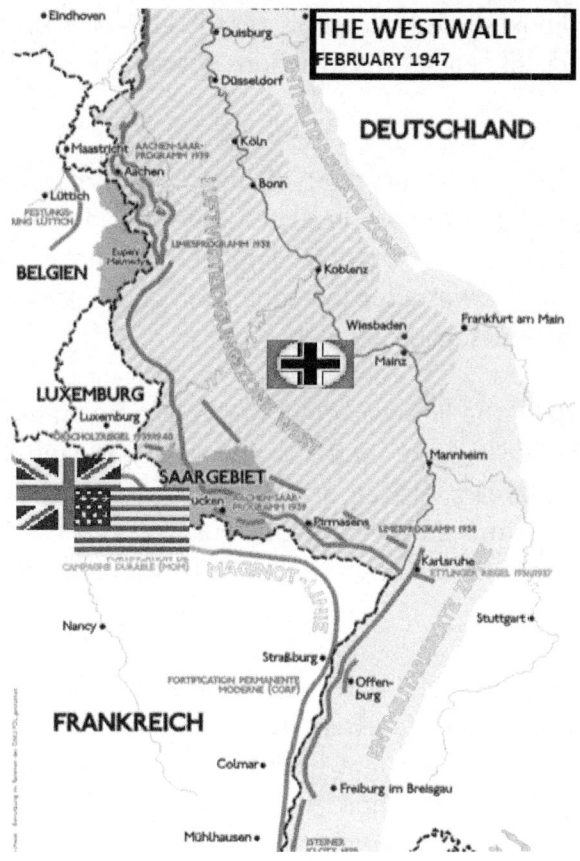

The Siegfried Line, known in Germany as the West wall, was a German defensive line built during the 1930s opposite the French Maginot Line. The build was in-trend with the other armies of the time and supposed a defensive-minded thinking that the Wehrmacht thought would not need anymore after it destroyed the French and British armies in 1940-1941.

It stretched more than 630 km from Kleve on the border with the Netherlands, along the western border of Nazi Germany, to the town of Weil am Rhein on the border to Switzerland – and featured more than 18,000 bunkers, tunnels, and tank traps.

The large numbers of bunkers were built in several different types, from the smallest (for machine gunners and riflemen) to the largest (for anti-tank guns as large as the PAK 43,44, and 45's). Smaller concrete "pillboxes" and "dragon's teeth" anti-tank obstacles were built as part of each construction phase, sometimes by the thousands.

Czech hedgehog, another tank obstacle, was made by welding together several bars of steel in such a way that any tank rolling over it would get stuck and possibly damaged. Where it was doable, water-filled ditches were dug instead of tank traps and, on the other side, ringed with defensive bunkers.

For a long while, the line was quiet and even in a state of disrepair, as the Third Reich conquered far and wide, expanding its might across the European, African and Asiatic continents. But by 1945-1946, it became more and more obvious that the West wall might finally fulfill the grand design it was built for: the defense of the Fatherland.

Over 30 000 forced workers (French and British POWs), in addition to 15 000 young kids fourteen to sixteen of the Hitleryoungen (Hitler's youth), were brought back to the Siegfried to work round the clock to prepare new, more modern defenses. Weaponry had advanced far and wide during the conflict, and not all the West Wall's bunkers and fortifications were adapted to it. So several were redone, and thousands of guns, artillery, and anti-aircraft weaponry were brought forward.

Army Group West lofty forty divisions bolstered the whole defensive apparatus, including several Panzer Divisions and experienced troops. As per a direct decision from the Fuhrer, all of the "V" rockets weapons were also given to the old general for tactical uses.

Some of the men amongst Rundstedt officer staff that had been at some point part of the by now famous Dnieper-Lovat-Volkhov Defensive line in Russia even claimed that the West wall was stronger. And no wonder. The Wehrmacht had a great defensive position, narrow front to protect, tons of full-strength units, sufficient air cover, and still enough willpower to resist forever.

Somewhere in Slovenia
February 21st, 1947

He looked right. Looked left. "No," he thought. It wasn't what he was doing. He was turning his head from right to left. That's what he was doing. Gaston was lying flat on his back. The sky was full of falling snow, and he could see his rasping breath thru the vapor it produced in the cold. He sat up. He seemed to be in a field, but his world rocked and turned. He was utterly dazed, perhaps even stunned. Maybe he was dreaming.

The field was some kind of farmland, for it seemed to be somewhat square and was surrounded on all sides by towering forests. It was uneven as when the ground had been plowed before winter. In the distance to his left, he thought he saw a river or a stream, but he wasn't sure because it seemed covered in ice, so he could not tell. His eyes focused on something bright. Yes! It was his fighter's wreck, fiercely burning at the end of the field to his right. He thought it odd that the aircraft had crashed near where he landed. For there was no mistaking it now. Lamirande had been shot down, but he'd survived. He unbuckled the straps on his parachute that lay sprawled behind him. The fine linen was flapping into the gentle wind, and some parts were already being buried in the falling snow.

Eventually, his ears started working again. At first, he heard what seemed like a distant rumble of thunder. But, as he focused more and more and his mind got back to normal, he finally concluded that the boom was the roar of battle. He tried to look from where it came from. No luck. The noise seemed to be all around him. Then, he noticed quick flashes going from one side to the field to the other. Then again, he finally registered that they were bullet and shell tracers.

Suddenly, the whole dreadfulness of his situation hit him like a sledgehammer. He'd just crashed and was in the middle of a field. In the middle of a fire exchange between Axis and Allies. Both sides were shooting at each other from the forest edges. Several explosions rocked the ground and shredded trees. Several of them were on fire, and mounds of dirt and snow rose and fell as the ordinance impacted the ground and forested area.

Looking for his side gun, he patted it with his hand. It was resting in its holster, as he'd left it. He stayed as immobile as possible, as the combatants didn't seem to have noticed him. Which he thought odd since he'd probably landed with his parachutes and been quite obvious about it. What Lamirande didn't know what that again, he'd been incredibly lucky. He'd been shot down and had had to bail out of his plane, but he made landfall before any of the soldiers slugging it out on both sides of the field arrived. So when they started to shoot at each other, all they saw was a burning jet and some "dead pilot" lying in the snow. The French Canadian had indeed been out cold for over an hour since he'd landed awkwardly and hit his head.

Gaston turned on his belly to try to stay as invisible as possible. From where he was, he didn't know which sides were which. He could only see explosions and tracers. He wondered what to do. There weren't many solutions to his predicament. Stay where he was and hope for the best, or else take his chances and run toward one side. He had a 50% probability of throwing himself in enemy hands. Quickly surmising that the odds were not good enough for his situation, he decided to wait some more.

Another twenty minutes into the firefight, a loud whistling noise started to be heard from the left. Left was what it was since the sky was white with snow and clouds, so he could not figure out any direction (north, south, east, west). He wondered what it was for a moment, and then the whistle sounds morphed into explosions. A lot of explosions everywhere across the field and forest on his right. It was an artillery barrage.

Since he was out in the open, the shells landed near him, and he quickly started to be showered with dirt. He had no choice. He stood up, hesitating for another second on the direction to go, and he sprinted. He ran like the devil possessed him. It didn't take long for the soldiers on both sides to notice the crazy men running in the field amidst the falling artillery. But not one of them targeted Gaston since they didn't know if he was Axis or Allied.

His proverbial luck held again on that day, and he was not hit by any shrapnel. As he approached the forest's edge, he started to hear shouts of encouragement. The men were cheering him. And it was then that he realized that he would be saved since they were English voices. He'd chosen the good side! If he'd run the other way, he would have been taken prisoner, and his next destination the POWS camps in Germany.

He ran directly into the arms of happy, smiling American faces that had all stopped to shoot. In fact, the whole field had stopped firing, and for just a fleeting moment, there was peace between the two sides. Apparently, even the Germans had rooted for the pilot's survival.

Lamirande was brought back to the rear by the G.I.s, where he was rapidly put on a jeep back behind the Allied lines. On his way back toward the nearest airfield, he had a lot of time to think about what had happened. He'd been shot down; that was quite obvious. He couldn't remember the last few hours before his crash. He recalled the mission but nothing else. The squadron had been tasked with another air-to-air superiority mission. And then the rest were vague images at best. He wondered if he'd been shot down by his nemesis or else by some other German pilot.

A Luftwaffe ace named Adolf Galland was having a good day several kilometers away. He'd finally shot down the hockey sticks pilot. He surmised that his duel with the man was now over. He'd circled the field where his plane had crashed and had seen the British pilot strewn about o the field near his parachute, unmoving.

Their dogfight above Slovenia had been another epic struggle, but the German bested the French Canadian in the end. Galland was happy but sad at the same time. He'd sort of enjoyed their little game. After all, their rivalry had been going on for years on end, without any clear winners.

He hoped to see the man in the afterlife. Little did he know that he would get to see him a lot sooner than that, for four days after being shot down, Lamirande was deemed fit for duty, and while he could have had a leave to get some rest, the Canadian ace insisted on getting back into a fighter as soon as possible.

Weapon development – United States of America
Super Pershing, M18 Hellcat, Phantoms, P-80

Left: M46 Super Pershing. Right: M18 Hellcat

As the war dragged on and took a turn for the duration, all major countries accelerated their weapon developments. As it became obvious that the USA would have to shoulder several more years of war to end the conflict, many more projects were brought to fruition during the 1945 and 1946 years.

Advances in all fields were tremendous, and none were more obvious than the atomic bomb. While it represented a game-changer for ending the war, it wasn't like the U.S. Armed Forces had neglected the other areas.

The initial shock of German tanks on the battlefield produced changes for the thinly armored and outgunned U.S. forces and their medium Sherman tanks. By 1943, the U.S. Army had cause to regret one of its most fateful choices: the decision not to build heavy tanks. Its M4 Sherman medium tank was a decent enough armored fighting vehicle when it entered combat in 1941-1942. Yet by the end of 1943 and middle of 1944, the thirty-ton Sherman had repeatedly been pulverized by heavier German tanks like the sixty-ton Tiger and its heavier version, the Konigstiger, which had bigger guns and thicker armor.

The American response was the heavy but slow T29(35km/hour), with its 105mm guns and 102 mm frontal armor. The M26 Pershing also entered service with its 90mm gun and a 48kmhour speed.

Produced in impressive numbers by the start of 1946, it was well on its way to replacing the American tanks already at the frontline. While the T29/M26s were not necessarily as adequate as the IS-2 Russian tanks, they represented an adequate counter against the Panzerwaffe. They were not perfect, but they were becoming numerous enough to make a difference against German armor that was no longer untouchable.

By 1944-1945, new projects to make a tank more suited for the European battlefield were accelerated. The result was the Pershing II (or the Super-Pershing) with better speed (49 Km/hour), improved frontal armor (102mm), and almost 60 tons. The tank still sported the 105mm gun as well. Production was launched in Detroit, New York state, and Pittsburgh by the middle of 1946, and by February 1947, the first models were arriving in the newly liberated French ports.

Another exciting development for the American Army was the M19 Hellcat, a superb, light, and versatile tank destroyer. It was the fastest U.S. armored fighting vehicle on the road (89km/hour), so it could dance around its heavier and consequently quite slower German counterparts. This speed was attained by keeping armor to a minimum and using an innovative automatic transmission. The designers equipped the relatively light vehicle with the same main gun used on some variants of the much larger Sherman tank. So if the Hellcat dueled with Tigers, the trick was to move since the super-thin armor (25 mm frontal) did not permit it to sustain a 88mm round. Compared to the 41km an hour that the Tiger II could make (and even the 50km/hour for the upgraded version with the 1000hp+ naval engine), it was quite a game-changer for the Allied forces. The gun was a respectable 75mm, enabling U.S. tank commander to kill a lot more German tanks than its small size entailed at first glance: The Hellcat moved fast and wide and could outmaneuver any Panzer to fire at their softer sides or rears.

P-80 shooting star

In the air, the Allies had been lucky to get the Gloster Meteors operational by the time they did. The Americans and the British version of the aircraft shouldered much of the air fighting burden by the middle of 1946. While U.S. companies like Boeing and Lockheed had been outclassed by the German ones in getting jet technology to the battlefield, they redoubled their efforts once it was realized how far behind the Americans were compared to the Germans and even the British.

The Lockheed P-80 Shooting Star was the first jet fighter used operationally by the United States Air Force. Designed and built by Lockheed in 1945 and delivered just 143 days after the start of the design process, production models were flying by the end of that same year. At the beginning of 1947, the new aircraft was deployed in all American-occupied areas and had already fought several battles against the Axis Horten wings and ME-262s. Some were also rushed to Japan to face the developing situation against the Russians in Manchuria / China.

The plane compared itself advantageously to the Meteor or the ME-262 and was close enough or better in all aspects of performance (turn rate, turn radius, climb rate, dive rate, roll rate, acceleration, top speeds, etc.).

In short, dogfighting performance would boil down to individual pilot skills and tactics, but at least the Allied pilots had another similar plane with which to fight the German Luftwaffe. The P-80 was on paper a superior fighter, and it remained to be seen how it would fare in combat in 1947. Given the speed difference despite similar thrust, it was a "cleaner" design aerodynamically than the German one, so the American planners were reasonably confident that it would do well. After all, most U.S. pilots had combat experience in jet fighters, having been equipped with Glouster Meteors for the better part of two years already.

F-84 Thunderjet fighter-bomber

Another aircraft development was the Republic F-84 Thunderjet, an American turbojet fighter-bomber aircraft. Originating as a 1944 United States Army Air Forces (USAAF) proposal for a "day fighter," the F-84 first flew in 1946, and by 1947 it was looking like it would enter production, as the war didn't seem to be ending anytime soon.

Mcdonnell Phantoms

The U.S. Navy was not neglected. The McDonnell FH Phantom was a twinjet fighter aircraft explicitly developed for carrier-based operations. Its first flights were in 1945, and production had started in the last few months of 1946. The first aircraft were arriving to replace the older propeller-driven fighters of the U.S. Navy. Shipment to the Pacific Fleet (Nimitz) was prioritized, given the challenging situation developing with the Soviets in the Far East.

With many other developments in the pipelines in terms of larger bombers, new infantry weapons, significant advances in sonar and radar technology made the US planners, including President Truman himself, confident that the Us Armed Forces were up to the coming challenge: Finish the Axis and face the new, lurking Red menace.

Extract Of Heinz Guderian 1952 Book, Panzer Leader
Brest Litovsk Fortress, February 22nd, 1947

View of Brest Litosvk central citadel, 1947

After the Lake Balaton counter-offensive concluded, I pulled back my forces from Hungary and Slovenia. We had much cause for celebration. We'd given another good drubbing to the Soviets and even had had a chance to show the Americans that the war was not over.

From the two-pronged offensive poured thru over half a million battle-hardened soldiers from the Balkans. Surprisingly enough, the going had not been difficult. Our forces cut thru most Allied defenses, either be Russians or Americano-British. Several historians have tried to figure out why we were able to be so successful in so complicated a situation and facing such overwhelming odds. I must say, many years later, that the only answer I can give is that we had the most superb army in the world at the time and had top-of-the-line equipment.

Added with solid air cover from the Luftwaffe jets and Arado blitz bombers, our new and improved Tigers II (with the naval 1000hp+ horsepower engine) sliced thru the Russian units like a hot knife thru butter. Perhaps it was because the Red Army was at the end of a prolonged offensive that had started in the heart of the Ukraine after we decided to cancel Operation Citadel in 1946. Or perhaps a combination of the two factors. I cannot say for sure.

But the attack we executed on the Western Allies was different, in the sense that for the first time, the U.S. and British forces encountered an "eastern army" with its full complement of heavy tanks and splendid artillery units. The war on the Ostfront was of an entirely different size, and our attack came as an utter shock to the over-confident Western Allies. For months on end, they'd operated on the narrow Italian front, where they had a high quantitative advantage over Manstein's beleaguered forces. Furthermore, it was one of the first times in a long while (since 1945) that these troops ventured out of range of their powerful naval guns that had sort of compensated for their lack of field artillery.

For if one asks what are the main differences between the war in the east and the war in the west to an old general like me, I will always say that it was all about tanks (their staggering numbers) and artillery guns. From the start of Operation Barbarossa, the Wehrmacht got hammered with incredible numbers of Soviet ordinances. So we rapidly adapted and brought forward all the guns we could bear on them. What the American units encountered in our Slovenia counter-offensive was a taste of the mighty struggle being fought between the Reich and the USSR. A battle of titans that the Western Allies were ill-prepared for.

So once the Slovenia-Hungary offensive was ended and the troops were saved to help bolster our already considerable forces, we returned to a more defensive mindset, for we could ill-afford the losses during an offensive. In the case of the Balaton attack, the cost to benefit ratio was not hard to calculate since even if we lost many tanks and men, we saved hundreds of thousands of fighting soldiers that would otherwise have been lost.

Our frontline stretched from the northern parts of Hungary and southern Poland (Galicia) to the east of Konigsberg. I was responsible for the forces in Army Group Center (my forces were renamed as such by OKW when the Balaton offensive was over) from a few hundred kilometers north of Warsaw to Galicia.

On February 1st, I was touring the frontline in the Brest-Litovsk region and coming back to the area for the first time since 1942 before the start of Operation Barbarossa brought a stream of memories back to my mind. I remember feeling a mixed sense of dread and confidence in attacking the Russians. For if was certain in our ability to face the Red Army man to man and push them around as we did in the two years that followed, my uneasiness came from what I knew of Soviet production capabilities and the immensity of their land, resources, and factories. I was unfortunately proved right in my apprehensions. Russia ground down the Wehrmacht and the Reich of a thousand years' hopes fluttered to the winds in the immensity of the Russian steppe.

Although largely obsolete by contemporary standards, the old Austro-Hungarian fortress was still a pretty formidable position, as the Russians had worked extensively on it from 1939 to 1942. Still, much work had to be done to get it ready to receive the Russian attack since the defenses (bunkers, gun emplacements, and the likes) pointed the wrong way (west).

The ancient fortress held a strategic position at the confluence of the Muchawiec and Bug Rivers. Occupying the site of a medieval castle, it was strengthened and reconstructed in Napoleonic times then again in 1847 and also before the First World War. Heavily damaged in 1915-1916, the fortress was turned into a materiel depot by the Poles and its central part into a prison.

The fortress occupied a strategic position in the Polish lines, and its defense could prevent the Red Army from crossing into central Poland and toward Warsaw. By the start of the Second World War, it still had its original outline of a star-shaped fortification since its construction in the early 19th century. The citadel, the core of the fortress, was on the central island formed by the Bug River and the two branches of the Mukhavets River. The island was skirted by a ring of a two-storied barrack with four semi-towers. The 1.8 km long barrack comprised 250 rooms to accommodate 6000 soldiers within thick walls built from super strong red bricks. Initially, there were four gates to enter the Citadel, but only two remained after the heavy 1942 battle, and the rest had not been rebuilt. The place also used to house 12000 soldiers, but a lot had been demolished in our 1942 attack.

Three fortifications surrounded the citadel as bridgeheads made up of branches of the Mukhavets River and moats (ditches), fortified by earthworks ten meters high with redbrick casemates inside. The three fortifications were named after towns: Russian name for the city of Kobryn in Belarus, Terespol in Poland, and Volyn, a historical region of Volhynia majorly located in Ukraine. The Kobrin fortification was the biggest, located in the northeastern part, shaped like a horseshoe, featured four fortification curtains, three detached ravelins, and a lunette in the western part, East Fort and West Fort. The Terespol Fortification was the western bridgehead, featuring four detached lunettes. The Volyn fortification was the southeastern bridgehead, featuring two curtains with two detached ravelins. They were pretty obsolete (almost medieval-like), but they represented a serious strong point for my defensive setup with the right amount of guns, tanks, and men.

I toured Brest without thinking that it would be the focal point of the Soviet offensive. I was to be entirely surprised a few weeks later when the town was the exact spot where the Red Army chose to put the hardest pressure.

Weapon development – USSR
Enter the T-54 Main battle tank

T-54

The Soviet T-34 was an incredibly well-balanced tank, taking into account protection and mobility for its cost of any tank of its time in the world. Its appearance on the battlefield came as an utter shock for the Germans. It even sparked the making of the brilliant Panther and Tiger designs. The revolutionary Russian tank development never stopped throughout the Second World War, and it continued to perform well by being regularly upgraded with better guns and armor modifications. However, the designers could not incorporate the latest technologies or major developments as vital tank production could not be interrupted during wartime unless a firm commitment was made by the Soviet government. The other possibility was that the struggle at the front took such a positive turn that the Stavka could accept fewer numbers produced.

In 1944, under orders from Stalin to further the T-34's design, the Morozov Design Bureau (formerly in Kharkov but moved to Siberia on Perm to flee the German advance) resurrected the pre-war T-34M development project and created the T-44 tank. After encountering the heavily armored German tanks in their countless battles in the Russian steppes, Soviet designers concluded that the only way forward was to raise firepower. Thanks to a space-efficient torsion-bar suspension, a novel transverse engine mount, and the removal of the hull machine-gunner's crew position, the T-44 had a cross country performance at least as good as the T-34, but with substantially better armor and a much more powerful 85mm gun.

By the time the T-44 was ready for production, the T-34 had also been modified to fit the same gun, and the IS-2 Stalin tanks were present in great numbers on the battlefield. In short, the Russians had enough firepower to face the Wehrmacht on its own terms without that model.

Although the T-44 was superior in most other ways, T-34 production was in full swing by this time. The massive numbers of T-34s being built offset any advantage to smaller numbers of a superior design. So up to the middle of 1945, the T-44 was produced in only small numbers, around 500 being completed by the end of the year. Not many of them even saw combat.

So, the designers continued to use the design as the basis for further improved guns, experimenting with a 122 mm design but later deciding a 100 mm gun was a better alternative. Efforts to fit the 100 mm gun to the T-44 demonstrated that small changes to the design would significantly improve the combination. The main issue was a larger turret ring, which suggested slightly enlarging the hull. A new design prototype, about 40 centimeters (16 in) longer and only 10 cm wider, was completed in 1946. This model looked almost identical to the original T-44, albeit bigger with a much larger gun.

As the war was taking a very advantageous turn for Russia in 1946, it was decided to slow down T-34 mass-production to begin making the new tank that its designers believed would revolutionize mobile warfare. The vehicle officially entered service on 14th September 1946. Full production was launched in the giant Nizhny Tagil factory in November 1947. By the middle of that year, it was planned that over 4000 of the new tank would be made.

Being impatient as ever with his new toys, Stalin put all his weight into the project and made sure the T-54s would make their debut in the Goldap Offensive in February 1947. The 3rd Tank Guard Army would have the honor of going into battle with it for the first time. Hopes were high that it would be able to face the Tiger IIs without any problem.

Russians mathematics did not think they were faulty in their belief that, after fire testing, the T-54 would win over the best and strongest armor the Germans could offer. After all, the tank's D-10T high-velocity 100mm gun had a tested and confirmed penetration of 239mm at optimal range. Since the heaviest German steel plates ranged from 185mm(Konigstiger) to 220mm(Maus), they were right in their assessments, as the battlefield would soon confirm.

The miraculous recovery
One last lull before the fall February 26th, 1947

At the end of February 1947, the Third Reich had finally stabilized its frontlines. For a moment, in December 1946 and January 1947, it looked like the Wehrmacht would crumble and fall, but it was not yet to be.

The German forces operated what had been called, in many a history books after the war, "a miraculous recovery," as they were able to stop the Allies from advancing on all fronts. Even if only for a short period of time, it nonetheless was impressive.

First, General Von Rundstedt was firmly entrenched in the West Wall (Siegfried Line) and, with a little over 40 full-strength divisions, didn't look like he would soon fail. The defensive fight that the old general had to put up to retire his soldiers in an orderly and organized fashion was one of the most brilliant fighting retreats of the war. He saved most of his troops while exacting a severe toll on the advancing Western Allied forces.

Supported by a powerful artillery, V1 and V2 rockets re-purposed for tactical roles and with full air cover (jets, Wasserfall missile system), the units under Rundstedt command represented quite a challenge for the Americano-British forces.

In the south, the recovery was as remarkable. Erich Von Manstein, the theater commander, had fought and operated one of the best defensive campaigns of the Second World War, making the Allies fight for every inch of Italian soil they wanted to conquer. After a succession of grinding battles along well-prepared defensive lines, the General was able to entrench his 15 divisions into their last redoubt in the Italo-Austrian Alps.

It didn't look like the Western Allies would be able to break the masterful deadlock that Manstein imposed on them from his towering fortifications. In the east, the Wehrmacht came out of a challenging 1946 year that had seen it completely pushed out of the Soviet Union. After all, only eight months before the Germans had been firmly entrenched along their Dnieper-Lovat-Volkhov line.

But the Axis soldiers were able to pull yet another rabbit out of their hat and keep themselves in the field even if losing a tremendous amount of men, equipment, and territories. Bolstered by retreating forces and everything the Reich could muster in one last desperate push to get troops to the frontlines, Model (Army Group Prussia) and Guderian (Army Group Center) led a little over 100 divisions to try to keep the Communist hordes away from the Fatherland.

It would take something truly extraordinary to break the German might. Unfortunately for the Reich, the Allies had what they needed to do it: the Atomic Bomb and numbers that at least doubled the number of divisions that the German Army could field.

Weapon development – United Kingdom
Jets and heavy tanks

British Centurion heavy tank

The British Empire, much-diminished in power and seeing its American cousin taking the lead of the free world, still had some serious bite left. And besides, the UK scientific community was quite strong and had been able to evacuate before being captured in the 1940 invasion. Without men like Frank Whittle and his Powers Jets ltd company, the Allies would have had a lot of challenges against the Messerschmitt 262.

The country was temporarily weakened by the German conquest of the British Islands, but Churchill's dynamic move to Canada and the subsequent industrial buildup from there compensated for the loss. Once the British Isles were liberated, English engineers and scientists returned to the country and continued the developments they'd pursued while in the Dominion of Canada.

The Empire had at first relied on American tanks before rebuilding their own industrial infrastructure. By 1943, most British divisions were equipped with Shermans and then by their upgraded "firefly" versions. By the end of 1945, several units sported the Pershing tanks as well.

Still, that didn't mean that Churchill had given up on the UK making its own tanks. Development on a new, heavy model began in 1943 (in Canada), and the first prototypes were tested near Manchester in early 1946. The tank was called the Centurion. Initial designs called for the tank to weigh no more than 40 long tons (speed was thought more important than protection then). Still, after the first disastrous encounters with German Tigers and Panthers, armor thickness was revised upward by order of magnitude, increasing the proposed weight to 50 tons. New requirements also included a heavier gun and a larger turret to house it.

After the liberation of Great Britain, the old tank and automotive factories were either rebuilt, repaired, or re-purposed. The final version that came out of the assembly yards sported 150mm frontal armor and a 100mm high-velocity gun. Designed to go head-to-head against the best the Reich could offer, it was starting to arrive on the European battlefield, just in time for the final offensive against the Siegfried Line.

(DeHavilland Vampire jet (left) and Hawker Sea Hawk (right)

In the air, the Brits had been the Allied leaders in jets. The latest developments from the aircraft factories in Liverpool and Windsor (Canada) were great proof that the English scientist had improved on the Glouster Meteor design.

The DeHavilland Vampire was the second British jet fighter to be operated by the RAF, after the Gloster Meteor, and the first to be powered by a one jet engine. Development of the Vampire as an experimental aircraft began in 1943 during Canadian exile. From the company's design studies, it was decided to use a single-engine, twin-boom aircraft powered by the Halford H.1 turbojet. Aside from its propulsion system and twin-boom configuration, it was a relatively conventional aircraft. In November 1946, the Vampire entered operational service with the Royal Air Force. It was still relatively low in numbers compared to the Gloster Meteor, but it nonetheless represented a significant improvement.

The Vampire had a relatively good power/weight ratio and was reputedly quite maneuverable within the 400–500 mph (640–800 km/h) range. Heavy use of the rudder was required at slower speeds, during which pilots had to be cautious during shallow turns to avoid stalls. The Vampire was the better of the two as it was fairly small, very agile, and fast, especially at low altitudes, had good speed over a wide altitude range, and had outstanding firepower with its 4 20mm cannons. The plane best mimicked the characteristics of a similarly sized piston-engine fighter (most pilots still trained on various piston-engine aircraft, after all) and was probably the best dogfighter. But the plane wasn't produced to replace the Meteor, and in the end, both aircraft would remain operational during the next few years as the war continued to unfold.

The other novelty was the excellent Hawker Sea Hawk, the first jet fighter (along with the U.S. Air Force Phantom) to operate from an aircraft carrier. Design and prototypes were done in Canada (1943 to 1944) and testing on an aircraft carrier from the decks of Bonaventure in 1946. Production was still limited in 1947, but the Auspicious, the brand-new aircraft carrier being finalized in the Liverpool yards, would be equipped with the new aircraft.

The heavy hand of Soviet Diplomacy
Stalin meets with Molotov, February 24th, 1947

"So, comrade Molotov," said Stalin in his calm and menacing voice. "Let's review your instructions." The two men were in the small, austere-looking office that the Russian dictator loved to work in. So much in fact that he had it rebuilt almost the same as the one that was destroyed along with the Kremlin in the German offensives of 1942 to 1945.

They were alone, and it was well into the evening. The General-Secretary called the Soviet diplomat out of his bed for an urgent meeting. Molotov was none too happy about it (he had been sleeping, after all), but no one in the USSR refused a summon from the dictator. Nor could it permit itself to make the man wait too long.

Luckily for him, Stalin had sent a car, and it had been waiting in front of Vyacheslav's house. They'd driven quite fast to the New Kremlin, as most of Moscow's streets had by early 1947 been cleared of rubble and debris. The workers toiled days and nights to make the country's capital great again. Stalin had even ordered to use the tens of thousands of Axis prisoners of war to help with the reconstruction. "They destroyed it; they will rebuild it," was one of the Soviet leader's favorite quotes.

The drive to the meeting had been pleasant enough; the city had reclaimed the night with the end of the blackouts and curfew that had been in effect since the reconquest in 1945. It was considered that the Hitlerite forces were far away now, and besides, they'd stopped bombing Russian cities almost entirely. The Reich needed its planes and pilots at the frontlines, for the Fatherland was fighting for its very life by then.

Molotov had been brought to Stalin's office the moment he exited the car on Red Square. The famous landmark was also being rebuilt, and it would look similar to the old version, except that time, there would be more statues of the Soviet dictator.

Stalin handed out a folder with the mention "secret" on it. Vyacheslav took it from across the small desk that was separating the two men. They were both sitting down on a chair. The diplomat thought for a moment that the look of the place had a gloomy sense about it. Two small, green glass banker desk lamps provided the only lighting in the darkish room.

"First, let's talk about our official position in Asia, shall we, comrade Minister of Foreign Affairs?" "Of course, said Molotov eagerly, turning some page in the folder until he got to the Manchurian part of his orders. "What we want to convey to the Westerners is simple. We are here to liberate China and help our Communists brothers led by Mao." Stalin backed up comfortably in his chair, clapping his hands together. "Make the promise that we will evacuate Manchuria and North Korea as soon as the civil war in China is over and the Nationalist forces have been vanquished." Molotov took his courage and dared ask a question to Stalin. "Great leader. I do not want to contradict you, but I am not sure the Americans will buy it. Their commanding general in the Far East, Douglas MacArthur, seems to be the sort of fellow that won't...." "That won't what, comrade Molotov? Won't accept our position? The man will never dare attack us first." Vyacheslav continued since the dictator seemed calm and received his words well. "Our information points out to the fact that they have started to supply the Japanese forces still resisting our troops in the Pekin and Western China areas." "I agree, comrade Minister." And that is precisely what you will tell them. Turn the tables and let them know that we will not back down unless they stop helping our enemies. Be specific that we still consider them the enemies of the alliance between us and the western nations." Molotov silently nodded, so Stalin continued.

"As you know, you will be flying to Washington D.C. soon and will ask for a meeting with the U.S. President once we have detonated our atomic device on the Hitlerites." So the next set of demands that you will give them is that they evacuate all of Germany for the Soviet Union to occupy. Try to push a little for France and Italy, but let them think we let it go to give them the idea that they won something. Anyway, we don't have anything to justify those actions." "Yes, Comrade General-Secretary."

"Be as firm as you can, Vyacheslav. I am counting on you to scare them into believing that we will attack them with nuclear fire if they do not comply with our demands. They will fold, and we will have Europe and all the territories we want in the Far East as well." "Yes, Great Stalin." "Now, go back to sleep, and don't let me down, comrade Minister."

Stalin gave him a slight hand gesture before burying himself again in the tons of paperwork on the desk. Being dismissed, Molotov got up and left. On the way home, he looked absently at the outside thru the vehicle's window. The diplomat was lost in thoughts, and most importantly, in worry. He was not sure that Stalin was right on this one. He would obey the dictator's orders because he knew the cost of not doing so, but he highly doubted that the Americans would accept being pushed around by a new bully.

After all, they'd waged a global war against the Axis to liberate the free nations of the world. Not see them enslaved by another power, either by Russia or any other.

They had the atomic bomb, while the Soviet Union only had one and then would rely on a bluff to make the Allies believe they had more to scare them from using their own.

Molotov was a believer in the Communist dream. Also, he would do precisely as Stalin demanded. He just was not confident that it was the most brilliant move.

Weapon development – Germany
Tiger III, Maus II, ME 262.b

By late 1946 and as its empire dwindled (so resources were scarcer), Germany was beyond making new weapons that diverged too far from what was already being built. It simply couldn't stop production lines to meddle with new projects. But the Reich already had great platforms in tanks and aircraft, so it opted for improving its existing weapons.

The first to be improved was the Tiger II. The tank had become, by mid-1946, the Panzerwaffe main workhorse. The Konigstiger was present on every battlefield, but it had been noted that the 88mm gun shot glanced on sloped armor at greater range. Also, some of the heavier Russian tanks (IS-2, KV-2) were quite resistant since they were equipped with hefty frontal plates. So it was decided to make a running change on the Panzer with a new, more powerful weapon, the 128mm PAK44, that would significantly increase armor penetration from all ranges. Added with the new Simmering Sla.16 engine and transmission that solved the mobility issue, the Tiger II.b (or more commonly called the Tiger III) represented an even more potent threat for the Allies (as if it wasn't already the king of the battlefield!). The machines were present in ever-increasing numbers by middle February 1947, and the ministry of Armament and Production planned on replacing most Tigers with the new models by mid-1948.

Then came the Maus II, another incredible improvement over the first version of the super-heavy tank. The Maus' great mass (180 tons!!!) had made it as slow as a snail, and its engine/transmission had been totally underpowered for its size (20km/hour speed). So the machine had only been suitable for static defensive warfare. That major flaw rendered the tank un-useable in any type of offensive movement. So, the Porsche company designers worked hard in 1945 and 1946 to get a better engine, and they found one in the 1000hp+ Simmering Sla.16 engine that was also installed in the

Tiger III. With the modification, the tank was still slow (35km/hour) but could be considered for more than just an incredibly well-armored static gun. Its 12.8 cm Pak 44 anti-tank gun was the most powerful gun on any German armored vehicle, so it was hoped that the Maus would have a tangible impact on a battlefield where narrow movement was expected, like on the Western Front. The Pak 44 had short to medium-range performance similar to the 8.8 cm Pak 43. Still, the 12.8 cm Pak 44 better maintained its anti-tank performance over long to extreme-long ranges - 1,800–2,700 m (2,000–3,000 yd) and beyond - while also doubling as an effective field gun when firing high-explosive shells. Due to planned steel shortage, not as many Maus IIs were built by early 1947, but the Reich was still able to equip several heavy Panzer Battalions with it.

Overall, the Reich still felt quite confident that its incredible tank force (Panzerwaffe) would do a carnage on the frontlines. With the amazing air cover that the Luftwaffe provided, the German Panzers could maintain themselves in the field, only worry about what was in front of them and disregard anything from above them.

The Luftwaffe, by 1947, decided to concentrate its production on the model it already had, as the ME-262s, Komets, and Horten's were so far ahead of what the Allies had that more development was slowed down to concentrate on making more planes and improving on the existing designs, like better rockets (new versions of the R4Ms), more range and better handling.

Anyway, who could bet on the Reich's chances to survive for long? So the Germans banked on what they had and hoped for the best.

The Tiger III
Walder gets a new toy February 28th, 1947

"Look, commander!" It was almost a yell. At least it was not born out of desperation, thought Erich; it was one of excitement. Walder's young and talented gunner, Hans Stromer, was beyond himself. He looked like he was a kid in a candy store.

The reason was the magnificent 128mm PAK44 that equipped their new ride. The Maus also had the same gun, but the machine was so slow that it was useless in any type of offensive operations. It was getting a new engine that would make it faster, but it was still too slow for offensive operations.

But the Reich's engineers had not only improved the tiger with a new engine; they now sent a brand-new tank with the mega gun. Every one of his men was happy that day. They all harbored broad smiles. The mechanics were busy reviewing everything there was to see about the new engine, Hans had his gun, Walder improved optics, the loader a little more space in the turret (the new Tiger had needed a slightly enlarged one to house the larger 128mm PAK44), and the driver marveled at some minor changes the engineers had made for the Panzer's control and throttle. It was all subtle, but real improvements for the battlefield were all that the Panzerwaffe crews needed, and the Reich had delivered it to these experience, tough men.

But for the tank commander, the main improvement was the gun, so he inspected it along with Stromer. According to the manual he'd read about the weapon, it was very potent. The 128mm PAK44 had been on the battlefield for a while and proved its capability to destroy any Russian tanks in the field with disconcerting ease. It had short to medium-range performance like the 8.8 cm Pak 43 but better maintained its anti-tank performance over long to extreme-long ranges - 1,800–2,700 m (2,000–3,000 yd) and beyond - while also doubling as an effective field gun when firing high-explosive shells. With a weapon like that, Walder figured that they would be able to pick up any Russian tank the second they saw it, even if only a tiny spec on the horizon. This would make all the difference in the world.

The gun was fed with two-parts ammunition, the projectile and cartridge making up separate pieces (it was the reason the Tiger's turret had been expanded). Because of this, the gun could be fired using three different sized propellant charges; a light, medium and heavy charge. The light and medium ones were usually used when the PAK fulfilled an artillery piece role, where they would launch the 28 kg projectiles to a muzzle velocity of 845 m/s and 880 m/s, respectively. The heavy charge was used when the gun was fulfilling its intended role as an anti-tank gun, where it fired a 28.3 kg shell at a muzzle velocity of 950 m/s. Since the Tiger IIIs would be called upon to battle against enemy armor, 80 of its 86 shell complements were for anti-tank purposes.

With the heavy charge, the Pak 44 could penetrate 312mm of 30 degrees sloped armor at 500 meters, 230mm of 30 degrees sloped armor at 1000 meters, 200mm (7.9 in) at 2,000 meters, and 173mm at 3,000 meters range. In short, nothing would be able to withstand a direct hit from that monster.

Walder moved from the gun's muzzle, where Hans still marveled at the thing, to the top of the Panzer turret. Standing up tall, he looked around. The unfolding scene with his crew seemed to be repeated everywhere he looked. The 1st Heavy Panzer Battalion had just received a new complement of Tiger IIIs for the coming campaign.

The unit had been ordered to the rear after their retreat from Budapest and the successful conclusion of the Lake Balaton counter-offensive. General Bayerlein, the Panzer Lehr commander, had wanted his best unit to be rested and refitted with the new, improved Konigstiger.

The battalion's men used the fifteen or so days of rest to replenish their forces and repair their Tigers. Little did they know that the Wehrmacht had new rides in store for them. Walder had even been able to get leave to go see Ingrid in the hospital. She was still there when he got to Berlin (the field ward was in Potsdam), and he spent the two days of his time off with her. She had been injured quite seriously to the head, but to Walder's great relief, she was well on her way to a full recovery. The girl lost a lot of her beautiful blond hair but assured him that she would regrow them. "By the time you see me again, my love, it'll all be mended, I promise." He'd come back with enough memories to last him for another six months of grueling battle.

The battalion was near Warsaw's primary rail node, and they were under orders to get ready to deploy within the next day. The Yvan's were again brewing up an offensive, and it was rumored that they would send a powerful thrust all along the line. Looking at his men's happiness and at Hans' glee for his new toy, he knew that the Panzer Lehr 1st Heavy Battalion would give the damned Reds a good run for their money.

The area was crawling with Panzerwaffe soldiers, as train upon trains laden with new Panzers arrived hourly, unloaded with the rail yard's big cranes, and were picked up by their crews. The Tiger III was the big novelty, but several Maus super tanks also arrived, and they would now be part of Walder's unit, for they had a somewhat decent speed with the new 1000hp engine (35 km/hour). Since they had the men and the material, Erich would now command not forty but fifty tanks (40 Tigers III and 10 Maus with the new engines).

Still standing tall on his turret, he fished out a cigarette from his front pocket (Ingrid had been able to get him some American Lucky Strikes from the black market). He lit it and dragged a long breath. The smoke he exhaled scattered thru the slightly cold breeze of February. He gestured to Stromer if he wanted one, but the kid did not even notice, busy as he was with his PAK44 inspection.

He wondered what the next campaigning season would bring. The Reich certainly was at the end of its rope. Walder wasn't worried about the Panzer's performance but more at the fact that they would soon run out of territory to retreat to. Taking another Lucky Strike puff, he decided that there wasn't much he could do about it but fight and hope for the best. Such was the way of the soldier.

Extracts from Von Manstein's 1958 book, LOST VICTORY
Visit to the frontline near Lake Garda, February 28th, 1947.

The final line of defense I commanded in Italy against the Western Allies was probably the strongest. Not necessarily by the fact that I had the most powerful troops. At fifteen division, my command was much-diminished from what it had been earlier in the Italian campaign. But my Army Group was greatly helped by the towering height it stood on and the re-purposing of the Italian defensive line.

So OKW had decided (and I concurred) that the additional troops were to be sent to other fronts; to the east, in particular, where there was never enough troops against the damned Communist hordes.

As part of my command responsibilities, I often took it upon myself to personally tour the frontline. In this, I was not as forward-savvy as a Rommel or a Guderian, for example, because I believed that a commander's job was to plan and manage, not to fight alongside the troops at the frontline. But visiting the troops that fight and bleed regularly was, in my view, an essential part of the theater commander's job.

Upon arriving in one of the major bunker complexes in Austria (between the Tyrol and Italy), I was again pleased with the soldier's morale level. Were these men not the ones who had fought, bled but constantly retreated and thus were defeated? It didn't appear so. The most substantial incentive for the German soldier was not necessarily ideological, as by now, even the most enthusiastic Nazi supporter understood the war was lost. It was about defending the homeland, and the war was going badly on all fronts anyway. So why worry too much? There were still enemies to fight in front of them.

That day, the position I visited blocked Lake Garda's access in the Austrian Tyrol. This area was ethnically German but officially part of Italy since the end of the First World War. The pass was called the Brenner Pass, and it was one of the Austrian Tyrol's main access routes, so we had it strongly defended.

Dairy cattle grazed in alpine pastures just below our towering bunkers and defenses in the valley beneath the pass and on the mountains above it.

The central section of the Brenner Pass covered a sizeable paved road and a double railway track connecting Bozen/Bolzano in the south and Innsbruck to the north. The village of Brenner proper was where our men were billeted. It needed to be defended at all costs. The 7th Mountain Division was entrusted with the responsibility, and I was impressed by their readiness status.

Over 55 PAK44 guns were well camouflaged and dug in, covering firing positions, while many bunkers and trench-likes hideouts dotted the landscape. Two artillery regiments were positioned just north of Brenner, ready to pound the Allies to oblivion.

The road itself had been completely gutted, and a huge anti-tank ditch had been built by our forces. 7th Division commander General Gaspar Blumeritt also had a heavy Panzer battalion (Maus IIs) at his disposal for a counter-attack if the enemy broke thru.

The General himself escorted me, and we went about visiting most of the PAK44 emplacements. I was thus able to chat with the soldiers handling them. We, therefore, discussed the gun's capabilities, and the men were happy to see their commander.

The reason for my visit to this specific area was that the 7th commander had asked me to come to verify his claims that he didn't have strong enough forces. An hour into my tour of the Brenner Pass, I gave orders to the staff accompanying me to send more troops to Brenner, as we had not near enough. Upon my return to theater HQ, I even asked OKW (and got) an additional heavy Panzer battalion for the position was critical and could not be lost.

These additional forces would come in handy when the Allies came hard at us later in the year.

CHAPTER 4

The Goldap Offensive part 2
Frontline, near Eastern Prussia, March 3rd to March 8th, 1947

The Russians regarded East Prussia as the seat of German militarism. Many of the Wehrmacht's top commanders came from the area, which had produced highly trained soldiers for centuries. It was from East Prussia that the Teutonic Knights launched forays into Poland and the Baltic regions in the 13th and 14th centuries. The Prussian state also had produced warrior Kings like Frederick the Great. For the Soviet victory over the Reich to be complete, it needed to be erased from the map.

During World War I, the Russian Army invaded the province and had suffered decisive defeats in the 1914 Battle of Tannenberg and at the 2nd Battle of the Masurian Lakes in 1915. Driving the Tsar's army back, German forces moved into Russia, eventually destabilizing the country enough to plunge it into a bloody civil war.

Detached from the rest of Germany by the Treaty of Versailles, East Prussia was reconnected with the Third Reich after the defeat of Poland. The German Fuhrers, first Hitler than Goering, had directed the war in the east from the Wolfchanzze (wolf's lair) in the Masurian woods, south of Konigsberg.

During the opening days of the invasion of the Soviet Union in 1942 (Operation Barbarossa), East Prussia served as the jumping-off point for Army Group North's drive to Leningrad. By March 1947, Army Group North no longer existed, and Cherniakhovski had received orders from Stavka (the Soviet high command) to continue his advance. It was time to enter the lair of the German beast.

On March 3rd, Cherniakhovski sent the go-ahead orders to launch the attack, following Zhukov's instructions to do so. The time had come for the final offensive against Prussia. The calm was broken at 4 am, when the Soviet artillery pieces opened up, lighting the dark sky with heavenly lights. A five-hour shelling hit the German front, raining a hail of steel and explosives on the Axis positions. The intensity of the bombardment and follow-up bombing from the air (an epic air battle also raged overhead) shocked the German defenders. Such firepower had rarely been seen on the Eastern Front. Men were buried alive as trenches collapsed or were blown apart by the heavy mortar shells fired by corps and army artillery units. Frantic calls for help were cut short as communication lines were blown apart and the force of the concussions from the heavy shells shattered eardrums.

A few hours into the mighty barrage of fire and iron, Colonel-General Kuzma Nikitovich Galitskii's 11th Guards Army, composed of nine rifle divisions and an armored regiment, was ordered to hit the Germans in an area around Edytkau, about 40 kilometers west of Gumbinnen. To his left, the 31st Army (seven rifle divisions) under Col. Gen. Vasilii Vasilevich Glagolev was to advance on the Rominte Heath to the town of Goldap. On the 11th Guards' right, Lt. Gen. Ivan Illich Luidnikov's 39th Army (eight rifle divisions, an armored brigade and regiment, and an assault gun regiment) would breach German lines around Schirwindt, located about 55 kilometers northeast of Gumbinnen, and head for Schlossberg. He would be supported by Lt. Gen. Aleksandr Aleksandrovich Luchinskii's 28th Army (nine rifle divisions, an armored division, two armored regiments, and two assault gun regiments).

Colonel-General Nikolai Ivanovich Krylov's 5th Army (eight rifle divisions and an armored brigade and regiment) were held in reserve to exploit any breaches in the German line. In addition, the 1st Baltic Front had Maj. Gen. Aleksii Semenovich Burdeinei's 2nd Guards Tank Corps (three armored divisions and a mechanized brigade) operated independently. It attacked northward on a direct course to Konigsberg itself, further spreading the German defenses.

In the south, the 2nd Bielorussian front also launched its offensive, but against Army Group Center and its leader, the famous General Guderian. The objective there was to prevent the Wehrmacht from sending forces north to help defend Eastern Prussia.

Facing Cherniakhovski were the superb divisions of General Walter Model's Army Group Prussia, tasked with the ultimate defense of the Fatherland. Since retreating into East Prussia, these troops had been busy repairing long-neglected fortifications. However, East Prussia was now the front, and the men worked feverishly to improve positions that might stop the Russians.

So as the Soviet bombardment moved to the rearward German positions, the Red Army troops advanced on the Axis divisions.

Because of the attack's powerfulness, they expected to find only corpses and dazed survivors and the shattered remains of the German defenses, but they received an entirely different experience. Rising from the rubble, the soldiers that had been fighting like the devil for the better part of the last nine years greeted the advancing Soviets with a withering fire. As the shelling passed on (artillery moved westward as the Soviet soldiers advanced), men struggled to right machine guns and mortars, while others dug up buried comrades, still alive. They rubbed off the excess dirt and picked up their weapons to shoot at the Russians. Two-man details were also sent to repair damaged radio lines that had been cut. As more men were put back into action, the divisional and corps artillery battalions, guided by surviving forward observers, brought down a wall of fire on the advancing Red Army. The Nazi guns were no pushovers and could give back equally what the Soviets sent them.

Within the first hour after the barrage, Model sent in two of his best Panzer divisions, the 11th and 12th. The battle's intensity raised up a few notches as the Red Army responded in kind with their own tanks.

While soldiers at the front struggled to hold a cohesive line, the Red Air Force struck German supply lines in the rear, again and again, incurring crippling losses to the mighty Luftwaffe. But they sent so many planes that they simply overwhelmed the German air defenses with their numbers, so bombs rained down on the beleaguered Axis defenders. The town of Gumbinnen felt the full fury of the Soviet airmen as fighter bombers smashed the rail line that ran through it. A follow-up by medium bombers caused more damage, almost destroying the entire town that was, by the end of the first intense day of battle, a big bowl of fire where hundreds of thick, dark smoke columns rose high in the sky and rubble covered its streets.

But the Germans held the line. By sheer luck, willpower, and a good dose of reinforcements, General Model was able to keep the situation under control, inflicting countless casualties on the Soviets and taking attrition he knew he could not sustain as long as the Red Army.

Frustrated by the first day's action, Cherniakhovski urged his generals to make better progress, and on March 4th, opened with another massive bombardment. The East Prussians of General Schittnig's division, which occupied positions in and around Schirwindt, were once again the object of Luidinikov's 39th Army. The 1st Division stopped the initial attack of the day dead in its tracks, and the Russians fell back eastward.

Luidinikov then sent armor and infantry to outflank the town from the north and south. Once again, the antitank guns of the 23rd anti-tank battalion destroyed several Soviet tanks, but the move was effective. The Russians were able to enter the town, and the battle deteriorated into house-to-house fighting. The Germans had evacuated the city by evening, leaving many of Schirwindt's 1,000 inhabitants dead in the streets.

By the end of the second day, the Soviets had made decent progress, and the German forces retreated under the relentless pressure of too many guns firing on them and too much ordinance falling on their heads.

On March 6, heavy fighting erupted to an even greater level as Gumbinnen came under attack. Model sent an entire Panzer corps into the fury of the battle, while the Soviets responded with their new toy, the T-54 main battle tank. These new tanks weighed 45 tons fully loaded and had up to 205mm of armor for protection. They were armed with a 100mm gun, which made them dangerous opponents, as several Tigers and Maus found out that day, for they routed an entire German armored division for one of the first time in the war. The weapon's penetration capability was well over the best armor the Panzer had (239mm), so any of them hit by the ordinance lit up like a Christmas tree.

By the end of the day, the Soviets had pushed even farther westward. Cherniakhovski, frustrated by the continued German resistance, released his reserves, Burdeinei's 2nd Guards Tank Corps. Moving quickly, Burdeinei's 25th Guards Tank Division and 4th Guards Mechanized Assault Division swept toward the Angerapp River and took the crossing at Nemmersdorf. After occupying Nemmersdorf, the Soviets set up defensive positions on the western edge of the village.

Gumbinnen fell on March 8th, and by then, Model let go and retreated westward to a new line of defense, while more reinforcements were rushed to his aid. The Russian spearhead was finally less than 80 kilometers from the Fuhrer's headquarters at the Wolf's Lair. Some of Goering's aides urged him to evacuate it, but he refused. He was worried about the effect on the troops' morale if it appeared that he had abandoned them. But on the morning of the 9th (the very next morning), his courage disappeared, and he climbed in his armored train to leave for Berlin.

The outlook was not good for the Third Reich, and while the Fuhrer's HQ was in danger, it was the same for Konigsberg.

The Battle for Anatolia
March 2nd to March 6th, 1947

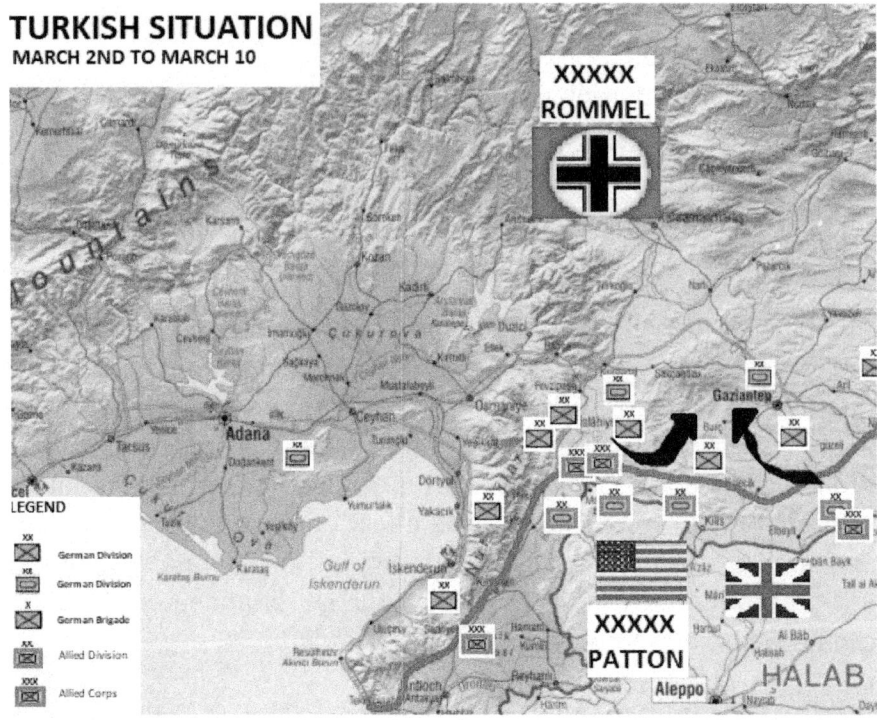

As foreseen by German General Rommel, Patton's offensive did indeed go for Gaziantep. The Americans planned to take the city and then swing west toward the mountain passes and spill out into the valleys beyond to take the city of Adana ultimately. Once there, it was only a short hop to Ankara, the Turkish capital, and their surrender.

Fortunately for the Axis forces, their defenses were well-prepared and in very rugged terrain. Anatolia and its mountains were not the best places for a modern war. The Germano-Turkish forces could use every stream, ravine, mountain, or rocky outcrop as a strong point. Tanks would have great difficulty moving thru the rough, rocky ground, and only infantry could attack in many places.

Patton 11th Army included three full corps of American troops (one armored), two Brazilian divisions, one Indian, and two Canadian units. Over 600 planes, including Meteor jets and half of them tactical bombers like the B-26 Mitchells and the Thunderbolt tank-killers. Some more units were also part of the offensive, namely the 6th CAV division and several other units formerly of General Bradley's defeated Army at the Battle of Alexandria the year before.

His forces were scattered along the frontline from the Mediterranean Sea (by the Golf of Iskenderun) to the rugged Syrian/Iraqi hinterland, all the way to the Anatolian foothills.

Patton concentrated five of his divisions and two of his armored for the Gaziantep drive. But the battle for the mountainous terrain slowed the Allies considerably, and after a couple of days of a grinding and attritional struggle, he returned to his starting positions. The Germans had solid defenses and heavy artillery, so they could not be pushed back. In some Allied units (especially the two Brazilian divisions that participated in the assault), casualty levels reached staggering numbers, with over 30% dead or wounded.

The Germans won the exchange for once since they lost no ground and had very few losses. The Turkish government rushed three additional divisions from his reserve army near Ankara to bolster the line.

The Allies renewed their assault on the fourth, even coordinating their efforts with Auchinleck's British forces near Mosul that tried to break out near Lake Van. The Germano-Turkish forces proved too well prepared and too strong there as well for any gains to be gained for the English and Indian units.

By the 6th of March, both Allied commanders and their armies reported back to Eisenhower in London that they could not move the Axis defenses one inch backward with the state of their forces and the strength of the enemy's defenses. Strong reinforcement and better supplies would be needed (artillery shells were in short supply). Or perhaps (in their opinion) the attack should be conducted elsewhere in Auchinleck's sector.

While the Western Allies certainly had potent armies in the Middle East, they just didn't have the planes or artillery to pulverize firmly held fortifications. The overall Allied commander didn't worry too much about it since these forces were cut off from the Reich and bottled up in an area that wasn't critical for the war's conclusion.

Rommel's forces could rot for all he cared. So he decided that he needed his best offensive general back in Europe. On the 7th, he sent down the orders to recall General George Patton back to France, where Eisenhower deemed him more beneficial for the conflict's conclusion.

British General Auchinleck was named overall commander of all Middle East Theater forces, from the Mediterranean to Persia, and was tasked with safeguarding the border. He also received loose objectives to somehow break into Turkey. The British officer would certainly try, and there were reasons to believe he had better chances of success in the Lake Van sector of the frontline.

The assault on the Brest-Litovsk Fortress
The Russians attack, March 3rd to 7th, 1947

The storming of the fortress, the city of Brest, and the capture of bridges across the Western Bug and Mukhavets were entrusted to the 45th Rifle Corps and the 119th Tank Guard Corps under the command of Major General Constantin Popov (about 80 000 soldiers) with reinforcement units. To conduct artillery preparation during the first two hours of the assault, mortar divisions of the 31st and 34th infantry divisions of the 12th Army Corps of the 2nd Bielorussian front were attached. Several battalions of Katyusha rocket artillery battalion were also brought forward to bombard the old Austro-Hungarian fortress.

In addition to the impressive gun line-up, nine light and three heavy batteries, a high-power artillery battery (two super–heavy 400-mm self-propelled mortars), and a division of 210-mm were also called to the fore. The total planned consumption of artillery ammunition amounted to over twenty thousand rounds with a caliber of 100 mm and above.

Soviet artillery began their massive bombardment of the western outskirts of the city of Brest, and at 04:15, the fire was transferred to the fortress and the northern town. The destruction brought about by the massive attack was incredible. Warehouses were destroyed, the water supply system was damaged, communication was interrupted, and severe damage to the garrison was inflicted.

At 03:23, the assault on the Volynsky, Kobrin, and Terespolsky fortifications began. The attack led to the garrison's inability to provide a unified, coordinated resistance because of the heavy shelling and was split into several separate centers. The Soviet assault detachments of the first wave, advancing on the fortress, stormed the northern gates of the Kobrin fortification against withering fire, and it was repulsed. However, their second attempt succeeded in overwhelming the defenders in a gory battle where horrendous casualties were taken on both sides. In the end, it even came down to hand-to-hand bayonet attacks.

The 35 000 strong Axis defenders (there were two Ukrainian volunteer divisions in the central fortress itself) fought toes and nails to stay alive and stave off the Red Army's powerful assaults. Brest-Litovsk held a strategic and critical position within the Guderian's defensive setup, but at the same time, the famous general had not put all his eggs in the same basket. His views on the matters were that the fortress was old and the Wehrmacht was better served with defending it but keeping most of its force mobile and out of range from a possible encirclement.

The German plan was quite simple. Let the Soviets attack the fortress and hope the assault would grind down its offensive power. Army Group Center was well stocked in Panzer divisions, so Guderian's overall intention was to counter-attack the Russians after they took the Brest if they ever did. To make this happen, he'd kept an entire Panzer corps and six infantry divisions (mostly mechanized) about twenty kilometers at the rear. The goal was, of course, to retake the fortress but to avoid the initial shock of most Red Army offensives: the artillery and air shelling.

What the German general could not prepare for was what kind of reserves the Soviets had behind the forces that stormed Brest-Litovsk.

And indeed, Zhukov was far from being a stupid man. He'd learned that the Germans liked to send counter-attacks, like the recent disaster encountered by his men at Lake Balaton and Budapest. So Voronezh Front (the front responsible for the whole Central Poland and Bielorussian areas) was instructed to wait for any German counter-stroke and then send its 8 Rifle and 6 Tank divisions into the maelstrom once the enemy was fully engaged with the forces attacking the fortress.

Meanwhile, by the end of the 4th, the battle inside the cauldron continued. The fortress became utterly isolated, encircled by Soviet forces attacking aggressively every hour. The Ukrainian troops defending (1st and 2nd Galician) within its battered walls knew what was in store for them if they laid down their weapons, so there was no question of surrender even if their situation was desperate. They would be considered traitors to the Soviet Union and shot after the battle. So for them, it was a fight to the death, which was the exact reason Guderian put them there. He needed troops who would resist their utmost capabilities while coming to their rescue.

By midday on the 6th, the fighting was concentrated chiefly around the citadel on the island in the middle because the Russians had stormed the rest of the German positions.

Knowing that the end was near if he didn't do something, Guderian launched his planned counter-attack, even if by then he knew he was going to come up against serious enemy forces. The air reconnaissance flights reported large enemy troop concentrations just east of Brest-Litovsk. It was almost like the Russians waited for him to launch his men into the fray.

And they were. While the battle for the citadel reached its crescendo on the 7th, a significant armored battle was fought just on the Bug River's bank, where the Soviet forces mauled the German mobile forces, prompting them to retreat in disarray.

After hearing Guderian's radio message that he would not be relieved, the Ukrainian commander shot himself as the Communist soldiers were nearing the room he was cowering. The citadel fell a few hours after the Axis forces turned back westward.

Not many prisoners were taken. Either because the Soviet soldiers killed them or because by the time they stormed the last Axis position, they were already dead.

Armored might on the Bug River
1st Heavy Panzer Battalion, near Brest-Litovsk, March 6th, 1947

"Wow, just wow!" said Stromer enthusiastically. "Good work, kid," added Walder. Everyone else in the Panzer was ecstatic. "Did you see commander! We hit the thing square in the faceplate, and it opened like a tin can. It's a thousand meters further than my best shot with the 88!" added the young gunner with his usual high-pitched and excited voice. With his long war experience, Erich had seen tanks destroyed from that distance with the 88s, but Hans was right. The new 128mm PAK44 gun was indeed a fantastic weapon.

With their older Tiger II, three shots out of four glanced on the enemy's armor when they fired anywhere further than 1500 to 2000 meters, But the new wonder maintained its anti-tank effectiveness up to 2500 meters. He wanted to try if it would perform from even further away. "Hans. Do you see that Soviet machine further away, about another 250 meters down the river's bank?" "Yes, commander." The youngster knew what Walder meant. "Here you go..." the kid adjusted the turret, traversing it a couple of degrees. He angled the gun to the desired distance he wanted and pushed the firing pedal with his foot. A muffled clang was heard. It was the satisfying sound of their gun firing.

The shell shot straight on its flat trajectory, and for the half a second that it took to get to its destination, the crew was able to follow it as it arced slightly. The round hit the Soviet tank right on the turret. It was an IS-2 tank, but that didn't matter one bit; its 200mm steel thickness was cleanly penetrated. The round seemed to enter clearly thru a glowing red hole. It appeared that the tank would survive for a fleeting instant, but then its ammunition ignited. The explosion excited the blowing-up machine from a weird angle, and a column of fire and debris erupted from the rear, skyrocketing high in the air. Then, two more columns, this time of dark heavy smoke, shot out horizontally from both sides, and then the tank disappeared from view in a catastrophic cloud of debris.

Erich was impressed. "Wow, Stromer. Another great shot and the round just entered clean thru the enemy's armor." The Russian guard division was advancing from the south, hugging the Bug River bank, but it was still out of range and didn't shoot at the German tanks yet. He paused, looking further away. "You guys wanna try something even longer range?" His question wasn't directed at anyone in particular, just his crew in general. Most of them just yelled an enthusiastic yes. Tankers just loved it when they could fire at the enemy while he was out of range. No wonder, since it meant they were safe from the fiery death promised by the Russian anti-tank shells.

The heavy Panzer battalion had been ordered to rush to the battle scene just south of Brest-Litovsk. Their job was to counter-attack the advancing Soviets that crossed the river further down south and now advanced to close in on the city and its defenders. They'd moved fast enough, and anyway, they had been near the frontline. Guderian knew that the Red Army was coming for the Fortress and had prepared a defense that involved another sharp counter-attack like the one they successfully executed at Lake Balaton.

So for the last fifteen minutes, Walder's unit had finally come into visual range of the Communist tanks and so had initiated battle. The Tiger IIIs and the Maus in the battalion fired away with everything they had. One keen observer could already see several (dozens) smoke columns rising into the air, proof of destroyed machines on the Russian side. And, so far, not one of his Panzers had been destroyed. Some had received glancing hits, but the out-of-speed Russian shells just bounced off their thick armor. More enemy ordinance sprouted in the dirt in front of the Germans. Erich decided that the battle's outlook wasn't good for the Yvan's.

Hans spotted another enemy armored machine driving hard on some muddy patch of ground by the river through his targeting sight. It was spurting dark, wet earth on each side as it sped thru the muck. The young gunner adjusted his sight a little, traversed the turret another degree, and the moment the loader told him that the gun was loaded, he pushed the fire button. Another red tracer shot out of the 128mm and ended up hitting the Yvan right on the side in some weird but destructive angled shot. The explosion's blast was so powerful that it toppled the tank over on its turret, left track wholly destroyed. It also horribly scarred it, but the round didn't look like it penetrated inside. It didn't matter to Walder; the damned thing was out of commission anyway. "Good job, Stromer." "Thank you, Colonel.", answered the talented gunner.

The happy crew continued to pick off Soviet tanks from a distance until such time that the enemy's multitudes finally got into range themselves. Several big mounds of earth were churned just by the Tiger III, showering it with half-frozen and wet dirt. It was the middle of the morning, and some snow started to fall from the sky, reducing gunners' visibility. Germans optics being a lot better than their counterparts, Hans and the rest of the battalion continued to have hits. But the Russians also were able to score some.

After another twenty minutes of fierce battle, four German tanks out of fifty had been destroyed, and Walder was surprised to hear that the enemy had penetrated even a Maus. Facing the Soviets from the front, it was a bit baffling how such thick armor could be penetrated, but he rapidly got busy again with the needs of his own tank and momentarily forgot about it.

Then the Tiger III just beside him exploded catastrophically, large pieces of it hitting Erich's tank, and everyone in the machine felt the concussion from the blast. "Damn!" said the driver. That was one hell of a hit." "Commander," said Stromer a bit hesitantly this time, for it was the first time the youngster had used this tone in combat. "Yes, Hans?" Well, I think that the enemy has a new tank of some sort...." He was interrupted by a powerful noise. The tank on their other flank had just exploded as well. "Commander!" said Stromer in an urgent tone. "We need to move." Said Walder, trying to stay as calm as possible." Back up full speed," he said to the driver.

The man didn't need to be asked twice, he could see that something terrible was going on, and the normally invincible German tanks were being picked off quickly by the Yvan's. Erich picked up his radio. The whole affair felt like a disaster in the making, so he decided that his Panzers would be better off a longer range. "Battalion, retreat. Follow my lead."

The Tiger III rumbled backward, just in time to avoid being hit by another high-velocity shell, the same kind that destroyed its two flanking tanks. Still, the explosion rocked the Axis machine even if it only hit the ground. "The Commies have a new gun for certain, commander," confirmed Hans' in a worried tone of voice.

And indeed, they did. For the T-54s main battle tank also made an appearance against Walder's unit. In a sense, the Germans were lucky that day because most of the new weapons were attacking in Eastern Prussia. But Zhukov had decided to try the machines in Poland by sending a few detachments to bolster the advance near Brest Litovsk.

Back to battle
18th Imperial Division lands in Tsingtao, China, March 5th, 1947

Private Ichiro Tanaka, a soldier in the elite 18th Imperial Division, walked down the ramp to the pier in the harbor of Tsingtao in Jiaozhou Bay. He wondered why the hell they were stopping there and thought for a moment that it might be because of supply problems. The freighter they'd been on had sailed from French Indo China a few weeks back, and it had to stop in the Philippines (in an American base of all things) to refuel because Japan had barely enough oil at the end of the war. What had simply been a transport ship bringing the soldiers home looked like it had become something else. Ichiro hoped he would get to know for once, as no one ever told private soldiers anything in this damned army. The only thing they were instructed was where to point their bayonets and where to die. The coastal city was located in China and was one of the main

Japanese base in its war against China.

During the First World War, Japan had conquered the area and taken it from the German Empire. It then left it for several years but re-occupied it by 1938 when the war with China started in earnest again. The harbor and the surrounding had been, from that moment forward, an important Japanese land and naval base.

For a brief moment, it looked like the city would be returned to its Chinese owners, but that was not to be after the electrifying news of the Soviet attack on Manchuria and against Japan that had already surrendered to the Allies.

The move triggered a reaction from the Americans and the beleaguered, staggering Jap armies left in the area. Most notably, the leading commander in the Kwantung Army, General Yamada, called every Japanese soldier still in China or Manchuria to his banner. Many flocked to him, and some semblance of resistance started to take shape. But the Soviets advanced on one side, the Nationalist Chinese from the west and even the Mao Tse Dong's Communists from the north. So without something drastic, the Imperial forces that were in an advanced state of disintegration would simply fold under the pressure.

General MacArthur, the American Far East theater commander, had other plans. He had no intention of letting the Soviets grab the land they were so blatantly attacking and, to do so, had decided that he would deal with the lesser of two evils. The American General planned to help the Japs rearm in China and everywhere they could resist the Communist hordes.

So while many supply ships had docked in Tsingtao lately, several ships bringing the defeated imperial soldiers home had been re-routed to Tsingtao. Most, like Tanaka, did not even know why they were disembarking in the Chinese harbor.

So Tanaka walked a few meters further from the ship to several long lines of soldiers as they were instructed to wait their turn. At the end of the lines sat tables with Imperial Army officers in full uniform. Tanaka decided that it looked like something was brewing up.

In fact, it almost looked like they were being put back to work again. He wasn't sure why or how, but his guess, along with several of his comrades nearby, was that the Americans had re-directed their freighter to China for them to fight against the damned Soviet Communists.

He wasn't certain how he felt about that, but he sure was ready for more fighting, as it had been the only thing he had known for the last ten years. A soldier's life was simple, and he liked it very much. So if they told him to shoot at Russians, he would gladly do so. Well, as long as they fed him, paid him, and that he could do some good old looting and raping, of course. In short, he was fine with the whole concept of renewed war.

Meeting with the Fuhrer
Carinhall, March 15th, 1947

Famous commando Otto Skorzeny was sitting in the black Mercedes' back seat, looking out the window. The car drove along the long, winding forest road leading to Carinhall, the Fuhrer's retreat and home.

The snow was finally gone, and spring was in full bloom. The sun was shining on that beautiful day of March, and he felt good. The lengthy preparations for his operation were done, and he was ready to go. One last meeting with Goering, and he would get his final go-ahead. The German leader had decided that the small German bomb would be exploded on the Americans.

He'd been asked to go and present his plan personally to the Fuhrer. He had a couple of spots to propose for the site, as it was impossible to launch it from planes. The devices needed to be ignited from the ground, either remotely or with a timer.

As he was lost in thoughts, the vehicle entered the large clearing that housed Carinhall. It used to be a simple hunting lodge, but Goering had put a lot of work, money, and energy into making it the most luxurious mansion in all of Germany. Its front side was covered with expensive stones and marble columns. The entrance was a long driveway with soldiers lined up in a file.

The car screeched to a halt, and a smart-looking Wehrmacht officer opened the door to the car. He excited rapidly, and the officer clicked his black boots and made the Nazi salute. "Heil Goering!" "Heil Goering!" was Skorzeny energic response.

Torches had been lit all along the path to the main double doors, and all the soldiers were at the ready. "A full honor guard just for me," whispered Otto to the officer. "Yes, Herr Skorzeny. Just for you. The Fuhrer is pleased with you and has hopes that you will continue helping him."

Goering noticed that the whole Carinhall mansion was now covered with enormous camouflage nets. He knew that, unfortunately, Allied bombers (especially Russians) were now in range of the place, and since it was Goering's HQ in many a given days during the week, it was a possible target.

The large wooden doors (carved wood, with intricate Viking symbols on them) opened as he approached the entrance. They gave way to the large and obese Hermann Goering, leader of the Reich. The man was dressed in his usual white uniform, laden with medals. He was flanked by Frantz Halder, the head of OKW, that looked austere in his grey military uniform.

"Ah! My dear Skorzeny!" said the Fuhrer in an enthusiastic tone, arms open wide. "Come here, my dearest commando!" Otto approached, embracing Goering. "Mein Fuhrer." "Bah. It's Hermann for you", said the German leader. He tapped Skorzeny on the shoulder and gestured him in. "Shall we, my friend?" and they entered the building.

The walk to the Viking-style grand hall that the SS commando remembered was again rich with paintings, arts, and expensive rugs looted from all over Europe. Goering was said to be a great art collector, and Carinhall showed it in all its glory. They chit-chatted on unimportant matters all the way to the meeting. Halder stayed formal and didn't speak, content to follow the other two men from behind.

"So everything is ready?" said Goering as two guards quickened to open the last double doors (they were also intricately carved wood pieces). "Yes, Mein Fuhrer." "Good, good. Let's have a seat, shall we?" A couple of servants were waiting by the table, and the fire was blooming with flames, creating a pleasant atmosphere. The hall was as big and impressive as Otto remembered. A large table in the middle, capable of housing over a hundred people for diner. A large fireplace, surrounded by many plush couches and chairs. Marble statues (he noted they seemed to be from Italy), expensive red rugs, paintings, and medieval weapons attached to the walls completed the visual setup.

The three men sat down at the head of the table, closest to the fireplace. Some maps were laid down on it. Servants came by and offered drinks. Goering and Skorzeny took one, while Halder stayed quite formal and refused while on duty.

Goering started the serious conversation. "Herr Skorzeny. Halder here," he gestured toward the General, "has selected a couple of sites to get our revenge on the Americans. We would like you to look at them." The Fuhrer was done talking, and Halder finally warmed a little to present his plan. "Herr Skorzeny. First of all, let me thank you for your services so far. Your achievements are quite impressive." Otto just nodded solemnly, still listening. "So we have selected a couple of sites we think could be interesting to detonate our device. The frontline is now pretty static, so since it's not possible to drop the bomb with planes, we needed to find a place where the Allies could advance into." He picked up one of the folders besides the map and handed it to the commando.

"We have this one," Skorzeny listened as he opened the folder, "northwest of Aachen, in Belgium, where the Allies will soon move into since our forces are in a bulge over the Siegfried line. So if we retire those troops to the east behind our fortifications, it won't look suspicious to the Allies. So when we retreat, they will advance." The commando nodded, reading the paperwork presented in front of him—the town of Eupen. Interesting target.

Halder continued, handing a second folder to Skorzeny. "The other area is in the Vosges, near Belfort. There we also have a bulge that we could retreat from. The defensive position we hold is quite strong, but it's in a forested area, so it would do the trick in order to avoid being detected." "Thank you, Herr General," said Otto harboring a thin smile. "I like the two sites. I'll need some time to review them a little more if you don't mind." "Of course, he doesn't mind," said Goering laughing. "He will be back here tomorrow night, and by then, you'll let him know which option you like most. Now, we need to get some food, and after that, my dear friend, we are going hunting!"

Far Eastern American HQ
Army/Navy meeting, March 13th, 1947

"Sutherland, what about the news out of Korea?" asked the American commander in his commanding, calm voice. "Still the same, General. The Soviet forces are quiet on the Heijo-Gensan line. They are moving reinforcements by the thousands, but apart from that, things are calm."

MacArthur sat down on his chair, facing Admiral Nimitz, U.S. Navy overall commander, to discuss things over with the Admiral. "Well, Chester. Looks like we've got ourselves a bit of a weird situation here." The Admiral nodded. "Agreed, Douglas. The enemy buildup is obvious, and they continue to attack on land in China. The Japanese are hard-pressed, I heard?" "They indeed are," answered Sutherland, the General's chief of staff. "While we've landed several infantry remnants that were being repatriated from the south, we don't think that simply sending men with rifles will be enough." "Why is that?" said Nimitz. "As I remember, the Nipponese are hardly a pushover."

"Chester," answered MacArthur. "It's pretty simple. The Japs are good fighters, but they are up against a modern army, and they don't even have a decent tank with which to fight the Ruskies. It is not going to be simple for them. Beijing (Pekin) is threatened and should fall soon. General Tanaka is hard-pressed and won't resist long." "I see," answered Nimitz, realizing that the situation was not looking good.

"Admiral," started Richard, "What is the status for the Kuriles Islands?" The Soviets had invaded the southern part of the Japanese-held Sakhalin Island a week before, without the Americans doing anything about it again. They'd protested thru diplomatic channels, but the Soviets had remained deaf to their pleas. And then the damned Red had tried to get bold and sailed from their Vladivostok bases to attempt an invasion of the Kuriles Islands Chain, another

Japanese territory. But the U.S. Navy had been ready for that move at least and presented a firm wall against the Soviets that didn't go as far as provoking the Americans. So the Soviet ships turned around back to port.

"My forces are heavily patrolling the area, and trust me, there aren't any Russian trickling thru our fleet," said Nimitz in a convincing manner. "Speaking of the fleet, Admiral," interjected MacArthur. I trust that the show in force we've organized on the Korean coast, the Bohai Sea, and the Yellow Sea have been obvious enough to our Commie friends?" "Yes, General. I've got most of my big ships sailing around on maneuvers. We've even had a few battleships shell unoccupied rocks in front of Gensan to show them the firepower and our seriousness."

And indeed, the U.S. Navy was showing its heavy hand in the Far East. The Americans hoped that the Russians got the message. They would not be intimidated.

"We have just received several reinforcements from the American mainland, the Philippines, and Borneo, where our land campaigns are over there. Our command is now 25 divisions strong." "What of the armored divisions we've asked for, Richard?" Macarthur was particularly worried at the Soviet tank strength, and the Allies didn't have much to oppose them. "Two new divisions, sporting the M46 Super Pershings, are slated for transport from San Diego base to Tokyo within the week." Sutherland leafed thru some papers on the table in the meeting room. " And two more Marine divisions are on the way. The Aussies are sending three divisions, as per your request. The British government also confirmed that they would sail their fleet (several battleships and carriers), along with about ten Indian divisions."

"Well." Added Nimitz, whistling softly. "Someone's been busy." "Thank you, Richard. I am happy for the helpers. We'll be ready when and if the Commies decide to make their moves." He paused before changing the subject. "What of the Nationalist Chinese? As I remember from his last communication, Chiang Kai Shek was none too happy about our help to General Tanaka?"

And indeed, the Chinese leader wasn't. He'd been fighting the Japanese for the better part of his life and had been trying to evict them from China for the last twenty years. But, at the same time, the man was a realist. The sudden appearance of Soviet troops in Northern China meant that his other sworn enemy, Mao Tse Dong, the leader of the Chinese Communist forces, would be significantly reinforced. The Russian's arrival on the scene meant that the Commies would probably take power in his country.

"After his initial shock, the man relented. After all, the Japanese are nothing more than a fighting rabble now, however useful. Their not a threat to the Nationalists anymore. He's agreed to sign a truce with them until we've resolved this issue with the Soviet invasion."

"Thank you, Richard," said the General. "Good to know that Chiang is on board and sees the greater threat here. And anyway, let him know thru unofficial channels that we'll take care of the Chinese Reds once we're done with the ones with the big guns. "Of course, General."

The meeting continued for well over an additional hour, and the two American leaders left each other with a renewed sense of hope that they would weather the storm, even if the Red Army attacked.

Winston Churchill's address to the American Congress
British Premier visit to the US, March 15th, 1947

(...)

On the eve of our victory in Europe and over the Nazi tyranny that cast so much shadow on the free world, the United States, the British Empire, and the Soviet Union stand near-total victory. It is a solemn moment for world peace. For with success is also joined an awe-inspiring accountability to the future. If you look around you, you must feel not only the sense of duty done but also you must feel anxiety lest you fall below the level of achievement. Opportunity is here now, clear and shining for all of our countries. To reject it or ignore it or fritter it away will bring upon us all the long reproaches of the after-time. Constancy of mind, persistency of purpose, and the grand simplicity of decision must guide and rule the Allies'. We must, and I believe we shall prove ourselves equal to this strict requirement.

When American military men approach some serious situation, they are wont to write at the head of their directive the words "overall strategic concept." There is wisdom in this, as it leads to clarity of thought. What then is the overall strategic concept that we should inscribe today? It is nothing less than the safety and welfare, the freedom and progress, of all the homes and families of all the men and women in all the lands.

To give security to all, they must be shielded from the two giant marauders, war and tyranny. We all know the frightful disturbances in which the ordinary family is plunged when the curse of war swoops down upon the bread-winner and those for whom he works and contrives. The awful ruin of Europe, with all its vanished glories and of large parts of Asia, glares us in the eyes. When the designs of wicked men or the aggressive urge of mighty states dissolve over large areas the frame of civilized society, humble folk are confronted with difficulties with which they cannot cope. For them, all is distorted; all is broken, even ground to pulp.

When I stand here this quiet afternoon, I shudder to visualize what is happening to millions now and what will happen in this period when famine stalks the earth. None can compute what has been called "the unestimated sum of human pain." Our supreme duty is to guard the homes of the common people from the horrors and miseries of another war, as this one isn't even over yet. We all agree on that in the west and ask ourselves if they think the same in the east?

Before we cast away the solid assurances of national interests for self-preservation, we must be sure that our faith and resolve are built, not upon shifting sands or quagmires but upon the rock. Anyone can see with his eyes open that our path will be difficult and also lengthy, but if we persevere together as we did in the two world wars-though not, alas, in the interval between them-I cannot doubt that we shall achieve our common purpose in the end.

We cannot be blind to the fact that the liberties enjoyed by individual citizens throughout the Western World and so long overshadowed by the dreaded Nazi Empire are not valid in a considerable number of countries, some of which are very powerful. In these states, control is enforced upon the ordinary people by various kinds of all-embracing police governments. The power of the State is exercised without restraint, either by dictators or by compact oligarchies operating through a privileged party and a political police. It is not our duty when difficulties are so numerous to interfere forcibly in the internal affairs of countries we have not conquered in war. But we must never cease to proclaim in fearless tones the great principles of freedom and the rights of man which are the joint inheritance of the English-speaking world and which through Magna Carta, the Bill of Rights, the Habeas Corpus, trial by jury, and the English common law find their most famous expression in the American Declaration of Independence.

While still pursuing the method of realizing our overall strategic concept, I come to the crux of what I have traveled here to say. A shadow has fallen upon the scene
of our impending victory over the German tyranny. Nobody knows what Soviet Russia and its Communist international organization intend to do in the immediate future or what are the limits, if any, to their expansive and proselytizing tendencies. I have a strong admiration and regard for the valiant Russian people and for my wartime comrade, Marshal Stalin. There is deep sympathy and goodwill in Britain. I doubt not here also-towards the peoples of all the Russia's and a resolve to persevere through many differences and rebuffs in establishing lasting friendships. We understand the Russians need to be secure on her western frontiers by removing all possibility of German aggression and the Japanese or Chinese in Asia.

We welcome Russia to her rightful place among the world's leading nations. We welcome her flag upon the seas. Above all, we welcome constant, frequent, and growing contacts between the Russian people and our own people on both sides of the Atlantic. We also welcome its victory over the Third Reich to become a reality as soon as possible. However, it is my duty, for I am sure you would wish me to state the facts as I see them to you, to place certain facts about the present position in Europe and Asia.

From Konigsberg in the Baltic to Hungary in Central Europe, an iron curtain is descending across the Continent. Behind that line lie all the occupied capitals of some of the ancient states of Central and Eastern Europe. Budapest, Belgrade, Bucharest, and Sofia. All these famous cities and the populations around them lie in the occupied Soviet zone, and Warsaw, Berlin, and many others shall soon be under their heels once the German Wehrmacht is no more. And now the Asian theater, which had so recently and so happily ended its conflict, is ablaze again with what can only be called a Soviet aggression in Manchuria and Northern China. What should the Western Power do against this blatant act of war and disregard for the Grand Alliance that helped us all to vanquish the Axis tyranny? Suppose now the Soviet Government tries, by separate action, to occupy and conquer as much land as possible before the shooting stops. In that case, this will cause new severe difficulties to world peace and give the defeated Germans and Japanese the power to put themselves up to auction between the Soviets and the Western Democracies. Whatever conclusions may be drawn from these facts-and facts they are-this is undoubtedly not the Liberated Europe or Asia we fought to build up. Nor is it one that contains the essential prerequisites of permanent peace.

The world's safety requires a new unity in Europe and an immediate return to peaceful intention from the Soviet Union on its easter border. It also needs a clear message from Russia on its European plans, for the Western Democracies have no intentions of letting all of the old continent, as Stalin asked us so forcibly, to fall to Soviet occupation.

It is from the quarrels of the strong parent races in Europe that the world wars we have witnessed, or which occurred in former times, have sprung. Twice in our own lifetime, we have seen the United States, against their wishes and their traditions, against arguments, the force of which it is impossible not to comprehend, drawn by irresistible forces, into these wars in time to secure the victory of the good cause, but only after frightful slaughter and devastation had occurred. Twice the United States has had to send several millions of its young men across the Atlantic to find the war; but now war can find any nation, wherever it may dwell between dusk and dawn. Surely we should work with a conscious purpose for a grand pacification of Europe. We now ask Stalin to let us know his intentions, and clearly.

Again one cannot imagine a regenerated Europe without a free France, Italy and Austria, even Poland or Central / Eastern Europe. I say this today: We will never relent any of the free nations of Europe. I have worked for liberty all my public life, and I never lost faith in it, even in the darkest hours. I will not lose faith now. I have felt bound to portray the shadow which, alike in the west and in the east, falls upon the world as the light finally was about to show itself back with the Axis power's eclipse. I was a high minister at the time of the Versailles Treaty and a close friend of Mr. Lloyd-George, who was the head of the British delegation at Versailles. I did not myself agree with many things that were done, but I have a very strong impression in my mind of that situation, and I find it painful to contrast it with that which prevails now. There were high hopes and unbounded confidence that the wars were over and that the League of Nations would become all-powerful in those days. I do not see or feel that same confidence or even the same hopes in the haggard world at the present time. Russian intentions need to be clearly declared toward world peace and freedom.

On the other hand, I repulse the idea that a new war is inevitable; still, more that it is imminent. It is because I am sure that our fortunes are still in our own hands and that we hold the power to save the future that I feel the duty to speak out now that I have the occasion and the opportunity to do so. We still need to destroy the giant and ugly ogre that is the German Third Reich. The damned Fascist state that enslaved millions upon millions. That killed even more.

I do hope dearly that Soviet Russia does not desire war. I hope they do not desire the fruits of war, conquests, and the indefinite expansion of their power and doctrines. But what we have to consider here today while time remains is the permanent prevention of war and the establishment of conditions of freedom and democracy as rapidly as possible in all countries. Our difficulties and dangers will not be removed by closing our eyes to them. They will not be removed by mere waiting to see what happens; nor will they be removed by a policy of appeasement. What is needed is a settlement, and the longer this is delayed, the more difficult it will be and the greater our dangers will become.

From what I have seen of our Russian friends and Allies during the war, I am convinced that there is nothing they admire so much as strength, and there is nothing for which they have less respect than for weakness, especially military weakness.

Last time I saw it all coming, I cried aloud to my fellow citizens and the world, but no one paid any attention. Until the year 1933 or even 1935, Germany might have been saved from the awful fate which has overtaken her, and we might all have been spared the miseries Hitler let loose upon mankind. Conclusion: there never was a war in all history easier to prevent by timely action than the one that has just desolated such great areas of the globe. It could have been prevented, in my belief, without the firing of a single shot, and Germany might be powerful, prosperous, and honored today; but no one would listen, and one by one, we were all sucked into the awful whirlpool. We surely must not let that happen again. This can only be achieved by reaching now, in 1947, a good understanding on all points with Russia.

Let's hope that Stalin is listening.

(...)

Standing applause

The Goldap Offensive part 3
The Germans compress into a narrow area, March 8 to 15th, 1947

The Soviet offensive continued unabated for seven grueling days, as countless losses were tallied on both sides. The Germans had no intention of giving anything to their hated enemies, now that they were defending their homeland.

The Soviet offensive, which had so much impetus in the first few days, ground to a crawl by the 9th and transformed itself into a war of attrition. Cherniakhovski found himself in a rather precarious position. Some units were beyond Gumbinnen since the town was in Soviet hands, but his flanks were exposed until the neighboring armies overcame resistance in their sectors. In the Schlossberg area, the German 1st Infantry Division still resisted all the 5th Rifle Army efforts to break its line. Farther south, the line ran across Ebenrode to Gumbinnen. Model sent reinforcement to that line and strengthened it with two Panzer divisions and General Hans Lippert's 5th Panzer. The arrival of Brig. Gen. Günther Sachs's 18th Flak Division (directly from the Berlin area) added a deadly array of antiaircraft guns, including the renowned 88mm, which were also used in artillery and antitank capacity, to fight the Russians.

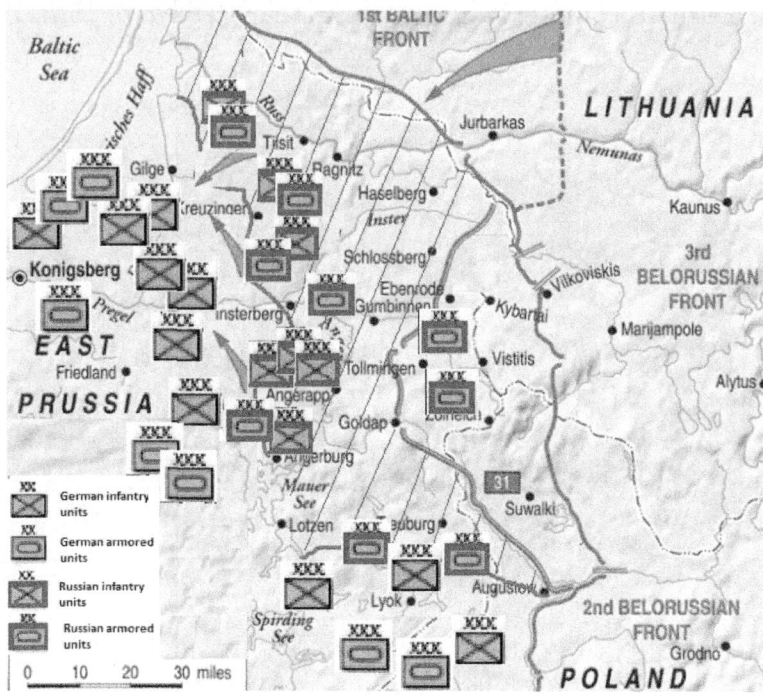

THE STRATETIC SITUATION, EASTERN PRUSSIA / POLAND
The Drive to Konigsberg March 8th to 15th 1947

Combat west of Gumbinnen and Trakehnen was particularly fierce, to the point that both sides got exhausted fighting by the 11th of March. And as is often in war, the side that wins is the one that can bring reserve to bear faster than his enemy.

Elements of Model's Army Group Prussia were forced to give way— under pressure from a new rifle, corps railed in near the frontline from 1st Baltic Front, as ordered by overall commander Zhukov. As the Axis infantry retreated, it ran into Panzers from the 95th Division, reinforcing the sector. A swift counterattack pushed the Soviets out of their newly captured positions and restored the line but only for a moment, and the Wehrmacht retreated westward toward Konigsberg.

Heavy attacks west of Gumbinnen were repulsed by reinforcements from the 5th Panzer Division. In a series of sharp engagements, the

Russians took substantial casualties. German losses were also severe to the point that they could not be sustained. The German defense fast became another vortex in which they threw everything they had with no tangible results. It seemed that the Panzers and infantry sent into the gap just melted away and came back broken.

On the 12th of March, two hard-pressed German units, the 131st and 170th Infantry divisions, bore the brunt of the attack. A Soviet armored column managed to break through the 131st's line. Still, disaster was averted by the timely arrival of a Sturmgeschutz anti-tank mobile guns brigade (the 179th), which destroyed several Russian tanks and forced the rest to retreat. A second breakthrough met the same fate. Gumbinnen itself fell the next day when the 170th was forced out of its positions within the town.

After another two days, Angerapp and Insterberg were stormed by the Soviets. The surging Red Army also took Tilsit, Haselberg, and Gilge along the Baltic Coast.

On the 15th of March, Marshal Zhukov, within his forward HQ near the front, received the message he'd been looking for when he launched the Goldap offensive: Cherniakhovski reported that the Germans were now compressed in a very narrow area of about 30 by 30 miles. For the OKW wanted to defend Konigsberg with everything it had, and under any military logic, they were right to put all their forces in that area.

The Red Army's counter-offensive would have ground to a halt in any normal circumstances. But Zhukov's plan was far from conventional. It was nuclear.

Rumbling back to the rear
1st Heavy Panzer Battalion, retreating westward, March 15th, 1947

Colonel Erich Walder tried to shrug off the growing sense of helplessness he felt. Again, the 1st Heavy Battalion was retreating along with its parent division, the Panzer Lehr. The Tiger III's engine purred weirdly, as it had not been the same after the hit they received in the battle on the Bug River's bank. It had only been a glancing hit, but it had still exploded on the rear armor plates and near the engine proper.

The new Soviet tanks were definitely something to be wary of. Their gun and range were not as good as the KWK 128mm, but it certainly packed a mighty punch once it got under 1800 meters. Damn. They'd lost several units on the 6th of March on their encounter on the Bug River, and he should have reacted sooner. He could not stop thinking about it.

But he knew that he was hard on himself since it wasn't like the Russians had given any clues about their new tank. And besides, they only lost five units on that day. The following days after that had been worse, and by then, he'd learned to be careful.

Since they still entertained better range than the enemy weapons, he'd instructed the battalions tank commanders to try to stay over 2000 meters to make sure that the Soviet shells wouldn't be as lethal as they could be. Even with these orders, the unit still lost another twenty-one tanks. So his strength was now halved since he'd started with fifty. No Maus had survived, being too slow compared to the lightning-fast Russian tanks. They'd all been caught up and destroyed. Walder couldn't do much about that. It wasn't his fault if the big tanks were too slow. The Yvan's overcame the big Panzers and destroyed them piecemeal even with the improved engine.

The last nine days had been more of the same recipe he'd

experienced over the previous three years. Russian attack, German counter-attack, and then German forces retreating in disarray, overwhelmed by the innumerable numbers of the damned Communists.

It seemed like he was living the same thing over and over again. There just wasn't anything that could be done. The last battle had finally broken his motivation and morale. He knew now that the war was lost. On an intellectual level, he'd already known for a while (ever since he was on the Dnieper Defensive Line in 1944). But his heart had told him otherwise. That the Fatherland, Germany, the Third Reich would find a way. And for the better part of those last three years, he'd kept hope, for Teutonic genius came up with new weapons in the air, new tanks, missiles, and all sorts of wonder weapons. Their equipment was ten times better than the Yvan's. Their tactics were better. But the Ruskies had something going for them. Numbers. Incredible numbers. And, Erich had to give them that; the bastards were crazy brave and knew how to fight.

Maybe all that bullshit propaganda about the superiority of the Aryan race was the other way around. The Slavs were the ones that would still stand on their feet once the shooting stopped.

The Panzer hit a large pothole, yanking him out of his daydreaming. The Heavy Battalion was heading westward, recalled to Central Poland for the eventual defense of the city of Warsaw. The tanks from his unit were advancing in a single file on the muddy road (it was still early spring, and it was raining almost every day). Their tracks and the countless Panzers, half-tracks, or trucks before them had dug a large trench in the mud that was difficult to master even for the powerful Tiger III.

Walder was standing half out of the tank's turret, thru the cupola, and could see the German troops around him in retreat as he was. They seemed steady enough, he decided. Walder turned around toward the east, where towering smoke columns and a rumble of rolling thunder could be heard. He wondered if he would get to face those new Soviet tanks once more. He dearly hoped so because they were worthy adversaries for his powerful Tiger III. Turning back toward the west, where the sun was finally peering thru the white-bluish clouds gave it some space, so its warm rays basked Erich, and for a moment, he felt that everything would sort itself out as it always had since the start of this ill-begotten war.

Nuclear fire on the Hitlerites
Konigsberg, March 19th, 1947

The Goldap offensive pushed the Germans back toward the Prussian city of Konigsberg. Walter Model's objective had been, all along, to retreat into the city that possessed impressive fortifications.

And incidentally, the Soviets wanted the same thing. In a different time, Zhukov would not have been happy with Cherniakhovski since he'd let the enemy retreat to better defenses. But it had been part of the plan all along.

Since the start of the attack, the Soviet forces had many occasions to encircle or destroy more German troops. But it could have meant a complete German withdrawal westward and a bypass of Konigsberg. Zhukov, as well as Stalin, wanted the enemy to hunker down in its large fortress. So they pushed their enemy, but not as hard as they could have since they wished to them concentrated in one spot.

The fortifications of the former East Prussian capital consisted of numerous defensive walls, forts, bastions, and other structures. Built in 1626—1634 and 1843—1859, the impressive medieval and renaissance constructions were largely obsolete by modern standards. Nonetheless, they included twelve bastions, three ravelins, seven spoil banks, and two fortresses surrounded by a water moat. Ten brick gates served as entrances and passages through defensive lines and were equipped with moveable bridges.

But even if outdated, the Wehrmacht still wanted to use it to defend the city and thus had prepared them as best they could, with new bunkers, gun emplacements, trenches, minefields, and everything that the industrious Germans could make in terms of protective works.

The new line that Model was working on ran from Konigsberg in its northernmost point to Guderian's position near Warsaw. The

German General crammed his defenses with over two corps of mostly infantry units and some Panzers. As he did so, he unknowingly played right into Zhukov's hand. In a sense, no one could blame him, as Germany could not expect the "backward Bolsheviks" to have any kind of nuclear technology.

So for a while, the Russians played a siege game and pretended to assault the place. The Germans felt good about their renewed successes against the enemy hordes. From the 16th to the 19th, they bloodily repulsed no less than five major assaults. So nothing could have prepared them for what was coming.

As the sun rose on the horizon, the German forces were ripe for slaughter on the 19th of March 1947. All Red Army forces had already been secretly withdrawn back ten kilometers during the night, which was considered a safe distance from the planned explosion. A large Soviet airstrike approached the city. In fact, it was the most significant Russian aircraft concentration of the war to date. Over six hundred planes of all sorts showed up, guns blazing. Sporting just a little over fifty bombers, it should have given the Luftwaffe some clues that something was wrong since the numbers of fighters protecting them were so staggeringly high that it didn't make any sense to commit so many of them for such a small number of the slower planes. But again, like the commander on the ground, why should they have doubted or suspected something was wrong? The Yvan's had fought a pretty straightforward war to date (even if dirty as hell), and it wasn't the first time they did something weird. So the German pilots went about their business of shooting downs some Red Amy planes.

Little did they know that the large, repurposed B-50 bomber in the center of the formation, protected tightly by the other smaller ones so no Axis planes could approach it, contained the third nuclear bomb ever produced in the world. The bomb that the Americans had lost in their failed raid on Berlin. The Superfortress had ended up crashing into Soviet territory, and of course, Stalin and his henchmen repurposed it – and its potent cargo – for their own designs. No one knew that the bomb and the plane had survived. Washington had deemed it lost and destroyed. The beautiful aircraft was repainted grey with the red star of the USSR on the fuselage's side and had been completely repaired.

If it survived its maiden flight, he would head straight back to Siberia, where Russian scientists awaited it to copy its engines and technology for the glory of Stalin and his plans of world conquest.

As the fiery battle raged all around it, the B-50 opened its bay doors, and the operator, poorly trained as most Soviet airmen were, awkwardly looked thru his sights. He could hardly miss, especially since the bomb was so powerful that it would vaporize everything within a large radius.

The device plunged right over the main part of the German defenses – not that it mattered, it only needed to fall within the city to destroy them – and exploded on the ground. In a second, half of the town just vanished in a blinding light reminiscent of heavenly power. The blast packed a destructive force equivalent to about 15 kilotons of TNT.

The epic explosion literally vaporized everything standing within a radius of two kilometers. The resulting secondary detonation produced a supersonic shock wave followed by extreme winds that remained above hurricane force over three kilometers from ground zero. Furthermore, every building within a ten-kilometers radius was leveled.

A secondary and equally devastating reverse wind followed, flattening and severely damaging homes and buildings several kilometers further away.

The intense heat of the bomb reached several million degrees Celsius and scorched flesh and other flammable materials over three kilometers away. Simultaneous fires were started throughout the blast-damaged area by fireball heat, overturned stoves, and furnaces, electrical shorts, etc. Twenty minutes after the detonation, these fires had merged into a firestorm, pulling in surface air from all directions to feed an inferno that consumed everything flammable. It leveled all of the fortified areas and the civilian parts of the city that had been "lucky enough" to be only partially damaged by the blast itself, killing more Wehrmacht soldiers trapped under fallen debris.

By the time the enormous mushroom cloud rose high in the sky, the city of Konigsberg had ceased to exist. More than 60 000 civilians were killed in the blast. If that wasn't already an immense tragedy for the Reich, the military losses were even higher. 7th Corps, 170th and 131st, (all infantry) simply ceased to exist. Furthermore, the German Army lost two of its best armored divisions, the 5th, and 95th Panzers. Konigsberg 100 000 defenders were gone. Not all dead, of course (those were the lucky ones), but all military cohesion disappeared instantly, as every soldier in the defenses was burnt, blinded, or severely wounded by the blast/shockwave itself.

Cherniakhovski men were instructed to launch the final attack five hours later. But they didn't, so appalled by the size of the large cloud that ignominiously rose over the German city. The Soviet General didn't try to enforce his instruction and instead cabled Zhukov to tell him that it would be crazy to ask the men to walk into such a vortex. After his subordinate described his strategy's success, the Russian Marshal relented. Like Genghis Khan before him, the man understood that it was dangerous to give an order that soldiers would not obey.

The Red Army troops would only get on the move the next day, but it hardly made a difference. It would take more than a day for the Wehrmacht to recuperate from such an epic-proportion disaster.

Maybe it never would.

The USSR makes its play
Molotov presents Stalin's ultimatum to the Allies, Washington DC, March 19th, 1947

A minute after the arrogant Soviet diplomat left the oval office, everyone in the room stayed silent. It was a sort of solemn silence. Not one of the men in the room dared speak, or maybe they were just completely stunned. Churchill, McKenzie King (Canadian Prime Minister), US President Truman, Secretary of State Cordell Hull, and General Marshall were all given the lowdown by Molotov.

The diplomat had arrived a few days ago in the U.S. capital under the pretext that the USSR wanted in on the discussions that were taking place in the American city. Tensions had been running high between the Allied powers lately, and apparently, Stalin seemed to want to play it nice.

But the whole thing had been a sham. Molotov had been there in anticipation of the nuclear attack on Konigsberg, and his Washington visit was for a particular reason. The man had just given them Soviet demands for a postwar world. All of Germany, Austria, Czechoslovakia, Poland, the Balkans, Turkey, the Middle East. China to the Communist Mao. All of Korea to be under a Soviet administration and a Communist government. Hell, they even demanded that the Allies evacuate Italy and France but said that this part could be negotiated. How nice of them.

Molotov continued stating that the Soviet Union also possessed nuclear fire and that for every bomb dropped on them, they would retaliate in kind. And then he'd just left, claiming that all these discussions would need to be done after the Third Reich was destroyed. "The arrogant, little prick evil bastard," thought Truman, just before Churchill decided to talk finally.

The man harbored his grave face. The U.S. President had seen the same look on him after the 1940 defeat in the United Kingdom.

"Gentlemen," he said, taking a cigar from his front pocket. "I think we have just found a new enemy."

"Damn right we have Winston," added the Canadian Premier. Truman finally decided to talk. He pushed himself backward on his chair, looking at the room's ceiling for a moment.

"Well. That man put on a good show." His anger was seething and threatened to boil to the surface. It was the same feeling that he'd felt after the dastardly Japanese attack on Pearl Harbor. He had not been president then but still felt the shame and frustration of it all, like every other American in the land of the free. "Stalin wants to play tough guy, well, we can also do the same."

By now generously puffing on his cigar, Churchill looked at Truman in his most serious stance. "Harry. We need to discuss what we are going to do. Obviously, the war against Germany isn't over, and the Russians won't do anything before that ends." He put his smoking cigar in the ashtray in front of him on the table by the couch he was sitting. "Comrade Stalin is dirty. He plays dirty, he things dirty." Winston smiled. "Well, good old England has its share of deviousness in its own right." "What does that mean," said the President. "It means we need to whatever is in our power to face the USSR and its dictator, Stalin." He paused, taking his cigar between his two fingers, pointing at the map on the Oval Office's wall representing Europe. "I also mean that we'll have to talk to the Germans in some form or the other." "No way," said the American, and the Canadian Prime Minister nodded silently in agreement. "Winston, this cannot be. We need to get rid of the damned Nazis, not work with them." General Marshall stayed silent but didn't react to Churchill in the same way as his leader. "Mr. President. Lord Churchill might have a point here." "Truman looked at his commander in chief awkwardly, clearly not pleased. "No. I just won't. We will finish this war first and then see how we can deal with the Reds. We'll do what we have to do to present a strong front and not be intimidated, but I won't talk to the damned Germans."

CHAPTER 5

Change of plans
Carinhall, five hours after the Konigsberg bombing March 19th, 1947

"I need to talk to the Fuhrer," said Skorzeny to the two large bulky guards in front of Goering's room. He was deep within the mansion, where the German leader slept. "The Fuhrer is not available at the moment," answered the nervous-looking man. Otto could feel his friend Sturm tensing just beside him.

No wonder he was nervous since Goering had been brought to his room upon the bombing announcement with some sort of problem. The man had seemed livid, catatonic. Skorzeny was also in his quarters after another nice hunting day with Hermann, and it had been a great time. The area around the hunting lodge (if it could still be called like that) was full of game, and he'd enjoyed his moment in the forest. For a while, the war had seemed far away.

The SS commando had been enjoying some downtime in Carinhall, as it seemed that Goering was still set on the bombing of the USA in Aachen, as suggested by Halder. He'd brought Marco Sturm over to finalize the whole affair, and they'd been hard at work since the 16th. On the 18th in the evening, they also had diner with the Fuhrer again, as Goering was quite busy with the running of the state during the day. He was also often required in Berlin proper. The news from the east wasn't good, as the Soviets had again pierced the line, and the Wehrmacht was retreating toward Konigsberg. But Hermann had told them to keep the faith since the city was heavily fortified and Model concentrated enough troops there to stop the enemy.

The two SS commandos worked a little more before going to bed, and that was that. They were both woken up by commotions and loud noises in the mansion in the morning. It seemed that the whole place was in a state of uproar.

Quickly putting his uniform on, he exited his room almost at the same time as Sturm did. A servant, running in the hall, tried to zip past them, but Skorzeny grabbed him by the arm and stopped him. "What's happening?" the man looked nervous, panicked. Otto shook him a little to loosen his lips.

"Herr Skorzeny... There has been a terrible incident in Konigsberg.", he stammered. "And," the SS man said in his menacing tone, tightening his grip on the servant's arm. "And the Fuhrer has not taken the news well." A cold feeling swept down Otto's back. This wasn't good. "What do you mean?" "The Fuhrer has had some sort of stroke or something similar; he is incapacitated." The man tried to free himself from Skorzeny's grip. "I really need to get going, Herr Skorzeny…." And he let him go. The servant quickly disappeared down the hall, going toward the Fuhrer's room.

Sturm looked at his friend. "What the hell?" "What the hell, Marco, is that we need to know what happened in Konigsberg." Let's go down and see the soldiers in the basement. They walked quickly toward the large stone stairs that went down the building. Two guards were standing by it but let the two SS men pass, as they knew who they were. They clicked their heels and made the Heil Goering salute.

The whole Carinhall basement had been transformed, after Goering became the Reich's Fuhrer, into a military HQ. It had become necessary because the man had wanted to be able to direct the war from his Carinhall mansion. So the whole basement had been redone into a complete radio communication room and operational center. It also doubled as a bunker if the place was bombed and Goering needed protection.

And so there they'd learned of the Russian nuclear bombing on Konigsberg. Countless soldiers were simply gone, and the frontline was torn open. It was a disaster of epic proportion. And they'd learned thru some of the soldiers there that apparently Goering had not taken the news well.

And so they'd doubled back to the Fuhrer's room to talk to him and were stopped by the two burly guards by the door.

"I will say it one more time, soldier," said Skorzeny, in a tone dripping with menace, with Sturm also ready to explode into violence. "Open that fucking door!" The two SS commando's reputation was established everywhere in Germany. So the guards were finally intimidated into opening the large double doors to the Fuhrer's room.

The scene portrayed in front of them was of a richly furnished room, with rugs and art statues everywhere and several paintings. A large fireplace was slowly burning out with its red embers, and in the middle stood a white-robed doctor, hovering over Goering that was lying down on the bed. "What is the matter of this! I have said that the Fuhrer is not to be bothered; he needs……," yelled the doctor as he turned to see who the intruders were, stopping himself in mid-sentence.

The two SS commandos approached the bed to see what was Goering's condition. "You cannot…" said the white-robed man, mustering some courage. Skorzeny waved him away with a quick hand gesture. "Get out."

"Colonel…." Said Sturm as he approached the German leader. Their leader was white as a sheet of paper and had open eyes that seemed empty. He wasn't moving. "Mein Fuhrer." Said Otto, without getting an answer. He touched the man, again trying to establish contact, but to no avail.

The German Fuhrer was utterly gone. He was still breathing but wholly incapacitated. Goering suffered a significant stroke upon hearing of the destruction of Konigsberg and the 100 000 men going along with it. His heart then just gave out. It was not like he was in good shape anyway. "Let's go," said Skorzeny in his determined voice. The famous commando knew what needed to be done.

The Generals take over part 1
Halder makes his move, evening of March 19th, 1947

As Skorzeny's car sped thru the long winding road out of the forest where Carinhall was located, he crossed several troop transports going toward the mansion and several staff cars. The SS commando didn't doubt that the Fuhrer's stroke had spread like wildfire and that the Reich's leadership was in an uproar. He didn't stop and was gone from the scene, leaving the people in power to deal with this while he and Marco would deal with the damned Yvan's.

The soldiers quickly disgorged from the Opel trucks and Hanomags while they quickly secured the area. General Halder, commander-in-chief of the OKW, had come in person to see Goering's condition. The country could simply not be left without leadership at this grave hour. The Soviets had completely gutted Army Group Prussia and would surely be soon pouring thru the gap created by their atomic bomb. And there was no telling if they would drop another one soon.

Things were in a state of flux in Germany on that day of March, as the Fuhrer was not at the helm. Some Nazi officials could have taken over rapidly, but one of the most prestigious was gone. Joseph Goebbels, the head of the Propaganda Ministry and one of the last of Hitler's cronies to still be in power after Goering took over, was reported missing (probably dead). He'd been in Konigsberg touring the area on a propaganda movie filming spree. Albert Speer was unreachable (he was said to be somewhere in Bavaria (southern Germany). Most of the other Nazi party members who had some influence during Hitler's tenure were already pushed out of the circle of power by the new Fuhrer after coming to power or dead even.

So it was not a time to wait to see what would happen. Things needed to move rapidly, or the Reich would fall like a house of cards. Halder issued some orders, recalling Von Manstein, Guderian, and

Rundstedt to Berlin. He also cabled Guderian directly to send as many troops northward as he could or organize some sort of counter-attack that would divert the Soviets from streaming thru the giant gap created by the nuclear explosion and the resulting chaos.

According to the preliminary reports that Halder received, even Model was reported dead or missing, as he'd been close to the main blast area. His visit to Carinhall was a short one. Upon seeing the Fuhrer's state, he ordered all military personnel out of the mansion and to report back to Berlin for further orders. He left the staff in place and called for more doctors to attend Goering. And then he left for Berlin.

More orders were issued across the Reich to get troops to East Prussia as soon as possible. Before he left his command post in the Austrian Alps, Manstein organized for the transfer of three divisions northward in a move that would surely give a great opportunity to the Western Allies, but it could not be helped. Rundstedt did the same, freeing eight divisions from the Siegfried Line's "quiet areas." The Anglo-Americans would not miss their golden opportunity.

And so, for a critical few hours, the Reich staggered and almost fell. But Halder and the other General's firm grip held things together. The rest of the story would then depend on what they did.

Somewhere over Bavaria
Another air raid, March 19th, 1947

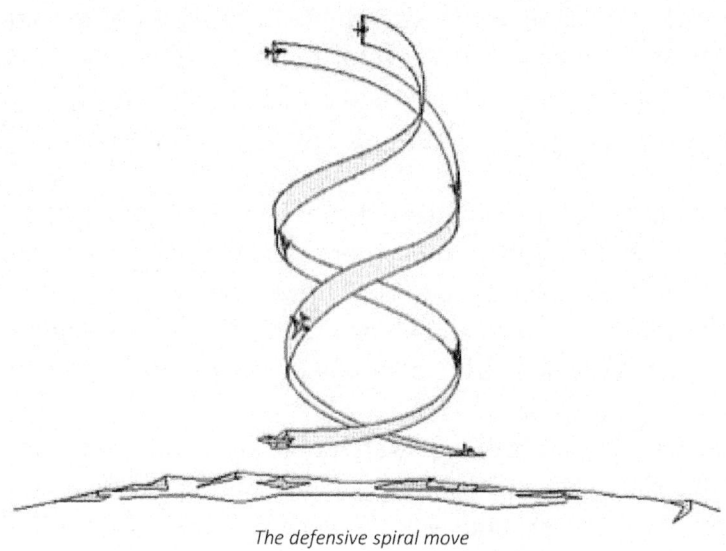

The defensive spiral move

The Meteor plane swooped low over the tall pine trees and scattered them in a thunderous roar, like a mighty wind blowing thru. 30mm shells from a German aircraft then raked Lamirande's wake. The ordinance shredded some of the old vegetation, splintering it in many directions, even starting a small fire on the ground.

After his little problem back in Slovenia, it was good to be flying again. After the crash, he'd been brought back toward the airfield and had been grounded for a few days to recuperate, under doctor's orders. If he'd been the one deciding, he would have simply climbed back into an aircraft and flown away to the nearest dogfight.

In any case, he was flying now, so it was the only thing that mattered. He was currently trying to shake off the persistent German pilot in a ME-262 trying to shoot him down. Pushing his aircraft throttle to maximum power, he climbed back high in the sky in what seemed the blink of an eye. The plane was fast, but so was

Gaston's tailing enemy.

The ME-262 followed the Meteor's move and tried to shoot down the French Canadian on the way up. Red tracers arced left and right of the plane, missing it by several meters. Lamirande decided to shake off his pursuer with a classic maneuver when he was high enough.

The defensive spiral was used by the defender when the kinetic energy became depleted, and other last-ditch maneuvers could not successfully be implemented. The move consisted of dropping the nose low during the turn and going into a spiral dive, using gravity to supply the energy needed to continue evasive action.

And so he positioned his aircraft down and started to do rolling scissors straight down. His goal was to stay out of phase with the attacker until the ground was dangerously close. And indeed, the forest greenery rapidly approached once he sped downward.

With the defensive spiral, the advantage usually went to the aircraft that could decelerate quicker. The best way to do this was by cutting power and extending the speed brakes to force an overshoot.

As he sped down and started to have a blurry vision (the G-forces he was receiving was relatively high), he waited to pull out of his dive at the last possible second. He hoped to cause the attacker to crash into the ground or in the forest. He mentally counted down from five to 0 and then pulled his control stick toward him, turning it in a slight leftward angle to speed thru two of the largest trees towering above the others.

The Meteor zipped past the trees, scattering some needles and shaking them heavily. The German pilot, trying to emulate Lamirande's maneuver, did not compensate fast enough, and his left wing hit one of the big branches. The German plane went into a tumble and crashed in a fiery explosion.

Lamirande throttled back up to high altitude and looked for a new target. He needed to find another German to kill. And then he saw him. The damned skulls and crossbones nemesis that he'd been trying to kill (and not be killed by) for the better part of the last three years. He was there, just below him. He veered hard toward him with a gleeful smile on his face.

Adolf Galland was having another great day. He was chasing his soon-to-be third kill and was shepherding it toward some of his comrades toward the north. The other two fighters were waiting for the Allied pilot some distance away. The German ace only needed to bring him toward them. He burst a few 30mm shells at the British plane without conviction. He kept concentrating on staying on the enemy's tail.

And so, for one of the few times in the war, he didn't see his enemy coming. To Galland's defense, he'd thought his nemesis dead after he'd shot it down over Slovenia and so had not been looking for him anymore in the sky.

Lamirande bored down on the German as a bird of prey on its last approach and loosed everything he had on the ME-262. The flurry of tracer shells crisscrossed the sky and filled the air in and around Adolf's. Some of the ordinances were bound to hit, and they did. A shell exploded on the Galland's right wing, gutting the engine.

The hit sent the ME-262 in a horizontal spiral that lasted for a few seconds. Just enough time for the Nazi ace to figure out he was hit and needed to bail out. He opened his canopy and jumped out of the plane as it finally started to fall down to the earth. As his jet crashed hard and exploded, Galland opened his parachute and slid slowly down toward the forest below. As he did, he noticed that the plane that shot him down came back near him, circling his chute for a few seconds.

And then he saw it. The hockey sticks on the Meteor's fuselage and clearly painted in red. His damned enemy was not dead. The man wiggled his wings a little in a sign of respect before speeding away toward his next target.

The Generals take over part 2
OKW meeting, Maybach II bunker complex, March 20th, 1947

The three commanders arrived at HQ at different intervals during the evening of the 19th or early on the 20th. First, Gerd von Rundstedt, the Western theater commander, held sway over forty divisions. The old general had been instrumental in the Wehrmacht's early successes, taking upon himself to countermand Hitler's order (while he was incapacitated) in Dunkirk, enabling the Axis to destroy the entire British Army. Its disappearance gave the Germans the chance to invade the United Kingdom successfully.

The second was also instrumental in the Third Reich's early victories. It was Erich Von Manstein, the mastermind strategist behind the Ardennes attack, that outflanked the Allied armies in 1940 and led to the major Dunkirk victory. The same man behind the incredible recovery on the Eastern Front after the winter 42-43 disaster, and the architect behind the Dnieper-Volkhov-Lovat Line when things needed to be switched to the defensive.

The third was perhaps the most famous of the trio. Heinz Guderian, the flamboyant Panzer commander always at the head of his column, with godlike admiration from the men under his command. The father of the Blitzkrieg tactic and the General behind the great mobile offensives in France, England, North Africa, the Middle East, and ultimately Russia, with a short stint in Spain and Tunisia in the 43-44 defensive struggle there.

General Frantz Halder, commander in chief of OKW, towered above them all as commander. He was the man who had instrumentalized both Fuhrer's wishes and did the planning since the start of the war. Halder knew that the three commanders he'd recalled to OKW for consultations were weathered veterans of war and, as such came with a lot of popularity within the military, so he needed them to control the crumbling Reich.

The scene that was unfolding was near Berlin, at the OKW headquarter. The OKW(overall command) and OKH (land army command) decisional centers were stationed in two separate facilities in the forested area between Zossen and Wünsdorf, Brandenburg, just some twenty kilometers south of Berlin. Two nearly identical bunker complexes, Maybach I and Maybach II, were built between 1937 and 1940. Essential for both organizations' mutual relations, the complexes were separated by a fence.

The "Maybach I" was for the Army (OKH) and was not used as much in 1947 since most of the command power and decisional structure had transferred to the OKW from 1941 and 1942 onward, under the wishes of the two Fuhrers.

The "Maybach II" was the complex that housed OKW and that held the March 20th meeting. It consisted of various structures with twelve bunkers "houses" at its heart, with three levels above ground and two underground levels. The buildings above ground were made to look like local civilian houses, with shingled roofs and plastered walls to conceal their military function. Nonexistent window cells and doors were added, and steel armored bunker doors were decorated with wood to look like normal ones.

Underground the "houses" were interlinked by a so-called "Ringstollen," which was part of an even larger network of underground tunnels and underground bunker rooms. These tunnels were fitted with facilities like drink water wells, machine rooms, and air filter systems to survive an attack or siege.

The meeting proper was in the second basement, where the primary command bunker was located. Halder was quite happy to finally be able to hold a strategic meeting where it was meant to be held at OKW HQ. During the war up to that date, gathering with the Fuhrer (or decisional peoples within the Reich) had rarely been held where they should have been. Instead, they happened at the Wolfchanzze in Eastern Prussia or at Carinhall, Goering's luxurious manor.

The room itself was the typical military command center. Large enough place to house over dozens of people, an enormous table in the center, with situational maps plastered all over the walls, with the most up-to-date one sitting right on the table.

Also attending the meeting in the room's main bunker were Von Paulus and Von Leeb, Halder's two acolytes in the OKW. Albert Speer was one glaring absentee, as he could not be found. While he'd been touring the Southern Bavarian oil depots, something had happened to him. Reports were unclear at that point in time, but apparently, he'd been seriously injured in an oil tank explosion.

The Wehrmacht General's preliminary discussions just glanced over the subject of the Reich's leadership, as these men were not politicians, and all of them were utterly uninterested in power. The way they viewed it, they met to discuss purely military matters and was what they wanted to do: lead the Wehrmacht.

But the Third Reich was leaderless, and for this very reason, the men in the room on that day of March 1947 were about to take decisions whether they liked it nor not. Hitler was dead; Goering, Goebbels, Rudolph Hess (mental illness), and most importantly, Himmler were all gone. As said earlier, even Speer, a popular Nazi figure and influential man in his capacity as Minister of Armament and Production, was not attending the critical meeting. Nazi men like Speer or Ribbentrop didn't have the stature to take over, and the more minor Nazi officials, like the Gauleiters (regional leaders across Germany), didn't have the clout to move in and take over.

So it was either Goering came back from his predicament, or else the military stepped in. The discussions on the dire situation went on for hours on end, and the assembled generals in the room did not have any clue how to save Germany.

Halder and most of the men in the leadership meeting were not interested in taking power, but something had to be done to show the Nazi realm that it was not leaderless, for the news of Goering's stroke would soon trickle down to the country in general. And if one thing was certain in March 1947, it was that the Third Reich needed a show of strength. It was in enough of a problematic situation as it was encircled on all fronts and attacked from every angle.

So then a vote was held, and everyone agreed unanimously that Guderian should step in as the temporary leader of the German nation. It was also decided that he wouldn't take any title. It would just be announced that he would temporarily lead Germany's destiny while the Fuhrer was incapacitated and recuperating. While it wasn't clear he would come back, that was the only way the generals saw that the Nazi officials within the Reich could accept it. While not happy about it, Guderian understood that he was the only man in the room with enough popularity and prestige to takeover.

The Reich faced a grave situation, and only a miracle would save it from the pit of hell it was falling into. The Soviet nuclear attack meant that both of their main enemies had the atomic bomb, and the whole thing did not bode well for Germany. Halder informed Guderian and the rest of the assembled men of Otto Skorzeny's plan to trigger a German bomb, giving everyone hope.

The point they would make was that the Reich also had the bomb, which would entail the Allied nations to be a little more careful about dropping nuclear ordinance on the German heads, for, in theory, they could retaliate in kind. Of course, it was all a bluff since the Reich only had the uranium it had and wouldn't be producing more for a while. But it was what these desperate men had.

Since Guderian needed to step down from his theater command to lead Germany and that Walter Model was dead, the group of men named Erich Von Manstein to lead the new Eastern Front command that was still a very potent force with over 90 divisions. Von Paulus was thus named commander of the southern theater as he would step down from OKW. Halder was, of course, kept in place along with Von Leeb.

The military situation was very fluid in the east, and the next few weeks would decide if the Reich either survived or disappeared in a deluge of steel and fire.

The Battle for Warsaw
Fighting retreat for the Panzer Lehr, March 22nd, 1947

The Tiger III engine groaned as it struggled up the steep slope that the tank driver was trying to overcome. The Panzer's survival depended on it, as many enemy tanks' shells flew their way. The Panzer Lehr's 1st Heavy Panzer Battalion was down to eight tanks, all of them new Konigstigers. The fighting of the last few weeks had been grueling and very difficult for the men of the Panzerwaffe.

After the disaster at Konigsberg, their already difficult position on the Eastern Front had become an impossible situation. The nuclear destruction of Konigsberg meant that the Soviets poured thru in the north, so the whole Polish positions were threatened with outflanking.

Their brand-new overall theater commander, Erich Von Manstein, was issuing desperate orders left and right for German units to move out of the fighting they were entangled in to get fresh reinforcements on the Baltic Coast and in what used to be Northern Poland and the Polish Corridor near Dantzig. This meant that the Panzer Lehr, as one of the best elite Panzer units left, was to take a double workload in the fight against the enemy. Not only were they to disentangle themselves from the Russians attacking from the east, but the Steel Division also needed to be ready for the planned counter-attack against the northern Soviet breakthrough.

Things were not going well lately. They had not been going well for a while, in fact. But the last three days had seen the loss of over 100 000 men in Konigsberg, the city erased from the map, and the complete destruction or disintegration of Army Group Prussia (that was retreating in disarray and trying to regroup westward).

And then the news of the Fuhrer's illness reached the frontlines. Most did not receive it as a disaster, as not many in the Wehrmacht admired any of their political leaders, for they were responsible for their predicament. Whatever respect and admiration the soldiers had for Hitler and then Goering died somewhere in the Russian steppes in the wasted offensives of 1944 and 1945 when the German Army should have been concentrating on husbanding its forces.

Walder opened the Panzer's hatch to have a better view beyond the immediate farm field the Tiger had leveled onto after climbing the steep slope. He decided that the risk was worth it since they'd reached the top of the small hill and were driving downward, so the enemy would be more than extremely lucky if it could hit his Tiger. He saw the seven other surviving tanks from the heavy battalion on both sides of his own. All of them were driving full speed, churning earth and some fine dust on their sides. "Radio operator," he yelled down the hatch. "Yes, Herr Colonel." "Instruct everyone to head for that hedgerow a little on our left, at about 400 meters." "Yes, Sir."

He'd spotted a large hedgerow of thick vegetation with a small dirt track large enough for his Panzers to get thru. Once behind the thick pines and other branches, he would be safer than in the open like he was now with his men.

The leaves had started growing on the trees, as spring was in full swing in Poland at the end of March. He hoped it would be enough to hide his force so they could make their escape even faster. The hedgerow was a length of at least two hundred meters, so it was long enough to hide his forces for a while. Erich hoped it would be enough to get to the next hiding spot or feature in the landscape.

For it was the only way he could think of to escape the damned Communist hordes.

Extracts from Von Manstein's 1958 book, LOST VICTORY
Back to Ostfront Command, March 21st, 1947.

After leaving the OKW meeting in Wünsdorf, Brandenburg (twenty kilometers south of Berlin), I remember feeling a moment of elation as well as a moment of dread. I was finally back in an operational command where more than pure defensive warfare would be executed. At the same time, the Reich's situation was critical, and I would have to pull more than a minor miracle to save it from the Soviet juggernaut.

The discussions that took place during that meeting would have been considered nothing short of treasonous only months before. Goering would have arrested us outright and probably even shot us. But be as it may, there was no more Nazi leadership strong enough to either command the Wehrmacht or else tell us what to do. The demise of every significant political figure in the Reich forced us to play politics. It was not about taking power; it was more like someone had to take it to keep the country from disintegrating in its hour of dire need.

Even the Gestapo, typically quite restrictive and violent, received our decisions the next day with uncharacteristic apathy. I have long suspected that most Nazis officials were by then busier with either trying to erase their crimes or disappear to avoid Allied justice, which promised to be swift and brutal on war criminals.

I was pretty happy at Guderian's nomination as temporary head of state, as I highly respected the man and knew that he would do what was necessary to preserve Germany. Even happier that I was not considered for the position, as I have never had any political aspirations of my own at any given time during my long career.

While the Russian forces bearing down on the Reich's eastern border were numerous and substantial, I still entertained some hope to fend them off. After reviewing the order of battle I was given command of (90 divisions at least), I had cause for confidence. Near to ninety divisions were at my disposal.

But the dread I felt came from the highly fluid situation, a consequence of the Russian nuclear attack on Konigsberg, where over 100 000 soldiers perished in the fire of hell. Upon arriving at Eastern Command west of Warsaw on the 21st, I immediately confirmed Guderian's earlier orders from the day before for all forces in Poland to retire westward. I even issued additional instructions for units to move toward Dantzig, where I hoped to stop the enemy.

In agreement with our temporary leader and Halder at OKW, I also resolved to fight the Russians where they advanced and not hunker down on another defensive line, as there were no natural features and fortification lines that could save the current situation. We were out of time and out of space to retreat into. This final fight would be one epic, fiery end where it would either be us victorious over a pile of bodies or the damned Communists.

The following summer would be the most intense fighting period of the war.

Extract Of Heinz Guderian 1952 Book, Panzer Leader
In command of the Reich, March 21st, 1947

The two unexpected events of the nuclear attack on Konigsberg and Goering's stroke created a power vacuum in the Reich. In different circumstances, it could have been filled with other Nazi Party officials like Goebbels and Speer, but on the 20th of March 1947, one was dead, and the other one was reported missing and severely injured.

While I took the position upon the urging of my esteemed colleagues and because of the Reich's dire situation, I was not interested in any political power whatsoever, apart from becoming chief of the general staff, a position that every staff officer dreamed of.

The OKW decision that trusted me into Germany's leadership role was born out of desperation because we just didn't know what to do. Decisions had to be taken, armies moved, and frontlines needed to be defended.

And besides, everyone presents on that day though the arrangement would be temporary, and the Fuhrer would soon resume his duties. But alas, as events would soon show, things did not go in that direction.

So after the OKW meeting in Brandenburg, I never returned to my theater command, letting General Manstein take back the place that had so unjustly been taken from him by a frustrated Goering.

I was instead ushered to Berlin by Halder and his suite, and it took us the better part of the next two days to assume full control of all of the Reich's political and decisional apparatus. For if the transition was surprisingly uneventful and without any reaction from the dreaded Gestapo, a lot of negotiation and "gun diplomacy" was needed to get everyone into line.

The country was in a state of uproar, especially with the nuclear destruction of Konigsberg, and most did not relent with happiness at seeing military men take the country's helm.

Others, like several of the Nazi Party regional governors (Gauleiters), did not understand why I was not seeking peace, as surely Germany could not win fighting two powers with atomic weapons. Little did they know that something was in the works on our side as well.

Beyond March 22nd, I did not know what I was to do yet to try to save Germany from ultimate defeat. At that time, it was too early to formulate any plans beyond trying to re-establish the situation in the east while holding the rest together. The growing rift between the USSR and the Western Allies was not apparent yet, so trying to approach the Western powers for a separate peace did not enter my mind as I knew it had been tried several times by Goering since 1946, with no success.

Change of policy
Western Allied leader's meeting, Washington D.C. March 22nd, 1947

"This is interesting, to say the least," said Truman, picking up his morning coffee. "Indeed, Mr. President," added Churchill also with a coffee in hand. The two men were again in the Oval Office in the White House.

The Western Allied discussions continued after the Soviet explosion of an atomic bomb and the USSR's foreign minister Molotov's visit. The man had come to tell them of Stalin's demand on a postwar world. The damned Russian diplomat had drawn a world where the Communists held sway in most of old Europe, Asia, the Middle East, and China, with Mao's Tse Dong's Communist eventual rise to power with the help of the Soviets.

And, most unsettling, he'd left for Moscow immediately after that, without any intention to participate in the Allied discussions that were to be held in order to talk about the war's end. Things looked quite grim from a diplomatic standpoint. Stalin gave the impression of wanting to fly away on his own and finish the war on his terms.

The two Allied leaders had just read the short transcripts from HQ Europe. Eisenhower had just reported that Goering was not in power and that a General had taken over the Reich's command. Not just a general; Heinz Guderian of all people. A highly skilled warrior and commander.

The electrifying news had been announced a few hours earlier over the radio waves. Goering, the German Fuhrer, was not dead but unable to lead for the moment, so the radio address to the Fatherland blared to all that would hear that a temporary leader had been named in this difficult hour for the Third Reich.

Truman was not an expert of anything foreign and didn't know Guderian other than by the reports he'd read. Churchill was better informed. "So, Winston. What about this Guderian fellow," said Truman, taking another sip of his coffee. "Well, Mr. President, for starters, he is a very decent gentleman. I have met him in the 1930s. Good fellow. Fair, smart, honest. Like most military people. Typical Prussian officer." Churchill sat backward on the couch. "He was the Reich's foremost expert of tank tactics and has since been a commander in most of their operations." "Wasn't he the commander in 1941 in our Middle Eastern debacle?" asked Truman. "Correct, Mr. President," answered Churchill.

The two men were developing the same idea at the same time. With the obvious deepening rift between Anglo-Saxons and the Russians, the General's arrival represented quite a change. Could they deal with the man? In fact, could they deal with Germany and its leaders? The obvious question glared at both men.

"His he a Nazi," asked the U.S. leader. "I don't believe so, Mr. President, but I am not certain I will need to have my people look into it," answered Churchill. "Do we want to deal with the Third

Reich?" added the Englishman. "Well, Winston. I am not at all certain I want to do that, but it is a definite possibility now that that pig Goering isn't in power anymore. We have not fought a war against Fascist oppression just to have it replaced by world Communism."

"Well, Mr. President, as I outlined a few days ago, I propose we send discreet inquiries thru our agents in Switzerland to see if we can start discussing with the Germans....." Churchill let his words hang for a second since he was aware of Truman's reluctance to think about dealing with the Nazis. The President didn't counter anything, so he decided that he was getting somewhere with Truman's state of mind. Churchill was many things, but like most British, he was a realist and was not as naïve as the Americans. The young nation only started to set out in the world and did not always understand the reality of politics in Europe. They were naïve. But once you got the Americans roused up about something, good luck...

Letting Stalin win was simply replacing an oppressive ideology (Fascism) with another one (Communism). While he wasn't sure if one was better (or worse) than the other, his long experience filled him with a certainty. You never let a bully get away with it.

In the 1930s, the democracies had let the Nazis get away with conquering territory. They'd even tried to accommodate the Germans and believed in their empty promises. They rearmed quickly, prepared for war, while France and the United Kingdom were content to have peace at all cost. And when it was too late to do anything about it, Hitler had attacked, and the free world had for a moment edged very close to the abyss. They'd been lucky to have the mighty United States on their side.

Back then, he'd told the British government (under Chamberlain) that something needed to be done against the Third Reich, but no one listened to him. Then the war came and the serious defeats of 1939-1941. Churchill was determined that history would not repeat itself with the Soviets.

"Mr. President. I think we both agree that we need to be firm against Stalin. We also need to be realistic. The world will not be safer with the Soviet hordes. We simply cannot accept anything else than a return to pre-war borders. Do we agree?"

Truman sighed heavily for a moment. The man was a little reluctant to the possibility of a renewed war, this time against the Soviet Union. "Damn stupid Stalin! We have a war to finish before we bicker for the spoils...."

Battleship Schleswig-Holstein fights its last battle
Gun duel in Dantzig Harbor, March 23rd, 1947

Battleship Schleswig-Holstein was the last of the five Deutschland-class battleships built by the German Kaiserliche Marine before World War One. The ship, named for the province of Schleswig-Holstein, was laid down in the Germaniawerft dockyard in Kiel in August 1905 and commissioned into the fleet nearly three years later. The ships of her class were already outdated by the time they entered service, being inferior in size, armor, firepower, and speed to the new generation of dreadnought battleships.

While most of the fleet was interned by the British at Scapa Flow at the end of the war, Germany was permitted to keep the Schleswig-Holstein as a coastal defense ship since it was anyway outdated in 1918 and not really a naval threat to the United Kingdom.

Schleswig-Holstein fired the first shots of World War II when she bombarded the Polish base at Danzig's Westerplatte in the early morning hours of 1st September 1939. And since then, it stayed in Dantzig proper as a coastal defense ship and because there wasn't any mission for the ship. But by the time the Russians approached the city, it again became helpful to the Germans.

After the explosion in Konigsberg that obliterated the city and the troops defending it, the Soviet forces waited several hours before launching their troops forward on the 20th.

The Russian soldiers found devastation of the likes never seen even by these hardened men. Most received high radiation levels, so they started to get sick after crossing the no man's land that used to he the German city of Konigsberg. These details hardly mattered to the Red Army leaders, pushing their troops onward. By the 23rd, they approached the town of Dantzig, where it all started in 1939.

After the German conquest during the early phase of the war, the Axis troops moved on and conquered new lands east, north and south. But the old battleship remained in the bay as a coastal gun platform because it just didn't have any other work. In 1946, the warship was also called for the evacuation of Finland. It transported some troops and escorted the barges and other transports, making Model's move from Helsinki to Konigsberg possible.

After the evacuation of Finland was over, the battleship was ordered back to Dantzig, where it was replenished with its shell complement (the Schleswig-Holstein shelled some Russian position on the Baltic Coast before sailing back to Germany).

And so, the Red Army finally arrived in Dantzig. When its first units showed themselves in the harbor or on the docks, the German sailors opened up with everything they had on the poor troops. Several hundreds of casualties were thus reported to Cherniakhovski's command. The General quickly ordered an airstrike on the Schleswig, but the planes called for the mission never made it to Dantzig. The Luftwaffe intercepted them over the ruins of Konigsberg and never made it thru.

After a few hours of taking casualties, the local commanders mustered all the artillery and tanks in the area, and an all-out attack was ordered on the old battleship.

The duel between the warship's 280mm guns and the hundreds upon hundreds of smaller ordinance lasted for over seven hours. While dozens of shells were fired at the Schleswig-Holstein every half minute or so in a flurry of tracers that seemed to buzz around it, most ricocheted high in the air, and while spectacular, didn't do much to weaken or destroy the steel behemoth.

Its armored plates, made to withstand heavy naval ordinance, easily shrugged off anything the Soviets threw at them. The duel took so much time that most of the city within a kilometer of the harbor was leveled by the battleship's guns. The area was also on fire, and Russian casualties were hefty.

General Cherniakhovski finally showed up personally in Dantzig to take over command of the units trying to assault the damned thing. Shooting a few divisional commanders in the head for incompetence, he sent several squads across the water to board the vessel like a good old assault, reminiscent of another century. Within an hour, a lot more Russians were dead, this time floating on the water in a rough circle around the Schleswig-Holstein. But while they suffered horrendous casualties, some were bound to get thru the German hail of fire. On the 23rd (at dusk), an epic fight unfolded across the great ship's bridge and access hatches. Soviet soldiers crawled everywhere on the boat, and as complete darkness fell around the bay a few hours later, the fight ended in a bloody massacre. The enraged Soviet soldiers took not one sailor prisoner.

The vessel was no more by 3 AM on the 24th, as Cherniakhovski ordered it scuttled. Explosive charges blew its sides, and it slowly sank at an awkward angle in the bay.

The ship that had started it all was no more.

Recon in the Austrian Alps part 1
141 Regiment assault a mountain, March 24th, 1947

Sergeant Jack Summers held his hand in a quick gesture to signal everyone to stop advancing. The American squad was somewhere high in the Austrian Alps, approaching the mountain's summit. Their parent unit, the Lone Star Division, was still stationed in Slovenia, as several other Allied units.

The battle for the south raged, but so far, the Germans held the line, well perched in their towering rugged terrain defenses. Things had been in a bit of a lull lately, as Allied command did not seem to make its mind to attack the Axis mountain defenses. The war seemed to draw to a close, and there were rumors that the Americano-British forces would just wait for it to be over instead of assaulting heavily fortified mountain defenses that would cost a lot of lives. In short, it was not believed that the war's end would play itself where Jack's unit was.

The Anglo-Saxon's reluctance for casualties was one of the reasons they were reluctant to launch themselves at the defenses. Still, it was mainly because of the Red Army's presence a few dozen kilometers east of the furthest British positions in Slovenia.

Things weren't going well with the Soviets, apparently. He didn't understand why since the fellows seemed decent enough. Jack had met several Russian soldiers since the two Allied armies met in eastern Slovenia and Southern Hungary a few weeks back. The Red Army soldiers had been allowed to roam free for a few days before their officers brought them back to their lines. He'd even exchanged some trinkets with them, trading American chocolate and cigarettes for a German Luger pistol that he'd been looking for to send stateside.

After the first few days of joy and warm camaraderie, both sides had retired to their trenches (the two opposing forces now had a clearly defined "border.") Jack and his men didn't understand what was happening and preferred to concentrate on the Germans and finish them. But diplomacy seemed to take a different turn.

They were all crouching low behind a small rock outcropping covered with wild bushes and with trees above them. The squad's mission was again a reconnaissance in force. Jack's job was to report enemy positions and the Soviet ones. For they were very close to the Ruskies and, of course, faced the Germans. The mountain they'd climbed for the recon was quite steep but possessed a convenient old Roman track that helped them climb a lot easier than they'd expected.

"Turnbull, get me the binoculars," said Summers, opening his hand. The soldier obeyed rapidly. "I've heard some voices," added the sergeant, taking the binocular to his face. "I believe they are Russians….." he surveyed the rugged land just to his right. And then he saw some movement. A helmet flashed by his view. The soldiers he'd spotted seemed to be in some sort of trench or hiding position.

"Sarge, are they German or Russians?" asked one of the new men (a kid, really). All of them had their rifle at the ready. They were so close to the enemy that everyone was nervous, especially the three newcomers (replacements) that arrived a few days ago from the rear.

"Shut the fuck up, private," said Jack, with his hand in the air, finger raised toward the recruit. He continued to survey the area where he'd seen movement. "Yes, now I can see...." He said out loud but in a muffled voice. And then, as clear as day, he saw that they were Russians. One of them exited the position, crouched low, and even laid on the ground and started crawling toward the left, where Summers was certain some German soldiers awaited. More Soviet soldiers advanced cautiously and laid on the ground a few seconds later, following the first man.

Summers turned his binoculars left in the direction the Ruskies were advancing toward but didn't spot any Germans or any kind of defensive positions. The Axis forces were quite good at camouflage and had gotten proficient at defensive warfare since it was pretty much all they had been doing in the last three years or so.

While he couldn't see anything, he knew they were there. The Russian officer that sent the crawling soldiers also knew it. But apparently, he was in the same position as the American soldier observing them; He didn't see anything. The poor bloke was in the same predicament, probably. Some asshole officer above him had ordered a recon.

"What do we do, sarge?" asked Turnbull. "We do nothing, Blair. First time I get to see the Ruskies in action, so we stay put and watch." The Red Army soldiers advanced slowly, and Summers wondered if the Axis forces somewhere near had spotted them. He tried to focus on the lead man that had first crawled his way out of the Russian position. The Soviet was busy cautiously unearthing a mine with his long knife. "The Germans are near," said Summers to no one in particular, but his men heard him, and that was his intention, so they redoubled in carefulness. Everyone in the squad sensibly tensed.

For if there was a minefield, it meant that the Axis forces line of defense was close.

Saving grace part 1
Skorzeny takes Germany into the nuclear age, March 24th, 1947

Otto Skorzeny and his right-hand man Marco Sturm could hear the approaching frontline. They were west of Konigsberg in a city called Gdynia. It was a major civilian and military port on the Baltic Sea and was an important industrial center in Poland before the war. The whole area still showed the signs of battle that happened so long ago in 1939, when the Wehrmacht invaded Poland to ignite the Second World War.

The Polish forces had valiantly resisted, but they were simply overrun by superior forces that attacked them simultaneously from the air and sea (Schleswig-Holstein battleship that first shelled Dantzig).

Old, scarred Polish tank hulks and burned-out bunkers still dotted the landscape since no one in the Reich had had time to clean up the mess, busy as they were fighting a world war. But the Luftwaffe had built an airfield by the coast, and that was precisely what the two SS commandos needed to execute their plan.

Their land convoy had stopped in Berlin for a few days for Skorzeny to meet up with the Fuhrer and finalize the plan. Goering had initially wanted the atomic device triggered against the Americans as revenge for their bombing of Wilhelmshaven. In this fashion, the OKW had chosen the city of Eupen in Belgium. The expected results were twofold; first, the Fuhrer's revenge, and second, it was a potential tactical opportunity for a Wehrmacht counter-offensive to destabilize the whole Western Allied dispositions.

But in the end, things did not happen as they'd been discussed. The Russians triggered their own device on Konigsberg, completely obliterating the city and the 100 000 men defending it. And then the Fuhrer had a stroke upon hearing the news, and Skorzeny was thus faced with a choice.

Without a leader, orders, and disastrous news pouring out of Eastern Prussia (the Carinhall radio room HQ in the basement had all the information the SS man needed to know what was happening), Otto decided to act independently.

And news from the east was awful. The frontline was torn open, and the Soviet forces were pouring thru the gaps left by the disintegrated German forces. And so he'd chosen to use the bomb on the damned Yvan's.

The two men rapidly drove back to their convoy and, upon reaching it, immediately set for a small city east of Dantzig called Gdynia. They arrived there on the 23rd of March. By then, they could already hear the rumble of Russian artillery and the sounds of battle emanating from Dantzig, the important port city twenty kilometers south of Gdynia. Large dark clouds rose ignominiously over the battle-raging area.

"Hurry up, damn you!" yelled the SS man, kicking the white-robed scientist in the ribs. The man turned to face the commando stammering. "Yes…. Herr Skorzeny. We are working as fast as we can. "Well, it isn't fast enough.

The bomb and the timer needed to be ready before they set out of the place. Because Otto had no intention of dying along with the bomb in one fiery end. The bomb would be rigged to explode with a timer, and then he would execute his crazy escape plan.

The airfield he'd chosen was huge, made to accommodate bombers. It also had several hangars, mostly empty by then, the Luftwaffe having moved their planes further to the rear. The modified Hanomag containing the nuclear device was parked in the middle of the place.

Skorzeny's plan was quite simple. Let the Soviet forces overrun the hangar and blow the bomb while they occupied the airfield and the town half a kilometer away. He didn't know if he would catch a lot of enemy troops with the blast, but the point that the Reich was trying to make was that to show the world that Germany also had atomic technology.

Recon in the Austrian Alps part 2
141 Regiment assault a mountain, March 24th, 1947

Summers and his men stayed in their hiding place for over twenty minutes as the sergeant observed several more Russian soldiers working on removing mines. They were lying flat on the ground, crawling inches by inches forward, and probed ahead with their knives, bayonets, or simple wooden sticks.

Jack had tried to find some sign of the German hiding places that surely lay ahead of the Russians and his own position. The heavily forested ground slowly sloped upward until it reached an area dotted with jagged rocks and cliffs, intersecting with trees and other vegetation.

"The damned Krauts are well hidden," said Turnbull, that had fished a binocular from someone in the squad. "I can't see any signs of…" he stopped mid-sentence as his surveying sweep slowed down to focus on one area. "Sarge," he added, tapping on Jack's shoulder, pointing up the tallest rockface that towered above the area where the Soviets were busy removing mines. Summers pointed his own field glasses at the spot that Blair had apparently spotted. He was skeptical since he'd watched that spot many times over in the last half-hour. "There nothing there, Turnbull." "Yes, there is sarge. Look by the bush that seems to be growing in one of the large cracks on the rockface. A gun nozzle is sticking out." Jack took a second look and focused his eyes as best he could. As his recruiter back stateside had told him, he did not have the best vision in the whole army. "No air force for you, kid," he'd added at the time, and he'd been stuck with infantry work ever since.

Blair was right. The unmistakable round end of a gun nozzle was sticking out of the bush. Either an 88mm or 128mm gun, Jack wasn't sure. "Looks like a PAK44 to me, sarge. And that crack is big, so probably more like either a cavity or a tunnel dug from the other side." He whistled softly. "Wow, cleverly hidden." "Sure is. How many more of those are there? Those poor Soviet blokes won't stand a chance once the Krauts open fire." From their vantage point, the Germans had a plunging view of the whole area. Since they spotted one gun, there surely were others. Once the shooting started, the Soviets would not stand a chance.

Summers wondered if he should warn the Russian commander, but then he figured that the man probably suspected that the Axis had defenses here, especially since he'd sent men to remove mines. Jack would have never sent men in such open terrain. It was like sending them to the slaughter, but he guessed that was not a problem for the Red Army.

A shot suddenly rang in the air, echoing on the mountains and forest all around. Jack focused his field glasses on the group of crawling Russians. One of them was dead, its head splattered all over the muddy ground in a gory and disgusting display. Then a second shot, hitting another soldier; a third. The last one was the signal for the men to start running for their lives, as German snipers picked them off one by one. The Axis shooters killed the Red Army men in a carefully rehearsed firing rhythm. In under a minute, it was all over. The Communists were lying dead, except one gravely injured one, that cried to his mother for help. But no one came. Any fighting man with a bit of sense and/or experience knew that it was a typical sniper strategy. Injure one and wait for his comrades to try and save him. Then kill the supposed savior, or injure him as well, and so on.

"What do we do now, sarge?" asked Turnbull. "Well. We wait. Maybe the Ruskies will send more men; I don't know. And then maybe we go down the mountain to the captain and report the enemy position. Tons of snipers here and plenty of guns."

Turnbull relayed Summer's word to the rest of the squad's men, and they laid low for another couple of hours before heading down the old Roman path they'd come up from.

Jack would not recommend the area for an attack, as first of all the Ruskies were in the area, but also because the Germans had a strong position here, and it would cost an excessive amount of men to take it. Better leave it to the Reds.

After all, that was what recon missions were for. Report and recommend to officers. It wouldn't hurt that, at the same time, his words would help them not to send the Division there for an attack.

Saving grace part 2
Skorzeny takes Germany into the nuclear age, March 24th, 1947

Skorzeny feverishly worked on the Type 17 electric clockwork fuze installed on the atomic device in the modified Hanomag. Just a little under 30 kilograms of enriched uranium was packed in the half-track, and the SS commando was about to lit the fuze.

The Type 17 was a time-delay fuze; It was made for the SC250 bomb and was designed to explode after the bomb had fallen. In this case, it had been modified to fit the needs of what Otto had planned. Put the bomb into the Red army's path, and wait for the Yvan's to walk in to blow it up.

It could be set for any time between 3 and 195 minutes. In order to play it safe, he decided to put a three-hour delay on the device. It would ensure that the bomb would explode within the Russian midst because Skorzeny would make sure to stay at the Gdynia airfield until he actually saw Soviet soldiers with his own eyes. It was risky, but at the same time, it would not have been really optimal to explode the Reich's only atomic bomb without blowing up Russians at the same time.

While the bomb was to make a statement to the Allies that Germany had nuclear fire and that they'd better beware before using another one, Skorzeny had decided that he would blow the bomb into the Soviet offensive's path to stop it dead in its track and give time to the military to salvage the situation and form up some kind of defensive front west of Gdynia.

The Type 17 was fitted with a Type ZUS 40 mechanical anti-withdrawal fuze to prevent the bomb from being defused by Allied bomb disposal personnel. It was a simple spring-loaded detonator fitted to avoid the removal of the fuze and resulted in instantaneous detonation if it were moved by more than 0.6 in (15 mm).

A bit off to the side in the vast hangar, Marco Sturm, Skorzeny's right-hand man, was also busy, going thru the pre-flight routine for their escape plan, the Fieseler Storch plane. The commando's idea was to wait until they literally saw Russians at the end of the runway before taking off and leaving the site. Only this way could they ensure that everything would work as intended.

The Fieseler Storch was a small liaison aircraft built for the German Army just before the start of the Second World War. It was used in every theater of war and even produced by other countries like the Soviet Union after Germany gave it the blueprints to build them as part of the Germano-Soviet pact in 1939.

The Storch was deployed in all European, Middle Eastern, and North African theaters of World War II. In addition to its liaison function, a number of them were used to fly a battalion of Infantry Regiment Gross Deutschland behind enemy lines during the invasion of Belgium in 1940. General Rommel still regularly used the aircraft for transport and battlefield surveillance during the North African desert campaign of World War II.

Skorzeny was also a believer in the plane. His commando team used the model during their Grand Sasso Operation to free the Italian leader, Benito Mussolini.

Its short take-off capability and sturdiness would also be a plus in the operation. It lifted off the ground in a dime and could take a beating.

As he was putting the finishing touches on setting the Type 17 fuze, Skorzeny could hear the rumble of explosions and other noises of war. They seemed to be getting closer by the minute. "Sturm!" he yelled. "Yes, Colonel?" "Go and see if there are Russians near. It looks like they are getting really close." Marco stopped working on the Storch and walked to the hangar's stairs, which climbed on its roof.

Half a minute later, he came back running like the devil downstairs. "Colonel! Soviet soldiers and a few tanks at the end of the runway eastward end!" "Damn!" swore Skorzeny. "Time to go, Marco!" He closed the lid on the bomb, exited the Hanomag, and locked it tight.

He ran to the Fieseler and arrived almost at the same time as Sturm. They started the engine, and the plane slowly rolled toward the building's exit. The second they were out in the open, several bullets sparked all around them, hitting the tarmac. "Must be closer than you saw!" Said Otto looking around from where the shot seemed to come from. And indeed, the Yvan's were close. They weren't just at the runway's end; they appeared to be all around the airfield. Several brown-clothed soldiers streamed out of the wooden area circling the Gdynia airfield. And all of them seemed to be fixing their attention on the small German plane. The two SS commandos turned the aircraft to line it up with the runway to take off. Bullets were zipping past from every direction, and the muzzle flashes of the guns firing could be seen from where the soldiers stood at the forest's edge. The Soviet ordinance inflicted some damage, but the Fieseler was not hit in any critical area, so it picked up speed. A powerful explosion rocked the ground near the Storch as it was about to lift off. A T-54 tank had just fired its main 100mm gun. The Russian gunner missed the plane but made a large hole in the paved area and scattered debris in every direction, showering the two men's small plane. Marco swerved the machine left to avoid the largest pieces of falling debris, and his move almost toppled the Storch. But he kept control with his firm grip. Skorzeny held on to the steel bar just beside him and was able to stay upright in the plane.

And then the aircraft lifted off the ground. Sturm pushed the throttle to maximum, and it climbed fast, followed by lines upon lines of red tracers from bullets fired at it. Within another half a minute, they were gone from the scene, flying low just over the forest, so the enemy didn't have any more angle to see them and fire. They flew off toward the western horizon, tapping each other on the shoulder in congratulations and smiles.

An hour later, Lieutenant-General Gasparov, commander of the 7th Tank Guard Division entered the hangar where the two SS men had been located. "We'll make this place our HQ and get me that German Hanomag operational; I want it for myself." He pointed toward the modified machine that Skorzeny had put the bomb in. Some of his staff officers walked toward it while some curious soldiers were already climbing it and noticing that the hatch was locked. None of them noticed that it was weird since locked German military machines were rare.

Russians soldiers were streaming into the place, guns at the ready, overturning the place to check for any enemies or valuables (The Reds were known to be experts at looting). All around the airfield, the Division was arriving, and the area had been chosen as a rest and refit area before the unit went on to the attack again the next day. Night was quickly falling, and Gasparov had ordered everyone to stop for the evening.

The 49th Rifle Division that was advancing along a parallel line as the 7th also approached the airfield on their armored trucks. Finally, Gasparov ordered the 245th Rifle to occupy the city of Gdynia, half a kilometer north of the airfield, since it was empty of German defenders.

The General thought that things were going well and that if they were lucky, they would move fast enough for the Wehrmacht never to catch its breath.

After another forty-five minutes, where he'd decided things were organized enough all around, he walked back to the Hanomag that his men had just finally entered after prying it open. "So, how's my new ride?" asked Gasparov, that was in a good mood. "Hehhhh... General, there is something weird in here..." What do you mean, soldier?" he answered.

The first German atomic bomb triggered itself, and the Soviets around it never knew what hit them as they were instantly vaporized. Within another second, the rest of the airfield was engulfed in a blinding light, erasing everything and everyone within a kilometer from existence. The blast expanded in a perfect circle to about a one-kilometer radius. Then the explosion made itself heard, and the earth shook like it was the end of the world. The forest just beyond the initial radius ignited like a match, and everything burned up, transformed in a fire vortex that engulfed over 45 000 Russian soldiers. Even the city of Gdynia was destroyed in the nuclear fury.

From afar and on both sides, the fighting stopped, every soldier looking up in the sky to watch the towering white mushroom that rose ignominiously in the air.

And just like that, Germany also claimed its place in the seemingly fast-growing club of nuclear power wielders.

CHAPTER 6

The death of Hermann Goering
March 25th, 1947

The man that had presided over the Reich's destiny for the last four years stopped breathing late at night between the 24th and 25th of March. Goering lived a long and eventful life. He was involved in most critical world events since he'd been a Red Baron's fighter squadron pilot during the First World War.

With him died the last of the top Nazi officials that had led Germany since they took power in 1933. First, Hitler and Himmler were killed in the plane explosion over Russia in 1943. Then Rudolph Hess developed a severe mental illness and was placed in a mental institution by the end of 1944. Goebbels death followed the destruction of the city of Konigsberg. Albert Speer was just getting back to Berlin after being injured during an Allied air raid on the Bavarian oil reserves hidden away in the mountain of Southern Germany. Martin Borman, the enigmatic and powerful Fuhrer's secretary (Hitler), had lost most of his power when Adolf died, and Joachim Von Ribbentrop had no credibility left after his diplomatic bungling's in 1939.

So the moment Guderian heard of Goering's demise on the morning of the 25th, he immediately went into action and moved fast to finalize the military takeover of Germany. Only this way, the man believed, that Germany could be saved.

The General knew deep down that the country had been poorly led since the start of the conflict. While it was too late to hope to salvage a win from the developing disaster that was the Third Reich's position, he held on to the belief that it was still possible to salvage the country and its armed forces before it was utterly destroyed and occupied by the Allies.

Most governmental agencies and organizations were under the Wehrmacht's control by noon. The Gestapo commander was relieved of command, and a General was put in his place (General Von Neurath).

Again, no real resistance was offered by any of the Nazi Party officials. It was like their will had died with the last few months of disasters and Hitler's death. After all, Goering had steadily trimmed down the SS armed forces and of any rival Nazi organization that could put any shade on his power during his reign. Maybe if Himmler had still been alive, things would have gone down differently, but as it was, Germany was ripe for a military takeover. Besides, the new man in charge was a famous General. Heinz Guderian had been the man that led the Wehrmacht to victory in France, Britain, Africa, the Middle East, and Russia.

No better solution could be offered to the frightened and almost beaten Germans than a famous and brilliant strategist.

Goering's body was brought back to berlin from his Carinhall mansion, where national funerals were to be organized for the man that had so gallantly taken over from Adolf Hitler.

This major political change within the Reich added with the Russian aggressiveness, and nuclear detonations of all three major powers still standing by 1947 would significantly change the diplomatic landscape in the next few months.

Recon in the Austrian Alps part 3
141 Regiment assault a mountain, March 25th, 1947

Jack grumbled as his squad walked up the old Roman path again toward the spot they'd been to the day before. The damned captain had ordered him to get in touch with the local Russian commander so they could figure out a way to get rid of the German position together.

Summers wasn't confident this was a good idea, for the Ruskies had not been too collaborative since the Allied armies joined together in Central Europe. All of his men had their guns at the ready since they didn't know if the situation had changed from the day before. For all they knew, the Germans could have moved up their trail to wait in ambush.

"Остановка!" The loud Russian word startled everyone in the unit. The three new soldiers fumbled with their rifles. At the same time, the rest of the experienced men put a knee on the ground and expertly aimed each in a different direction to cover all angles around the trail, just like they'd been taught to do in training back stateside.

Several Russian soldiers circled them from all sides of the trail in the woods and broken ground of the area. "ne volnuysya!" yelled the same voice. None of the American soldiers spoke any Russian. "I meant halt, and then don't worry," said a burly-looking Russian sergeant that casually appeared on the Roman track from somewhere above their position. His English accent was horrible, but they could understand him. "Damn, sergeant. You scared us big time!" said Summers. The Red Army non-comm officer didn't seem to understand, "Izvinite," he started, and then tried his English again "sorry for startling you." he added still in terrible slang-like English.

"No worries, sergeant," said Summers, trying to pick up his most confident voice. "My name is sergeant Jack Summers, of the 141st

Regiment, Lone Star Division.".. The Soviet man seemed to get what he said. "Yvan Visnevsky, sergeant in the 332nd Rifle Division." He finished his walk up and stopped right by Summers. None of the other soldiers on both sides had yet lowered their weapons. "What are you Americans doing here?" It was complicated for Jack to understand the man, but he thought he got most of what he said. "We've been sent here to make contact with you and discuss collaboration to take the enemy position up there, by the cliffs." The Russian officer seemed surprised by the American's words. "You've been up there?" he asked curiously. "Indeed, we watched your men trying to remove the mines get massacred by snipers. I even recommended to my officer that we should simply bypass this position because casualties will be too heavy to take it." The Soviet smiled at that, showing his rotten teeth. "Ja, sergeant. Same in every army. I've told my officer the same thing, but he still wants us to assault the German defenses."

Summers gestured for his men to lower their weapons, feeling the situation still very tense. His Red Army counterpart got the message and did the same. The tension dropped like a rock to almost nothing, everyone on both sides relaxing a little, some even smiling.

"Okay, Yvan. So what do we do now, you willing to work with us to take that German position?" The Russian non-com officer took Jack by the arm and brought him a little further down so his men could not hear him. "Sergeant, I am under direct orders not to interact with any American of British soldiers, whatever the reason. " He paused to look seemingly at empty air before boring directly into Jack's eyes. "But I don't like that order since it means more of my men and other friends from the Division will die because of stupid orders."

Jack nodded with a thin smile. "Okay, sergeant. So how do you propose we work this out?" "We are almost done clearout out the enemy minefield so that we can attack soon. Bring your men up; we'll attack together." He signaled his men to pack it up and go back up the Roman road. "He started walking, turning his back toward Summers. "In two days, we'll be ready for the assault. Bring your men up at dawn on the 28th." He smiled. "I just won't tell my stupid officer that we have agreed to attack together. It'll just be considered a coincidence that we arrived at the same time to assault the Hitlerites' lair."

And at that, he left, leaving Jack and his men in the trail. Turnbull walked up to Summers to find out if there were some orders for the men. "Damn, Blair. I know he's a damned Communist, but by god, I like that man."

Stavka meeting
Moscow, March 26th, 1947

Joseph Stalin tapped his finger on the table. He was annoyed but kept silent, while either Molotov, Malenkov, or Zhukov talked each in turn. It didn't matter if he spoke; he'd made sure to have their opinion already in individual meetings and had also given them their instructions.

The latest developments were not to his tastes. Things had been going so well for him—first, the complete success of the Manchurian invasion and total control of Northern China by his forces. Then the nuclear detonation of Konigsberg and the powerful offensive that pushed the Germans out of Poland. After the blast on the Baltic, the Wehrmacht seemed finished; even its Fuhrer was incapacitated.

But then Germany pulled another rabbit out of its hat and also detonated its own atomic bomb, obliterating over 40 000 Red Army soldiers in the process. It completely gutted the offensive going so well and poised to thrust at Germany's heartland.

The development came as an unpleasant surprise and showed the Soviets that the Germans still had some teeth. And besides, Stalin was not stupid enough to think that the Americans lost another bomb over the German sky, so the Reich must have developed its own. It meant that they would either have more or could build more. Not a good prospect for the USSR and consequently for Stalin's power. The country was years from attaining any kind of parity with the West in terms of nuclear technology. Until then, the Soviet Union was on its own to face atomic fire.

Hence, the situation gave the Russian dictator an even greater sense of urgency. Things needed to be resolved fast in Europe for the country to prosper. Only with the complete conquest of the old continent could it be safe. With Germany's conquest, it would also be possible to seize their nuclear technology or scientists and potentially accelerate their own development.

He knew from his spy network in the western world that his nuclear bomb had made a great impression on the Western Democracies and that they probably wouldn't dare use a bomb against the Soviets for fear of retaliation. Little did they know that Russia did not have any more atomic weapons. Not even close.

The Germans were an entirely different matter. The damned Hitlerites knew how to fight and were willing, as were the Russians, to die in troves to attain victory. He knew that telling the Germans that every bomb they would drop on him he would retaliate would fall on deaf ears. They just wouldn't care and would hope to launch more bombs than their arch-enemies could.

For all these reasons, he'd instructed Zhukov to launch an all-out attack. The man had a couple of weeks to prepare for the final assault on Germany, but he was instructed to leave nothing behind and send everything the USSR had. New units, partially built units, everything. One last desperate push to destroy the damned Germans. He would see how things looked from there, but he knew he would certainly be tempted to attack the Western Allies before they got too strong and had too many nuclear weapons.

Zhukov had told him that he would have to take troops from the Caucasus and dangerously thin out the Balkan occupation forces, leaving the recently conquered countries to their own devices. Thus he told Stalin that he would not be able to guarantee that these countries would stay within Moscow's orbit and that the pro-Russian Communist governments they were trying to install might fall rapidly.

The Russian dictator didn't care and had instead instructed Molotov to go on a tour of the Central and Southern European countries to tell them that if they moved against the USSR, there would be hell to pay once it was finished with the Third Reich. He believed the threat would be enough to keep the bastards in line.

The thinning out of the Caucasus armies meant that the Soviet Union would not be strong enough to destroy Turkey and the German forces there. Still, he figured that the Allies had a powerful Army in Iraq/Syria, so they would just have to do the job.

The argument between Malenkov and Zhukov heated up to the point that their yelling yanked Stalin out of his daydreaming. He didn't intervene, for he liked to see his underlings fight and bicker while everything was decided anyway.

State Dining Room, White House
Washington D.C., March 26th, 1947

"Nice meal, to say the least." Said Churchill, putting his scotch-filled glass on the table. "I agree, Winston," said President Truman. The two men were discussing the current European situation over a meal in the State Dining Room, the official White House guest dining place. It could seat as many as 140 guests, and they had a packed room that evening. The stately diner was held to mark the end of the Allied conference. So everyone on both delegations had been invited, along with many influential U.S. politicians, generals, and their wives.

The huge reception room was originally much smaller and served as a drawing room, office, and cabinet room at various times. In 1947, it incorporated the space that President Thomas Jefferson used as a private office. Tall and generously proportioned, the room had fireplaces on the east and west and during the day was flooded with daylight through tall south and west windows. When President James Madison and First Lady Dolley Madison took up residence in 1809, the room became a dining area.

During renovations in 1902, President Theodore Roosevelt greatly enlarged the State Dining Room. He mounted a large moose head above the fireplace and placed other game trophies on the natural oak panels. Roosevelt ordered the main stone mantel carvings to be changed from lions to North American bison heads. Late President Franklin D. Roosevelt hung George P. A. Healy's 1869 portrait of

Abraham Lincoln, donated to the White House in 1939, above the mantel. Truman added some renovations in 1946, adding rich oak-paneled walls painted a light celadon green.

In short, the room looked rich and was fit for a powerful nation like the United States of America. The mood in the room was festive, as much had been accomplished. The Second World War was drawing to a close, and hopes were high that peace would soon return. Many in the room did not want to believe that some sort of agreement could not be reached with Soviet Russia in order to avoid another epic confrontation.

But these people did not know the two leaders of the Free World. Both men were determined sons of bitches that would never back down from a fight, however dirty.

And Stalin seemed to want to have one. "This Guderian..." started Churchill, raising his hand so a British servant waiting by the wall could approach with a book he put in the Prime Minister's hand. "I've had his book brought to me. It was difficult to find in Washington, but my man here," he gave a slight look and a smile to the servant that quickly backed up to the wall behind the Prime Minister, "found it for me. Thank you, Alfred," finished the Winston with a smile to the British man.

He handed out the brick to Truman. The President picked it up with both hands and looked at the cover. It read "Achtung – Panzer!" It had been written by the General – now "Fuhrer" – in 1937. "It's a military book, don't get me wrong, Harry," added Churchill. "But I suggest you take it up and leaf thru it. It will give you a bit of what type of man he is". Truman was busy and wasn't planning on reading the book. Unlike Churchill, he liked to sleep and relax once in a while. "Give me the lowdown, Winston," he said with a smile. "Very well, Mr. President." Churchill took another sip of his Scotch before talking again. "It's just as I said. The man's military. Completely apolitical. The book only talks about tanks. According to my source in the Third Reich, Guderian is not interested in power." "And how should that help us, Mr. Prime Minister," asked a curious Truman. "Well, contrary to Hitler and Goering, we aren't dealing with a fanatic here." he paused to emphasize his words. "We are dealing with a cold-headed man that is a military professional. Not some sort of lunatic joke like the first two Fuhrers." He paused to take a breath, "So in essence, it means that the man can be reasoned with."

Truman took in the news the same way they'd talked about it the last two times during the conference. He felt disgusted at even contemplating discussing peace or anything else with a damned Nazi. He knew they might have to at some point but wasn't convinced it was now the time to do so.

"Winston. I understand what you say, and you might be right," Harry, giving a glance to the room, smiled at some of the people sitting down at the table. A President was always charming, even in the middle of a stately discussion with a legend like Lord Churchill. The mood was indeed festive, with a lot of cigarette and cigar smoke hanging in the air. He turned back toward the British leader. "I just won't do it. Not now anyway. If we do and the Soviets hear about it, it surely means war," he finished.

Churchill sighed and took a deep breath. "I am sorry to cut it out like this to you, Mr. President, but the only reason we are not officially at war with the USSR is because we haven't started shooting. But rest assured that comrade Stalin will do so in his own time." "That may be so, Winston. But I am willing to chance it and give time to diplomacy." His answer seemed to darken Churchill's mood. The sticking point was a sore one, and the two men completely disagreed on it. "But this doesn't mean that I am not going to flex my muscles for Stalin." Churchill nodded, calming himself again. "Very well, Mr. President, he finished." The British leader knew that the American President was no fool and that he understood that there were strong chances that war could break out with the Soviet Union.

And he was acting as such, sending reinforcements in the east, issuing orders for his generals to prepare and organize defenses where they were near the Russians and the likes. But the British leader had to accept that America would simply not deal with the Third Reich. Not unless it absolutely had to.

The Allied Washington Conference would close that evening, and the British delegation would fly back to the United Kingdom. The Western Allies had coordinated their following actions to finish the war. The talks had been quite bumpy, with incredible news landing while they were all together discussing—first, the Russian atomic explosion and Molotov's visit. Then, the German nuclear detonation. Finally, Hermann Goering's death.

The fact that every power on each side had the atomic weapon meant that the Western Allies could not simply count on the bomb to finish the conflict. In agreement with the Brits, the U.S. decided that they wouldn't use the nuclear devices for fear of retaliation by the Germans and even the Soviets if it came to war with the USSR. The war's closing would have to be purely conventional unless something drastic changed that.

It was also agreed that the planned offensive on the West Wall would start as proposed by Eisenhower's timetable on March 30th. All the while, the British would launch another offensive (under General Auchinleck's leadership) against Axis positions in Turkey near Lake Van in hopes of finishing the war in that theater.

Extracts from Von Manstein's 1958 book, LOST VICTORY
The Polish corridor offensive, March 27th to April 2nd, 1947.

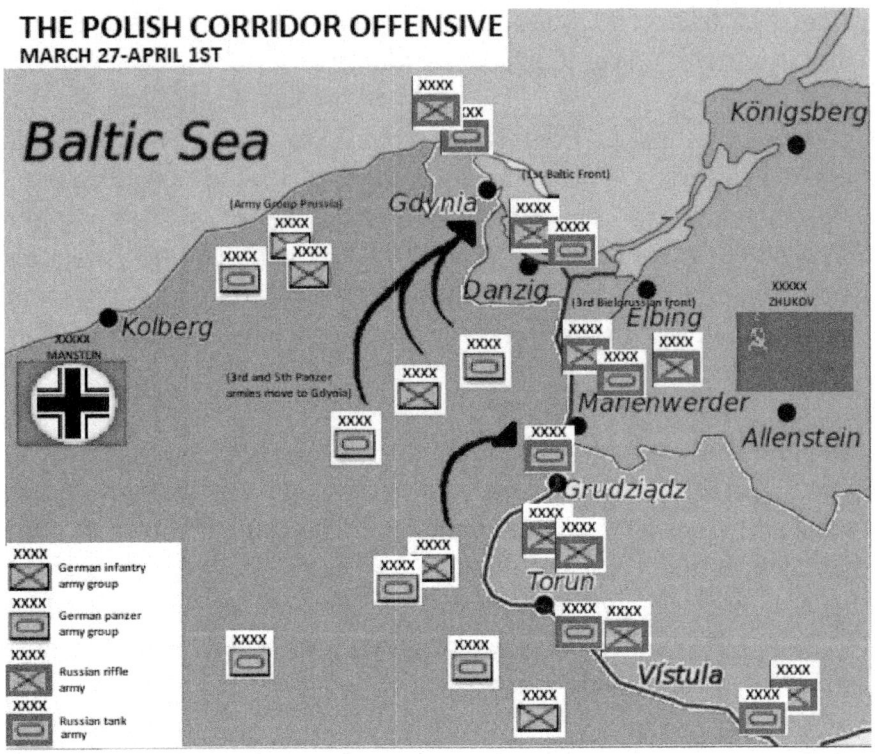

My arrival at my new command reminded me of a similar situation when I took over at the front during winter 1942-1943. The Axis forces were in disarray and needed to stop the Soviet offensive.

In agreement with our new leader and OKW, I resolved to stay on the offensive in order to offer the Reich its best defense. The ideal play would have been to organize a defensive line, but there was no more territory to retreat. The Wehrmacht was now fighting in Germany proper.

When I arrived at my command, Army Group Center was already evacuating Poland, executing a fighting retreat along the way. A few heavy battles happened in and around Warsaw, but I ordered the troops to retire westward.

The main problem that faced the Reich at the end of March 1947 was the Soviet offensive in Eastern Prussia. While the atomic bomb triggered by Otto Skorzeny gave the fighting troops some breathing room, it was not enough since two Russian fronts (over fifty divisions) were bearing down on the fatherland from that area. After all, the bomb (only!) killed 45 000 men. It gutted any offensive action on the Baltic Coast from 1st Baltic and 3rd Bielorussian for a few days. But by the 26th, the Soviets resumed their advance westward.

The attack's goal was to swing 3rd and 5th Panzer armies (twelve armored divisions and four mechanized) northward toward the Baltic Coast and attack the Russian forces of 1st Baltic front that had become over-extended as a result of its drive thru Dantzig and further west in Gdynia. The front was further challenged as it tried to organize the chaos created by the atomic explosion and the death of its commander General Gasparov. The attack would thus cut the Soviet forces in two.

At a minimum, I planned to disrupt the enemy's advance westward and force it to turn toward my forces, giving time to Army Group Prussia and reinforcement from the rest of the Reich to organize themselves after the Konigsberg nuclear disaster.

But what I wanted ideally was to cut off the two front's leading armies with a powerful attack thru the so-called Polish Corridor. On the 27th, all German forces on the frontline facing the enemy were ordered to disengage during the early hours of the evening and operate a movement west-then-northward toward the Baltic coast.

The 3rd and 5th Panzer armies, under the excellent General Herman Hoth, were entrusted with the drive that aimed at a point between the cities of Dantzig and what used to be Gdynia.

I also moved up several other units from Army Group Center northward to intercept the third Bielorussian front's armies that followed our backward movement.

For the first two days, fighting was inconclusive and very confused, but by the 30th, 5th Panzer Army reached the Baltic, amidst a deluge of steel and fire. The Luftwaffe provided excellent cover and bomber coverage throughout the whole operation, enabling my forces to move about freely and get strong support from tactical bombing attacks.

I fed more troops into the Polish Corridor to avoid the out-of-supply Russian Armies in Gdynia to re-establish their link with the rest of 1st Baltic and 3rd Bielorussian fronts. The Soviets tried hard for the following two days to push thru our defenses and come to their comrade's help.

During these critical days, I also visited Army Group Prussia's staff HQ and reorganized them as part of Army Group Center within my own command structure. I left several key people there to help bolster the troops and the command structure gutted by the nuclear explosion (Model and most of his senior staff were dead).

By the 2nd of April, I ordered the 3rd and 5th Panzer armies to disengage from the Baltic Coast and the Polish Corridor. Zhukov applied too much pressure for my troops to resist being attacked on both sides. By the end of that day, most of the German troops were beyond Gdynia, while the rest of Army Group Center withdrew almost entirely out of Poland in several mobile battles on the plains west of Warsaw.

The operation achieved what I wanted. It disrupted the 1st Baltic front's attack on the beleaguered Army Group Prussia (that by the 2nd of April had been incorporated into Army Group Center). It gave us the time to organize the next Soviet assault that promised to be quite a challenge.

General Auchinleck make a play against Lake van
Operation Bayezid, March 27th-April 6th, 1947

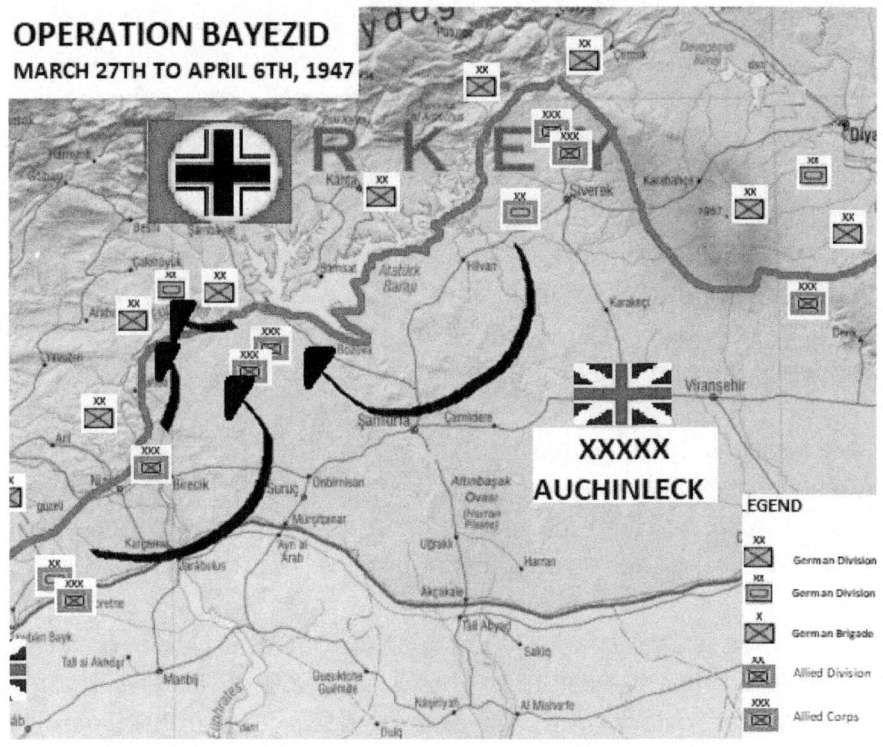

British General Claude Auchinleck gave the go-ahead for his grand offensive on the morning of the 27th of March. The operation, decided during the Washington Conference, named after an old Ottoman sultan defeated by the Mongols in the 15th century, called for the Allies to attack Axis defenses in the area and swing west around the lake to attack the Turkish hinterland and Rommel's position near Gaziantep. The offensive had been on Auchinleck's drawing board for a while. He sent his plans to Churchill in the UK and to Eisenhower, the overall Allied commander-in-chief of all Allied forces in Europe, but it had not been met with a lot of interest.

Claude was recently named theater commander of the Middle East and Anatolian theatres (March 6th). He was initially instructed to stay put and not try to be too bold until the war resolved itself in Europe (hence the lack of interest in his Bayezid offensive plan). But what had been one situation at the beginning of March wasn't anymore at the end of the same month.

Within that period of time, the Russians AND the Germans had exploded atomic devices. These grave events convinced Allied High Command that the Axis needed to be attacked everywhere possible, and the war brought to its conventional military conclusion as soon as possible. A better position in Turkey was also preferable for post-war positioning against the Soviets. It was no good to let the Russians conquer Turkey and control the Dardanelles Strait. And so suddenly, Bayezid was a lot more interesting to Allied command.

Lake Van was the largest lake in Turkey and the Armenian Highlands. It was located in the country's far east, in the provinces of Van and Bitlis. The saline lake received water from many small streams that descended from the surrounding mountains.

Its size was greater than 3,000 square kilometers (1,200 sq miles) and located at a high altitude (1,640 m (5,380 ft). So the weather was relatively cold for the area. But the body of water seldom froze because of its high salinity levels.

Lake Van was 119 kilometers (74 mi) across at its widest point. So without boats, pretty rare in the area (at least in the quantities needed for an army to cross it), it meant that the Axis defenses were greatly helped.

The Axis forces had extensively fortified the Lake's western end and defended it with two German (on infantry and one Panzer) and one Turkish division.

The land there was relatively flat and possessed a major city with a rail hub called Tatvan, at the extreme end of the body of water. The town was Auchinleck's primary objective.

The place was defended by the Turkish 45th Infantry, while the mountains around the city (they surrounded the Lake almost in its entirety) harbored the German 7th Mountain Alpine Division. The Panzer Unit (the 99th) was just a bit to the rear, ready to intervene against any Allied attack.

The British General decided that brute force would be his strategy. He had over fourteen divisions at his disposal (after amalgamating his and Paton's armies into one), three armored, the rest mechanized or motorized, and a couple of mountain divisions. All were ordered to move toward the city of Tatvan, and the attack was set to start on the 27th of March.

The offensive opened up with a fury, as Auchinleck used most of the available artillery in the theater in the first few days, expanding most of its shells complement to flatten the German defenses in the mountain passes that blocked the way to the Turkish city. The bombardment lasted until the 29th of March, and by then, the area was transformed into a lunar landscape.

On the 30th, several furious Allied assaults were launched at the German 7th division's position, without success. Casualties climbed rapidly, and Auchinleck had to retire the three units that made the initial attack to rest and refit. He followed up the failed assault with another day of heavy shelling and called in every available bomber and fighter to the area. Airstrikes followed one after the other, and a furious dogfight ensued that, for once, was won by the Allies, consolidating their control of the eastern Turkish sky.

On the 2nd of April, the English General launched six divisions at the mountain pass defended by the beleaguered 7th German, and this time it worked. His men overwhelmed the much-diminished Axis forces. Once the pass and the surrounding mountains were taken, the rest of Auchinleck's army poured into the plain by the city of Tatvan. Being vastly inferior in numbers, the 45th Turkish was rapidly destroyed in furious house-to-house fighting that pretty much leveled the city to dust. Even the 99th Panzer's counter-attack was easily repulsed since heavily outnumbered by the Allied forces. After another three days of furious battle, all Axis units in the Tatvan area surrendered to the Allies.

The whole frontline unraveled and was threatened with collapse. Even Rommel's forces, further west in Gaziantep, would not hold into their defenses since Auchinleck could now outflank them from the east and the north through the many mountain roads and tracks dotting the area.

The news of the defeat also rang like an alarm bell into the Turkish halls of power, where several people started to think that it wasn't the best of ideas to keep supporting Germany and that maybe surrendering was not that bad of an option. The Pro-German government, of course, didn't flinch, but its base was shaking and threatened to crumble to dust.

18th Japanese Imperial Division
Back to battle, March 27th, 1947

Tanaka stood up from the trench wall he was hiding behind and fired his Arisaka rifle at the enemy. A running Soviet soldier was hit right in the chest, and his body weirdly somersaulted backward in a spray of blood. The Japanese soldier was pretty sure he'd killed the bastard. The satisfying moment produced a thin, evil smile on his face

It was good to get a weapon again and even better to have people to shoot at. He'd dreaded the return to civilian life as the transport ships bringing back the Division to Japan sailed toward the Home Islands.

But then fate intervened, and the Americans had dropped Ichiro and his comrades on the docks at Tsingtao Harbor. Instead of returning home in shame and as prisoners, they were given new weapons and told they could fight the Russians attacking in Northern China and Manchuria.

The proud (and morally broken) soldiers of the 18th Division had been fighting since the 1930s (for the oldest among them like Tanaka) and didn't remember anything else than fighting and war. Most did not know what they would do once back in Japan and demobilized.

The Communist attack gave them the chance to redeem themselves and maybe die in battle with honor. When they landed in Tsingtao, they didn't see any Americans on land, only U.S. ships disgorging supplies and Japanese weapons. Japanese soldiers and officers were waiting for them with mountains of guns and ammunition, apparently dropped by the U.S. Navy several days before.

They'd learned that all of the returning Japanese troops were re-routed to Tsingtao and that soon the Imperial Army would have several hundreds of thousands of men to fight the Red Army. General Yamada, former commander of the Kwantung Army in Manchuria, had taken overall command of all Imperial forces in continental China and apparently worked hand in hand with the Americans to try and repulse the Communist aggression.

Tanaka was a simple soldier and did not understand the game at play or the reasons why the Russians had attacked Japan since it had already surrendered. In fact, he didn't care one bit, as long as it meant that it postponed his return to civilian life.

He prepared to get another shot at the Bolshevik assaulting their position by reloading his rifle. The 18th Division was fighting somewhere south of Pekin's suburbs area. Standing up again, he fired yet another precise shot at an enemy soldier, hitting him in the head and exploding it in a spray of gore and blood.

And in that perfect moment, all was right for Ichiro Tanaka, private in the (redeemed) 18th Imperial Division. All the shame of defeat was being washed away by the exhilaration of battle.

The offensive on the West wall – Operation Retribution
Final Allied meeting, March 29th, 1947

General George Patton overlooked the scene that was about to unfold in front of him. The field was covered in mud, dirt, and patches of green, as summer was well on its way. Artillery shells arced over them as a giant air battle was underway in the distance. They were near the recently liberated French city of Sedan, where the terrible defeats and suffering had started so long ago.

Behind him, the might of the American 8th, 9th, and 10th armies assembled under his leadership for the push against Nazi Germany. His men were about to be unleashed on the German defenses just over the border, on the supposedly invincible Siegfried Wall, the last German fortification in the west.

Besides him, many great generals of the war had also been recalled to be here on that day of March from other fronts. First and foremost, British General Bernard Montgomery, at the head of the British 1st, 2nd, and 5th Armies. General Juin, the victor of France and destroyer of the Pyrenes Defensive line, commanded the recently constituted French 1st army. General Crerar, the Canadian commander in chief, was also heading his country's 1st and 2nd armies. A plethora of other Allied commanders, Australians, New Zealanders, Polish volunteers, Indian troops.

They were all together, assembled one last time before the final assault on the West Wall. His friend from Westpoint, General Dwight Eisenhower, had named Patton the commander for the final offensive against the Reich, Operation Retribution.

A mind-boggling twelve armies and some change were about to unleash a deluge of fire and destruction on the forty German divisions handling the German defenses of the West Wall, under old and famous General, Gerd Von Rundstedt. 88 Divisions were fully armed with the best the Allies factories could produce. Over 21 000 artillery guns from all types and calibers were brought over for the four corners of the world all along the Axis line, ready to pound the Reich's fortifications to oblivion. Over 10 000 aircraft to win the skies above and destroy the Luftwaffe one and for all. And most importantly, the Allied will to win at all cost. The same will that helped the world's free nations keep hope against oppression and apparent German invincibility in the darkest days of the Blitzkrieg in 1941, when the Germano-Italian flags towered from Ireland to North Africa, all the way to the Middle East.

Now that will was finally about to get its reward; The defeat of the Third Reich and its world-conquering ambition. Patton turned around to face all the assembled officers he'd called for the occasion. "Gentlemen," started the man in his high-pitched voice. "We are about to embark on the final offensive against the Nazi hordes. I hope all of you understand the solemnity of the occasion. We finally have the chance to put an end to our enemy's power and capability to impose its will on other nations." He paused to turn toward the Sedan landscape and the Ardennes Forest behind it. "It was here that the disaster unfolded eight years ago, and it is here that we will redeem ourselves. Tomorrow, gentlemen, we launch the greatest Allied offensive of the war. Eighty-eight divisions will clash against the enemy's estimated forty." He put his war helmet back on his head (it was in one of his staff officer's hands that handed it out to the General in a carefully rehearsed move) and continued his speech. "You all know what you have to do. Go back to your command. We launch at 0500 tomorrow morning." And at that, the crowd of commanders left for their staff car and, ultimately, their command. The Americans had the Belgian sector to cover, along with the Canadian forces. The British were arrayed in Alsace and poised to attack Germany directly with the French. The Australians, New Zealanders, and other less numerous nations would also attack from the Franco-British sector in Alsace.

A storm was about to hit the Third Reich.

Juvincourt Airfield, Northern France
Transfer to the Western front, March 29th, 1947

Lamirande eased the throttle on his plane and lowered his landing gear. He cut the engine on his Meteor and smoothly touched the PHS asphalt that the United States Engineer Corps had freshly installed. He was at his new posting in Northern France, where he and his squadron's mates had been ordered.

The allied high command had decided to concentrate all of the available air force firepower into the coming offensive, as southern operations had ground to a halt since the Americano-British forces arrived at the foot of the Alp Defensive Line. There just wasn't enough incentive for Eisenhower to attack there, for the rewards promised to be scant even if the Allies broke the defenses. Southern Germany and Austria were filled with mountains and rugged terrain.

The plains of Western Germany were a lot more interesting for a commander that wanted to bring the war to a close. The only Wehrmacht stop-gap was the Siegfried Line, and once that was pierced, the Third Reich was done for; Nothing would stand in the Allies' way. Well, at least no natural obstacles apart from a few rivers like the Rhine.

Gaston slowly rolled his plane toward the gigantic and seemingly new hangars where the signalman was directing him. Built originally as a grass airfield by the French Air Force before the war, Juvincourt was expanded to become one of the leading German Luftwaffe airfields in France during the German occupation (1940–1946), hosting a wide variety of both fighter and bomber aircraft, including German jet fighters and bombers. Seized by the Allies in November 1946, it became a significant base for fighter, bomber, and transport units.

The airfield was an all-weather temporary field built by the XII Engineering Command of the United States Army Twelfth Air Force using graded earth compacted surface with a prefabricated hessian (burlap) surfacing known as PHS. PHS was made of asphalt-impregnated jute, rolled out over the compacted surface over a square mesh track (SMT) grid of wire joined in three-inch squares. Pierced Steel Planking was also used for parking areas and dispersal sites when it was available. Dumps for supplies, bombs, ammunition, gasoline drums, drinking water, and an electrical grid for communications and lighting were also constructed. Tents were used for billeting and support facilities, and an access road was built to connect the airfield facilities with existing roads. It was indeed an impressive sight, as Lamirande had been able to see for himself while he flew over it.

He parked the meteor, cut off all power, opened his canopy, and slid out of the plane's cockpit. He stepped on the ladder and jumped down on the ground. "This way, sir," said the signalman that had brought him to his parking space. The man had given Gaston the hangar's direction where many people seemed to buzz about. As he approached the hangar, another soldier walked by him: "Commander Lamirande," said the man, giving Gaston the military salute. "Your reputation precedes you." Indeed, he was now famous amongst all Allied pilots for being the man who shot down Adolf Galland not once but twice. That and also his 97 victories against enemy aircraft. "Thank you, private," answered the French-Canadian pilot. "The base commander awaits your arrival, sir." And the soldier gestured him forward.

He was brought to the commander's office, General Asternatch, a well-known World War One Fighter pilot. The man was sitting down at a table and seemed buried in military paperwork, signing form after form that a young staff officer handed out to him. "Ah! Welcome, commander Lamirande. I trust the trip was uneventful?" "Indeed it was, sir," answered Gaston, looking at the ceiling. A great way of not annoying a General in the army was not to look too bold and lock eye contact with superior officers. "Good, good. You and your team will be assigned to barracks B. You are one of the lucky ones, Lamirande; you don't get a tent but a proper roof over your head. Good luck and get me some kills, will you?" "I will, sir.", answered the French-Canadian ace.

After his quick discussion, he was directed to his barracks, reuniting with his mates. They would soon be into battle, as they'd been told to be ready for the very next day. Lamirande convinced himself that he would try to get a good night's sleep and not spend too much time with the boys at the officer's mess that night.

Operation Retribution Part 1
The offensive, March 30th to April 4th, 1947

The staggering number of artillery guns opened up on the German Lines in the early morning of the 30th. The whole night lit up with light from the North Sea to the Swiss border. It seemed like the God of thunder had descended on earth for the few hours it lasted (from 1 AM to 5 AM).

Several of the men in the forty defending German divisions had seen this kind of power since they'd fought against the Soviets that employed a similar number of artillery weapons and concentration. But whatever the soldier's experience, it was impossible to get used to it.

The poor men hunkered down in their trenches or bunkers and hoped to dear god that a shell wouldn't explode right on top of them, for if they were protected well enough, they would survive the shelling. Well, physically survive. It wasn't uncommon to have ben go crazy after such a powerful, earth-shattering bombardment.

The Allied ordinance overturned earth, exploded houses (the ones still left standing), and killed everything that wasn't protected or buried. A few cows, dogs, and other animals that didn't know better, of course, were shredded by the millions upon millions of shrapnel pieces that flew in every direction that day. Once in a while, it hit the top of a protective bunker, gutting it or mangling it severely. Men rarely survived a direct hit from a large artillery shell.

As dawn broke and the bombardment was still in full swing (4 AM), the Allied launched all available planes on one hell of an airstrike. The Luftwaffe dutifully took to the sky to battle it out with their enemy, but the constant attrition of the last few months of battle and the lack of space where it was possible to have airfields in "relative safe zones" was slowly taking its toll. The Allied air forces attacked in the sky and on the ground, and then some more. They had so many planes that they had fighters to escort the bombers that added to the artillery maelstrom hitting the poor Wehrmacht along the Siegfried Line and attacking the airfields from which the German pilots took off.

The combined attack from the air and artillery was so powerful and all-encompassing that at one point, the German commander, Gerd Von Rundstedt, was overwhelmed with problems and decisions. In a cable to Berlin (OKW) at 8h15 AM, where his frontline units reported that the Allies moved up to the Siegfried and assaulted all along the line, he called for reinforcements as Allied breakthroughs were unavoidable due to the state of his forces and the number attacking them.

Guderian, receiving the request and meeting with Halder at 8h30 AM, ordered to send everything available, which wasn't much. The Reich had pretty much everything directly on the frontline, and after that, well, that was that. A grand total of five additional divisions, located south of Berlin, were sent toward Alsace and Belgium. According to earlier air recons, the Allies seemed to have the most troops gathered in the two areas. The units were not in an ideal situation to go back to the struggle, being far from full strength, but it was what it was.

By 9h30 AM, the battle was joined from north to south, and the clash was of epic proportion. In Belgium, General Patton attacked with eight divisions directly at the Aachen defensive system, pretty mangled by the earlier shelling. Nonetheless, the Germans put up a strong resistance, and the Americano-Canadians advance ground to a halt below the fortification, and the men dug right on the spot. Later during the day, Patton came again with five powerful armored divisions, equipped with the new tanks (T28, T29, Super-Pershings). This time they advanced, followed by the beaten-up infantry that had been slugging it out with the Wehrmacht since the early morning.

In Alsace, the British and their Allies launched themselves at Saarbrucken and Offenburg. The going was slow at first, like in the Americano-Canadian sector, but numbers eventually took their toll on the German divisions defending both sectors. General Montgomery sent his infantry; it bogged down in front of the Axis fortifications, but the British commander followed up (not unlike Patton) with a powerful armored assault that broke through the West Wall defenses.

All along the line on the first day, the scene repeated itself. Powerful Allied formations were attacking in massed numbers at overwhelmed Germans, fighting like the devil to hold on to their fortification. Then, General Rundstedt sent several sharp Panzer counter-attacks to try and hold the line.

The fighting continued in a very confusing state of affairs all the way to the 4th of April, and the Wehrmacht held the line. Their performance was quite impressive. Outnumbered, outgunned, overwhelmed, they still held.

The only problem for the Reich was that they wouldn't resist forever. The West Wall was like a dam containing a great flood. Once it broke or the Allied spilled over it, there would be hell to pay for the Third Reich.

The final offensive preparations,
Friedland, Eastern Prussia, April 4th, 1947

Marshal Zhukov was overseeing the troop's final preparations for the offensive that he hoped would be the last one against the Third Reich. He moved everything the Red Army could bear down on the Hitlerites as per Stalin's instruction.

The assembled army was a sight to behold on an operational map: 1st Baltic, 3rd and 4th Bielorussian, 1st Voronezh, 1st and 2nd Ukrainian Fronts. There were a little over 255 divisions of all sizes and types, from infantry (foot, horse-drawn, mechanized, motorized) to armored (T-34s, IS-2s, T-54s, KV2s...) ready to launch at Germany.

In all, a staggering four million men, over 8000 planes (1000 of them jets), and 120 000 artillery pieces. The numbers seemed mindboggling and impossible even for the commander that oversaw it all. But they were true, and only a portion of what the Soviet Union had produced so far in the war.

The official production numbers by the end of 1946 were impressive. 35.3 million rifles, 1,9 million machine guns, 616,648 artillery guns, 397,900 mortars, 189,769 tanks and self-propelled guns, 335,600 army trucks, and finally, 283,742 military aircraft. Of course, many of the units "produced" by the USSR came from American sources, as the West sent a lot of equipment starting in 1944, but even if you didn't consider those (about 20% of the total numbers in trucks, tanks, and aircraft) what the Soviet Union had been able to achieve was nothing short of miraculous.

With the other Russian strength of quantitative superiority in terms of population numbers over Germany (170 million to Germany's 85 million), it meant that the Motherland was always able to have bigger numbers of soldiers and machines than the Hitlerites. For Zhukov, the whole affair was simple mathematics. Modern war was about the side that produced the most, the fastest, and the most efficiently with a reasonable quality ratio.

The Soviet Marshal's strategy was straightforward in its intention. Attack in force, attack everywhere. In contrast, this was not necessarily a strategy that had worked well for Russia during the war to date; for this final offensive, it made sense. The Germans didn't have any room for maneuvers, so it meant that the Red Army would not have to cope with fancy outflanking attacks or clever fighting retreats.

Their enemy would be just in front of them and pretty much defend in place. The Marshal was no stupid man and knew that his force's training levels were a lot lower than the Germans, and the same could be said about equipment quality.

But in the fight to come, he could count on some of the best qualities in the Russian fighting man: grit, determination, and an incredible capability to suffer under harsh conditions. The Germans weren't too bad in their own right, but the men of the Motherland were in a league of their own.

As he gave military salutes to one unit after the other from his vantage point (the troops were heading west in a great host, reminiscent of a Mongol horde…), he decided that he could simply not fail.

While he was not worried about the results against Nazi Germany, he was more concerned about the victory he would give Stalin. Once achieved, it meant that another war might erupt.

The man seemed intent on facing off with the Western Powers. While Zhukov didn't doubt that he could give the Americans a good run for their money, he was not sure that doing what the Comrade General-Secretary had in mind was the best of ideas.

Operation Retribution Part 2
Patton and Montgomery break out into Germany, April 4th to April 10th, 1947

The Canado-American offensive continued unabated for days on end from the 4th to the 10th of April. The German exerted extreme casualties on Patton's forces during that time, but not without steadily taking ever-higher losses. The fight around Aachen was particularly heavy, and by the 7th, four American divisions had to be taken out of the line to the rear, having received over 55% loss rate. The Germans, of course, didn't have the luxury of giving a break to their soldiers by sending them in the rear, as everything was engaged at the front, and nothing could be spared. Pervitin pills were given by the pallets, and injured men were sent back to the front with only minimal care. The only ones exempted from the frontlines were the ones unable to walk or hold a rifle. In short, you had to be knocked out to be given a free pass.

The North Americans, not used to these levels of casualties, almost balked at the horrendous attrition that their enemy was inflicting on them. Several divisional generals petitioned Patton to slow or stop the attack on Aachen to regroup and re-assess. But the gritty American General was not interested in half measures and wanted the Germans destroyed. He didn't care if some casualty-sensitive officers had a problem with his strategy. He knew that in the end, the Allies would win the day simply because the Reich was nearing the end of its rope and would run out of men to defend their West Wall.

Canadian General Crerar was of the same mind and wanted the battle to continue to its conclusion. The war needed to end, and he had sturdy soldiers. On the 7th in the evening, both commanders met together to discuss launching an all-out assault in a supreme effort to break the Wehrmacht in Aachen and the adjoining sectors. It was decided that beginning on the 8th in the morning, every available unit, even the ones in the rear, would assault the German position on a concentrated front within a radius of ten kilometers from Aachen. Patton also called his friend Eisenhower, who promised to send everything the Allies had in bombing assets.

On the other side of their guns, the Germans were nearing the end of their resistance capability, with most units down to 40% of their original strength. Rundstedt hoped for a miracle, meaning he hoped that the Allies would decide (as they'd done times and again in Italy and other theaters since the start of the war) that they'd had enough casualties.

The old commander would have held the line given only ten fresh divisions in reinforcement, but sadly for the Reich, they simply weren't available. The bottom of the barrel had indeed been reached.

So, when the Canado-American armies launched at dawn on the 8th, it quickly became obvious to both sides that the defensive line was buckling. On that day, the 56th American Division progressed over ten kilometers above the West Wall before being repulsed. More Allies incursions happened on the 9th. Then on the 10th, the whole Siegfried line unraveled like an exploding dam releasing its water.

A somewhat similar story played itself in Alsace, at the twin battles of Saarbrucken and Offenburg. Allied casualties reached record levels (even higher than on the worst days against the Gustav Line). But the slow, unrelenting grind of attrition also took its toll on the German forces. Launching his all-out attack on the same day as Patton and Crerar, Montgomery eventually pushed the Axis forces to their breaking point.

On the 10th in the evening, Rundstedt cabled Berlin to ask for permission to retreat his forces all along the West Wall, as the Allied had crossed it in Aachen, Saarbrucken, and Offenburg. Their victories meant that the rest of the troops defending the line would be outflanked if they stayed in their bunkers. With a heavy heart,

Halder and Guderian agreed to let the old General retire (they were not Hitler, after all).

The whole western front had just fallen apart for the Reich. With the soon-to-start Soviet offensive in the east, the end was near for the Third Reich.

However, Rundstedt had no intention of whimpering away in fear, and everywhere commanders were encouraged to engage the Allies while retreating toward the Rhine River.

Panzer on the Vistula
Wloclawek, Germany (former Poland), April 6th, 1947

Tank commander Erich Walder's Panzer recoiled backward as it spat another of its high-velocity 128mm shells. The shot produced some light smoke that exited from the gun muzzle. It also scattered some dust near the tank. The shells proper arced quickly to its destination: a poor transport truck. It looked like an American Ford model. The unarmored vehicle was pierced catastrophically by the German ordinance and exploded almost simultaneously, spilling its content in every direction. A secondary explosion rocked the ground around the truck and expanded the blast to an impressive size. "Commander! We hit an ammo truck!" said Stromer, his young and talented gunner. He had to give it to the kid; he was enthusiastic, that was certain. Walder remembered the war's early days when he'd been an idealistic youth like Hans. It was just about what would happen the same day and what orders he was given back then. Now that he got older and wiser, Erich was a little more difficult to keep happy. In short, he was war-weary and only dreamed for this wasteful, terrible conflict to end. No matter if the Reich won or lost. He just wished for the shooting to stop.

The ammo truck continued to spill its content and explode for a few more seconds, igniting three more trucks that rode beside it. Those were also full of tank shells, and again the same rhythm of catastrophic explosion started. The amazingly satisfying chain reaction continued for about another minute, engulfing more trucks and even a couple of T-34s that had been targeting the Tiger III after it shot its 128mm.

One thing was sure. The Soviets had not expected a lone Tiger to burst out of the woods by the Vistula river. The enemy had been casually strolling down a road, confident that German tanks were far away.

And most were. At least the ones sane enough to retreat as they were ordered. Walder's tank had broken down on the way, and they'd been stuck for the better part of the last two days in the small patch of forest located on the Vistula's west bank. It was located at the end of a farm field near the city of Wloclawek.

The transmission had just given out, and while it was repairable in the field, the men had needed some time. Since they were in a forest, he'd ordered the rest of the unit (there were only six tanks left anyway) to retreat westward with the rest of Army Group Center while staying to get the Panzer repaired.

And anyway, the Soviet forces had not crossed the Vistula River in force yet, but it sure looked like they would soon. After the Tiger III had been repaired, they set out for the west, but not before Erich gave his dear Communist friends a little parting gift. One of his men that he'd placed at the wood's edge to spot for enemy movement had reported that a supply convoy was driving by just within the optimal gun range.

In a snap decision, he'd decided that it was too good an opportunity to pass up. And besides, there were some enemy tanks, but they all seemed to be on the other side of the river. So he decided that sending a couple of shots at the unsuspecting enemy wouldn't hurt and that they would have time to retreat.

"Driver, back us up into the wood and toward the main trail. The Tiger groaned a little, for if the transmission was patched up, it was nothing more than a temporary affair. The Panzer would need a full overhaul when it got back to German lines. Several Russian shells crashed into the forest, exploding and splintering trees as they backed up. The Konigstiger rolled over some of the small fires and fallen trees caused by the enemy ordinance. And in a nutshell, they were back on the forest road. The thing was tight but large enough for their steel beast, which was something rare in a forest for the large machine. The shells continued to explode where they used to be, but as they sped out of the area, the sounds started to be further and further away. Within ten minutes, it was just some faraway grumbling noise.

The Panzer eventually exited the forest on its western end, and Walder ordered the driver to push the engine to top speed to get as far away as possible from the area. He suspected that while the bulk of the Soviet forces hadn't crossed the Vistula, some recon units and lone tanks were certainly roaming the land.

And as sure as rain, Stromer spotted an enemy. "Colonel!" he yelled. "Enemy tank bearing down on us from the north, at 2200 meters" Walder turned just in time to see the Russian gun's muzzle flash. The shell, however, fell short well before it reached Erich's tank. "The enemy sent of a range-finding shot. He will be coming in fast now," the commander said. Given the T-54 speed (almost 60km an hour), it would be in range in less than a minute. Fortunately for the Germans, their gun, the PAK 44, could fire now, since 2200 meters was well within its effective range.

Hans traversed the turret toward the north (the Tiger III was advancing on a perpendicular course, due west) and took a few more seconds to aim. Then the gun barked another 128mm shell.

Walder saw it race to its sought destination, and again the young gunner impressed him with a perfect shot on the enemy tank's gun mantle, obliterating the Communist machine in a spectacular explosion. "Good shot, Stromer! Enemy tank destroyed!" Everyone in the Panzer expressed their excitement with shouts of joy. "Driver, due west, keep going. That T54 cannot be alone. Hans, keep a watchful eye for more." Indeed, the damned Russians rarely acted alone, for there was strength in numbers, which was even more true with the Yvan's.

Under a minute later, Walder's suspicions were confirmed with several mounds of earth thrown into the air by enemy explosions near their Tiger III. The young gunner took two more Russian tanks with the 128mm, and then the enemy was in range. But since they were moving quite fast and it was difficult for the Russians to hit something that moved while they also moved (suspension and stabilization systems were a lot better on German tanks), all of the shells shot over the Panzer.

They eventually arrived at a depression in the ground where the road was dropping into, a sort of ravine with a dirt road. The Konigstiger sped into it at full speed, and enemy shells stopped exploding as the enemy didn't have any angle to attack. They would surely try to pursue the Germans, but for the most part, Walder decided that they would be okay since they'd been to this area before, and the ravine length was several kilometers across. The Tiger III would be long gone by the time the Ruskies got to the road and then drove down it.

EPILOGUE

Somewhere in the Austrian Alps
Russo-American Aftermath April 6th, 1947

Sergeant Jack Summers was sitting around the campfire along with his men but also with his newfound comrades, the Soviet unit they'd fought and spent time with for the last ten days or so. Their first meeting had been a little rough, but they learned to trust each other after a few battles.

In complete disregard for orders, the two squads met up the mountain regularly. At first, it was for trade, as the Russians were incredibly thorough pillagers and so had a lot of interesting trinkets that the American G.I.s wanted. And the US Army had chocolate, cigarette, beer even. Then, it was also for fun, as they threw big drunken parties up into the Slovenian wilderness.

After a few days, the word got around, as each side liked the other, and more men on both sides decided to come up for the weird nightly black market. It was a miracle that officers in both armies were still oblivious to the little fun they were having. It might have been because the war in the area seemed to be drawing to a close and because the frontline was quiet. Officers were also a little lax in these early days of April 1947. Things were a lot more active on the Siegfried Line and in Poland.

Jack still remembered their first day of fighting together. It was about ten days ago. They'd come up the mountain to again recon on their captain's orders and to find the Russians to offer collaboration to fight the Germans in the mountains. They then met with Yvan Visnevsky's squad, a sergeant in the 332nd Rifle Division. The high up in divisional command wanted to establish some form of local cooperation with the Soviets. Jack remembered not being happy about it, but now he was glad that at least one of the seemingly stupid orders had panned out all right for him and his men.

So they fought together and bled together and took the German defensive position they'd spotted. The Reds were tough, resilient fighters that made do with what they had on hand. Jack and his men liked their no-bullshit attitude toward war and the fact that they didn't fret at details like in the US Army. To them, war seemed the dirtiest business of all, like Summers and his men liked it.

After their success in the mountain, they found a cache of Schnapps that the enemy had stashed away in one of their well-protected bunkers. And so one thing led to the other, and by nightfall, they were still up the mountain and drunk as hell. It had been a fun night. The following day, they woke with skull-splitting headaches but agreed to meet again two days later to exchange stuff and maybe find more Krauts to kill (some of the Soviets called them Hitlerites, which Summers found hilarious).

And so, the little scheme continued after over ten days. "American sergeant," called Visnevsky, his counterpart in the Red Army. He always called him that way. Sometimes it was Jack when he was getting drunk. But when sober, it was "American sergeant."

"Yes, Yvan," responded Summers with a smile. He thought it extremely funny that the man's name was the moniker the Germans used for the Russians on the battlefield. "Another good day today. Are you happy about the gold we brought you?" "Indeed, my friend," and he signaled his approval with a gesture with the beer he held in his hand. It was crazy but true. In exchange for American stuff, the Ruskies brought gold stuff they'd looted in churches and houses from Hungary and Slovenia. A couple of ounces of gold was worth a case of beer. A box of chocolate the same and cigarettes (good American ones...) were in high demand and returned the best value for the G.I.s. Apparently, looting was a thing in the Red Army, while in the U.S. one, it was a crime. So Summers and his men figured that there was no harm in a little exchange, and to hell if they encouraged their Allies to steal to get what they needed to acquire the goodies the westerners had. They didn't even know if they would be alive in a week, so why the hell not?

Visnevsky looked at Summers with a smile, his face looking eerie on the large campfire they were all sitting around. It was the dark of night. "You think we are fools to bring you this gold, yes?" Jack just shrugged his shoulders, trying to look non-committal like he didn't have a care in the world. Of course, he thought they were crazy stupid bastards. "Well, that may be true in your country but in mine... Nothing is private. Anything that we cannot hide from officers gets confiscated. So better live life to its fullest while we can."

Again, Summers had to give it to Yvan. These Russians knew how to live and have fun. And, he smiled inwardly, we Americans know how to get rich. "That's what I like about you, Yvan. You are just the best goddamn realist I've met in my life," he said, adding a genuine smile. "za zda-ró-vye, American Sergeant!" said the Russian man. The Russian words were one of the first Jack and his men learned after drinking a few schnaps with the Ruskies. It was the Russian way of saying "cheers!"

The night promised to be another long and eventful one. It was quite peculiar how two diametrically opposed people could actually get along so well. But as they were, it was one of those perfect moments that these men would cherish one day, as their war was far from over.

Adana
Rommel's new command HQ, April 10th, 1947

"Herr general." Said the radio operator, handing out the telegram to Erwin Rommel, commander in chief of all German forces in Anatolia.

The scene was happening in the city of Adana, where all Axis armies were retreating to after the grave Lake Van defeat a few days ago. The city of Gaziantep, where Rommel had the bulk of his forces, had not been directly threatened yet, but the writing was on the wall. Hence, the General decided to retreat toward Turkey's interior as his position would be flanked soon.

The famous Panzer commander quickly read thru the paper and stared at empty air for a moment. He then tightened his grip on it, crumpling it partially. Colonel Blumeritt, one of his trusted staff officers, could not resist asking what was on the message. "Herr General...."

The man only needed verbal confirmation because the rest of the radio operation area within the HQ was in complete turmoil. Ignoring military etiquette and secrecy, the operators were jabbering about the news.

Blumeritt could simply not believe it. "No...." he picked up the paper from Rommel's hand without any ceremony, and the General let him. He seemed transfixed, far away.

The colonel opened the grossly mangled telegram and read what was on it. "Turkish Government surrendered unconditionally to the Allies.... Prime Minister Alp Asker under house arrest.... German troops in Ankara arrested and fired upon by Turkish soldiers...... Call for German surrender from new Turkish government....."

Blumeritt could simply not believe what was on the damned message. He turned toward Rommel. "Herr General. We cannot accept this. We need to fight.... We we... need to do something!"

But there wasn't much the famous man could do. The Germans were stranded and out of touch with the Reich. Without Turkish supplies and support, there was no more hope. The Axis forces in Anatolia were already cut off from the Fatherland by a thousand miles of Russian-infested lands.

Rommel had had enough. He just couldn't imagine any way out of it since the news from Germany itself was dire as well. It seemed that the Third Reich would fall within the next few weeks anyway. So why fight and lose brave German soldiers for nothing? The war was lost. "Colonel Blumeritt. The war is over," said Erwin, putting a hand on the other man's shoulder. "Get me a meeting with Allied General Auchinleck so we can put an end to this thing."

And just like that, another 250 000 Germans and Axis auxiliaries were to surrender soon. The Second World War was about to be truly over in the Middle East and North Africa.

OKW meeting
Berlin Chancellery Bunker, April 11th, 1947

"Mein Fuhrer," said Halder, as Heinz Guderian, former General in the Wehrmacht, entered the room in the bunker complex below the Chancellery in Berlin. It was early on the morning of the 11th of April. Halder noticed that the new leader seemed tired. No wonder, since he was no Goering. The man was in the field all the time, touring Berlin's air defenses, discussing with Generals, helping with morale in General.

"Ah, Halder." It's nice to see you, and I remind you again, do not call me Fuhrer. First, I don't deserve the title, and second I don't want it." Guderian tightened his fist in frustration. It was obvious the man wasn't enjoying himself. The OKW commander wondered what the Third Reich could have done with this man at the top instead of the two previous buffoons they'd had.

An orderly walked in from the other side of the room, bringing a tray with some coffee and breakfast stuff. The room they were in was well-tailored to manage military operations. The four walls could be pinned with maps as they were covered with cork, enabling the planners to pin whatever situation report they wanted on them. In the center lay a gigantic table representing Europe and where the frontlines were at that moment in time.

"You look like shit this morning, Halder." Indeed he did. He had not slept since receiving the bad news from Turkey. Added with the disaster in the making on the Western Front, no wonder he wasn't able to get some rest. "Indeed, Mein Fuhrer." Guderian gave him a vain smile. "General, I've told you not to call me that." "Sorry M…. General." "Ah, that's better." He walked up to Halder and put a hand on his shoulder before going to the coffee tray table, selecting some stuff for himself. Standing by the tray, the orderly poured him a hot coffee, staying silent as he was supposed to.

Heinz then walked over to the table in the center of the room while Halder also picked himself up a coffee. Taking a sip of the hot, burning liquid, the General-Fuhrer sighed in pleasure. "Ahhh. Nothing better than coffee in the morning. You know, Frantz, it's the only perk I like about this new job... Coffee isn't available in the Reich with the war rationing. So at least I have that" Halder, walking back to the table and also taking a sip, agreed with a silent nod.

"No one else at the meeting this morning?" asked the German leader. "No, General. Paulus is now commanding the southern front, Speer is still gravely injured and now in a Berlin hospital, and Von Leeb was sent, along with the 238th Division toward the west as the last-ditch reinforcement we talked about yesterday. It's just us for the duration, I am afraid. Well, for how long that duration will last...."

"Okay. Better get on with it then. So things are truly over in Turkey?" "Yes, we received Rommel's last radio message yesterday evening. The General announced that he was to surrender to the Allies." Guderian gave an ironic laugh. "No wonder. The man was cut off, retreating, and betrayed by the Turks. Not that I blame them, anyway." The German leader was ironic in a sort of way. He seemed to have accepted the inevitability of Germany's defeat. "Let's move on. It doesn't change our predicament as those troops were already lost." He signaled for Halder to continue since they needed to talk about the main subject.

"The Allies have cleanly broken thru our West Wall defenses in Aachen, Saarbrucken, and Offenburg. Rundstedt has asked, and I have, of course, given in, to retreat eastward to avoid the forces still defending the Siegfried being outflanked." He paused to take another sip of the hot liquid. "Rundstedt is retreating in good order toward the Rhine where he hopes to put up a scratch defensive line." The Rhine would probably be the last German defensive action in the west. If that failed...Guderian, still strangely calm on that morning bearing disastrous news, changed the subject. "What of our dear friend, the Soviets? They must be brewing up something." "Indeed they are, answered Halder in a grave tone." They are gathering an enormous number of divisions on the Vistula, and they seem to be ready to launch at any moment. According to our air recon over the Polish Plains, we estimate enemy strength at over 200 divisions." The Fuhrer seemed to balk for a moment. "And remind me how many divisions we have to defend against that?" "A mere 92 divisions, Mein Fuhrer. And most are not at full strength."

"Well," the Panzer leader said, taking a deep breath. "Let's hope our dear general Manstein pulls off another rabbit out of his hat." "Indeed," said Halder in return, with not an ounce of confidence in his voice.

"What of our peace overture to the Western Allies?" asked the OKW chief. "Not a bit of success, my friend. First of all, they won't deal with Ribbentrop. In fact, they won't even talk to the man. And then, they also said that no discussion with us is possible unless we surrender unconditionally. The Brits seem more realistic and want to talk, but the Americans are adamant that nothing can be considered unless we just lay down our weapons and surrender." Halder lifted his arms in the air in exasperation. "Don't they see that the Russian steamroller is just going to roll over them once done with us?" "It doesn't matter what they see, General. They are Americans. They think that all will be fine and that they'll win in the end anyway. I guess they want to finish one enemy before considering another one."

"Southern Front?" said Guderian, changing the subject. "All quiet. I have nothing to report, which is nice for a change. Some skirmishes, but nothing serious. It looks like the Allies had given up on that front." "Okay, let's gamble a little then. Tell Paulus to send five of his 15 divisions to France. He can do it the way he wants, but we just need more men." Halder nodded in agreement. "Indeed, Mein Fuhrer."

The Vistula-Oder Offensive
Soviet hordes launch the final offensive, April 12th, 1947

At dawn on the 12th of April, 225 Red Army divisions crossed the Vistula on the numerous still-standing bridges, pontoons, and boats. Some of the units had already been across for a few days, establishing solid beachheads and secure areas for the softer units to cross.

The Wehrmacht was nowhere to be seen, as Erich Von Manstein had operated a strategic withdrawal out of the exposed Polish plains. So the first day of the offensive was quiet, and nothing major happened apart from a few minor skirmishes.

What bore down on Germany was the most potent land force ever assembled in one concentrated offensive. Stalin ordered Zhukov to send everything the Red Army had. The Marshal had thus assembled a staggering four million men spread across six "fronts": 1st Baltic, 3rd and 4th Bielorussian, 1st Voronezh, 1st and 2nd Ukrainian Fronts.

On the other side of the coin, the Wehrmacht had 92 divisions to face the onslaught. They had arguably the best tactical general of the war in Erich Von Manstein. And they had desperation on their side. It would be the end if the German soldiers could not stop this mighty Russian offensive.

No more retreat. No more fancy maneuvering. No more excuses.

Just one last mighty battle for Wehrmacht to fight.

THE STORY WILL CONTINUE IN BOOK 10 OF THE BLITZKRIEG ALTERNATE SERIES:

SOVIET EUROPA

Thank you very much for reading my work.
*** Please go and review my book(s) on Amazon and Goodreads.com.
*** It helps me out and motivates me to write more books. Thank you in advance.
*** Send me an email at souvorov@hotmail.com if you feel like chatting about the books of the story.

www.maxlamirande.com

THE BLITZKRIEG ALTERNATE SERIES
BY MAX LAMIRANDE

Book 1: Blitzkrieg Europa
Book 2: Battle Europa
Book 3: Struggle Europa
Book 4: Fortress Europa
Book 5: Stalemate Europa
Book 6: Staggering Europa
Book 7: Faltering Europa
Book 8: Crumbling Europa
Book 9: Falling Europa (February 2022)
Book 10: *Soviet Europa*

THE PACIFIC ALTERNATE SERIES
BY MAX LAMIRANDE

Book 1: *Blitzkrieg Pacific*
Book 2: *Battle Pacific* (March 28, 2022)

THE NAPOLEONIC ALTERNATE SERIES
BY MAX LAMIRANDE

Book 1: *Austerlitz Alternate*
Book 2: *Friedland Alternate (March 2022)*

THE STORY CONTINUE IN THE PACIFIC ALTERNATE SERIES:

The year is 1942.

The world is at war. Almost every major nation has declared for the Allies or the Axis. Europe is occupied by the Third Reich, and the British Islands have been invaded and conquered by the Germans. Metropolitan France has fallen, along with its North African colonies. Spain and Turkey have joined the Axis. The Middle East is Axis. The USA and Soviet Russia are also at war with the Third Reich.

Only one major power is still on the sideline. Imperial Japan, already busy in its war of conquest in China, dawns to the idea of conquering the Pacific and Southeast Asia, following German successes in Europe and the subsequent weakening of the resource-rich Franco-British and Dutch colonies.

The United States, following Japan's occupation of the French colony of French Indo-China in 1940, froze all of Tokyo's assets, stopped scrap metals deliveries and is just about to stop delivering oil to the hungry Japanese military machine. A move certain to trigger a reaction from the warmongers in Tokyo.

President Roosevelt's decision to do so is about to have dire consequences for America. The Imperial Navy has set its sight on the main US base in the Pacific, Pearl Harbor. And all across the Japanese-held islands of the Pacific, the forces of the Rising Sun prepare for a full-scale invasion that they hope will give them control over the resources the country needs to continue on its expansion.

This is the story of the War in the Pacific.

Also from the same author:

DECEMBER 2ND, 1805
The War of the Third Coalition rages in Europe. Battles have been fought, and Napoleon Bonaparte's Grande Armée sweeps everything before it. With a big victory over an Austrian Army in Ulm, the French have occupied Vienna, the capital of the Austrian Empire.

The Russians have entered Austria to come to the help of their Allies and under pressure from the British. The Austro-Russians and the French are about to clash at a small, unknown town called

Austerlitz.

And then everything changes. The French are stopped trying to retake the Pratzen Heights, and the day's battle ends in a stalemate for both armies. Kutusov, the allied army's leader in the absence of young Tsar Alexander (who fell ill and is still somewhere in Galicia), decides to retire the army northward with the Austrian Emperor's approval.

The news galvanizes the Revolution's enemies and of the Empire, jealous of Napoleon's success and wanting him gone. The Prussians decided to join the war and move their troops into Austria to link their forces with the two other powers. The German states and other countries like Naples rethink their stances in the conflict. And the French Emperor's internal enemies, ever-wishing the return of the old regime, start to plot to overthrow the government in Paris.

All the while, the Ottoman Empire, convinced by the French several months earlier to enter the war, has decided to intervene in favor of Bonaparte and invade southern Hungary with an Army. Austria is on the brink of annihilation, but Napoleon's Grande Armée also has a big challenge ahead since it now needs to defeat three significant powers simultaneously.

Everything will come down to either Napoleon's genius to overcome the odds and win regardless of the troops arrayed against him, or else his defeat and the end of the French Empire.

This is the story of the Napoleonic Wars.

Printed in Great Britain
by Amazon